"I love you," Tessa whispered.

Passion smoldered in Denver's eyes. "I love you, too, Tessa," he avowed.

She believed him. With all her heart she believed he wanted to marry her, intended to spend the rest of his life with her. Her heart began to clamor, and her pulse jumped wildly when he circled the hollow of her throat with his tongue. His breath was warm as the summer wind, the honesty in his eyes clear as a mountain lake.

"You're sure about this?" he asked, swallowing hard.

"I trust you," she whispered. She smiled at him. "I'll love you for the rest of my life."

"Oh, Tessa."

"Love me," she whispered.

"I do— Oh!" he cried, his voice raw. "Oh, love."

Suddenly the smell of smoke wafted through the trees. Every muscle in Denver's body tensed, and his gaze darted through the surrounding hills to the valley floor far below.

"What?" Tessa whispered, reading the terror in his eyes. "Denver—?" Her throat was suddenly dry. She, too, smelled the biting odor of burning wood.

Fire!

Dear Reader:

Dreams, like flowers, can be fragile, but once they are pressed gently between the pages of a book, their colors and textures can be savored again and again.

This month, six wonderful authors—Ginna Gray, Lisa Jackson, Mary Kirk, Victoria Pade, Mary Curtis and Patricia Coughlin—bring you their versions of "the stuff that dreams are made of"... gently pressed between the covers of six Silhouette **Special Edition** novels.

Writer and dedicated dreamer Patricia Coughlin believes that "when you open a Silhouette **Special Edition**, you want to meet strong, compelling characters and be swept up in their unique adventure. You want to be touched emotionally, feel your heart race and ultimately be left with a sense of fulfillment. So do I," she confesses, "and I'm thrilled to share my dreams with you in the pages of a **Special Edition**."

For bedtime reading—anytime reading—our authors and editors hope you'll choose Silhouette **Special Edition**. These romantic novels are designed to bring you sweet dreams you can savor again and again, night after night, month after month. And the morning after, why not drop us a line? We always welcome your comments.

Sincerely,

Leslie Kazanjian,
Senior Editor

LISA JACKSON
Aftermath

Silhouette Special Edition

Published by Silhouette Books New York

America's Publisher of Contemporary Romance

SILHOUETTE BOOKS
300 East 42nd St., New York, N.Y. 10017

ISBN: 0-373-09525-2

First Silhouette Books printing May 1989

Printed in the U.S.A.

LISA JACKSON

was raised in Molalla, Oregon, and now lives with her husband, Mark, and her two sons in a suburb of Portland. Lisa and her sister, Natalie Bishop, who is also a Silhouette author, live within earshot of each other and do all their work in Natalie's basement.

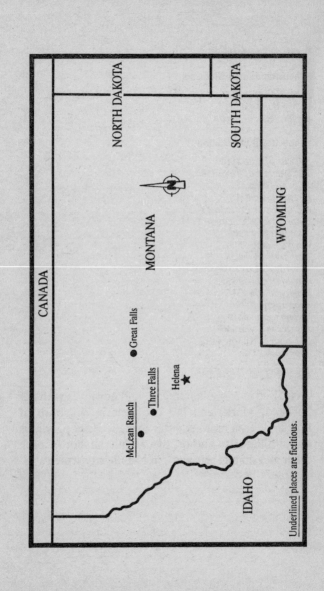

CANADA

NORTH DAKOTA

SOUTH DAKOTA

MONTANA

WYOMING

● Great Falls

● Three Falls

★ Helena

McLean Ranch

●

IDAHO

Underlined places are fictitious.

PROLOGUE

McLean Ranch, Montana

I love you," Tessa Kramer whispered. Lying on the summer-dry grass, staring into eyes as blue as the sea, she smiled, blushing a little at the boldness of her words. At nineteen she was certain she was in love. And no one, not her overprotective father, nor her suspicious brother, nor even Denver McLean himself, could convince her otherwise.

Denver's thumbs traced the arch of her cheeks. Passion smoldered in his eyes. "You're sure?"

"Absolutely." Her lips quivered anxiously. "So don't try to tell me that I'm too young or too naive or too...whatever, to know what I'm talking about."

"Am I arguing?" He kissed her softly again, his lips warm and filled with promise as they brushed tenderly over hers. Strong fingers tangled in her long, strawberry-blond hair.

Winding her arms around his neck, she felt the weight of his chest crush her breasts, could see blue sky through the shifting pine needles of the branches overhead. The summer sun hung low over lazy mountains, and insects hummed in the whisper-soft breeze that ruffled Denver's coal-black hair. Nearby, the horses, a buckskin gelding and a sorrel mare, were tethered together. The animals stood nose to rump, nickering softly and switching their tails at the ever-present flies.

The afternoon was perfect.

"I love you, too, Tessa," Denver vowed, moving gently above her.

Through her jeans Tessa could feel the heat of his body, the solid warmth of his legs entwined with hers.

Pressing eager lips against her neck, he groaned—a deep, primal sound that caused her heart to trip. Her breath caught somewhere between her throat and lungs as he said, "I want to make you mine."

She believed him. With all of her heart, she knew he wanted to marry her, intended to spend the rest of his life with her. Her heart began to clamor, her pulse jumping wildly as he circled the hollow of her throat with his tongue. His breath was as warm as the summer wind, the honesty in his eyes clear as a mountain lake.

"I trust you," she whispered.

She felt the buttons slide through the buttonholes in her blouse. The gauzy fabric parted, and sunlight warmed her bare skin. She smiled to herself, throwing caution to the wind. Today she would prove just how much she loved Denver, just how wrong her father was about him.

Shifting, he traced the sculpted lace of her bra with his tongue. Eager shivers darted down her spine. With ease he unlatched the fastening and tossed the scrap of white cotton into a clump of sagebrush.

She sucked in her breath. His hands moved protectively over her breasts, kneading each dark-crested mound until she burned inside with that same unsatisfied ache she felt whenever they kissed. He touched one nipple with the tip of his tongue and she moaned, wanting more and responding by instinct, holding his head against her, whispering his name as her blood, like wildfire, ran hot and fast in her veins.

She couldn't think and didn't want to. Her fingers moved to the waistband of his faded jeans and she released the button, pushing worn denim over his legs, feeling for the first time the downy hair on his thighs as he, too, stripped her bare.

Sunlight danced through the trees, dappling their naked bodies as they gazed upon each other in silent rapture. She wasn't embarrassed and met his hungry gaze with her own. He swallowed.

She licked her lips. "I'll love you for the rest of my life," she said softly. Touching his bare chest, watching the muscles of his shoulders ripple and strain, she smiled up at him.

Her fingers traced a feather-light line against his ribs, and he groaned. "Tessa, don't tease me—"

"Never," she vowed, devouring him with her eyes.

At twenty-three, Denver had matured into a handsome man. Long and lean, with tanned skin, flashing blue eyes and hair as dark as the night, he was rugged and charming. His features were no longer boyish, but chiseled into manhood. He was everything she had ever wanted, and unless she convinced him otherwise, he was leaving.

"Oh, Tessa," he whispered hoarsely, smoothing her hair from her face, his palms caressing her cheeks. "I want to make you happy."

"Do I look so miserable?" she asked, chuckling deep in her throat.

He grinned crookedly. "You're gorgeous."

"So, Mr. McLean, are you."

"I never want to hurt you," he said, growing serious again.

"You won't."

Slanting his mouth over hers, he moved until he was lying over her, his knees between hers, his thighs rubbing sensually as he entered her quickly. A swift flame of pain burned for a second within her, only to be extinguished by the gentleness of his strokes.

Tessa gasped, her arms circling his neck, her lips pressed to his as he began to move within her, enticing her to do the same. He kissed her eyes, her cheeks, her lips. The wild flames running through her blood leaped out of control and she was moving with him, riding on a storm as furious as a prairie fire, a tempest that swallowed them both.

"Love me," she whispered.

"I do—oh!" he cried, his voice raw as he stiffened above her, then fell spent into her waiting arms. "Oh, love."

The wind shifted silently, moving across the rugged ridge on which they lay, bending the dry grass and catching in Tessa's hair.

"Don't ever leave me," she begged, her mind still spinning in a kaleidoscope of colors as she clung to him and tried to still her racing heartbeat. She felt the dew of sweat on his arms, smelled the scent of lovemaking on his skin, saw smoky clouds swirl in a sky tinged with pink.

"I have to go to L.A."

His words were a cold dose of reality. "You don't *have* to," Tessa protested.

"Yes, I do, Tessa. I've got a job there in two weeks." Evidently seeing the disappointment in her eyes, he kissed the tip of her nose. "But you could come with me."

She swallowed back the urge to cry and looked away from him to the hazy heavens. "My dad—"

"Doesn't need you. I do. Come with me."

"What would I do in Los Angeles?" she asked, shifting her gaze back to his. "I train horses. I don't belong in the city. And neither do you." Blinking rapidly, she told herself not to cry, not this afternoon, not after loving him so completely. Clouds drifted overhead and the smell of smoke wafted through the trees.

"I'm an engineer, Tessa. I want to build bridges and skyscrapers and—" His nostrils flared and every muscle in his body flexed.

"And what?"

"Smoke!" he whispered, his gaze darting through the surrounding hills, to the valley floor far below. "Oh, God—"

"What?" she asked, reading the terror in his eyes. "Denver?" Her throat suddenly dry, she, too, smelled the biting odor of burning wood. *Fire!*

Scrambling into his jeans, Denver stared down the hillside, his face a mask of horror. "Oh, God, no!"

Tessa followed his gaze, only to see steel-gray smoke billowing from the stables of the McLean ranch. She felt the blood rush from her face as she scrabbled on the dry ground for her jeans and blouse and struggled into her clothes.

Denver ran barefoot to his horse and grabbed the reins. While the poor beast sidestepped and tossed his head, he swung onto the gelding's back and kicked hard. Leaving behind a cloud of dust, the buckskin tore down the rutted trail, his hooves clanging sharply on the rocks.

"Wait!" Tessa cried, cursing the buttons of her blouse as she yanked on her boots, then ran to her sorrel mare and climbed into the saddle. "Come on," she urged, shoving her knees into the mare's ribs. The little quarter horse leaped forward, half-stumbling down the rocky trail. Tessa slapped her with the reins, and the mare scrambled down the hill.

Wind tore at Tessa's face and hair, and tears blurred her eyes as she clung burrlike to her horse's neck. Denver was yards in front of her, cutting away from the trail and through the trees. "Wait!" she called again.

He didn't even glance back. Tucked low over the buckskin's shoulders, he streaked ahead.

"Giddap!" Tessa screamed, praying that the smoke pouring from the stables was from a fire already under control—trying to stop the horrid dread knotting in her stomach. Her game little mare sprinted into the pines, and Tessa had to duck to escape being scraped off by low-hanging branches. "Come on, come on," she whispered as they broke from the trees and raced across a long pasture leading to the stables.

The ranch was a madhouse. Stable boys, ranch hands and the kitchen help were running through the yard, yelling at one another, turning hoses onto the burning building. Thick, pungent smoke clogged the air, changing day to night. Flames crackled and leaped through the roof. Horses shrieked in terror, their horrific cries punctuating the ring of steel-shod hooves pounding against splintering wood.

"Dear God," Tessa prayed. "Dear God, save them!"

Denver yanked his horse to a stop, and as the buckskin reared, Denver jumped to the ground, then vaulted the fence.

"Stop! Denver, no!" Tessa cried, stricken as her sweaty mare slid to a halt near the gate. She leaped onto, then over, the top rail of the fence. Her eyes were glued to Denver as he raced, shouldering his way through useless ranch hands toward the stables. "Somebody stop him! Denver!"

Smoke burned her lungs and her eyes stung as she followed, stumbling forward. Somewhere in the distance she heard the wail of sirens. "Denver!"

"You can't go in there," her brother, Mitchell, commanded. He seemed to come from nowhere through the smoke.

"Like hell."

"Precisely." His gaunt face was streaked with soot, his hair grimy, his eyes red as he stared at the inferno. Hot, crackling flames knifed through charred shingles in the sagging roof. "Just like hell."

"Denver's in there!" she cried, still heading across the yard. But Mitchell had no trouble keeping up with her, taking one swift stride to her two.

"Listen to me, Tessa," he yelled over the roar of the fire, the shouts of men and the screams of terrified animals. "You can't—"

"I have to!" She was running now, only a few yards from the stables. Mitchell tackled her, his momentum pushing her to the ground. Her chin bounced on gravel, but she didn't care. She had to get to Denver.

"Damn it, Tessa," Mitchell's voice hissed urgently in her ear, "most of the McLean family's already trapped in there!"

"No!"

"When the fire broke out, Katharine and Robert tried to help save the animals and the ranch records stored in the office."

Struggling to a sitting position, Tessa clamped a trembling hand over her mouth and shook her head, staring at the burning building. Originally two stories, the stable had an upper floor used for storage and an office. The horses, the pride of the McLean ranch, had been boxed in stalls on the ground level. Tessa thought she would retch.

"The fire department will be here soon," Mitchell said, his voice rough from the smoke, his strong arms holding her back. "There's nothing anyone can do until they get here."

"We can't just sit here and watch them burn!" she choked out, feeling helpless.

Sirens screamed nearby and heavy tires crunched on the gravel. Red and white lights flashed through the smoke. A paramedic van ground to a stop, followed by a red car from the fire department. Three huge, rumbling trucks roared behind.

The fire chief threw open the door of his car and shoved a bullhorn to his mouth. "Everybody get back!" he ordered, his eyes searching the grounds as he waved to the driver of the pumper truck. "There's a lake around behind!" The truck tore around the main house to the large pond now reflecting scarlet. Firemen jumped from the trucks, dragging heavy canvas hoses toward the stables. "I want that barn contained and the surrounding buildings covered. We can't trust the wind today."

Water began jetting from the hoses, arcing high in the air before spraying over the burning building, sizzling as the first jets hit scorched timbers.

Tessa broke away from her brother and ran to the chief, Mitchell on her heels. "You've got to save them!" Tessa cried over the deafening cacophony of pumps, screams, the roar of the fire and her own, hammering heart.

"The horses, or—?"

"The McLeans are in there," Mitchell clarified, yanking a thumb toward the stables. "They might be upstairs in the office or on the ground floor. They were trying to save the stock—"

"Christ!" the chief swore. "How many?"

"Five—no, four. Denver and his parents, Robert and Katharine. And...and Dad, Curtis Kramer, the ranch foreman."

"Dad, too?" Tessa whispered hoarsely.

"That's it?" the chief demanded, his tired eyes narrowing on Mitchell. "What about John McLean and the other McLean son—what's his name?"

"Colton," Tessa murmured, thinking of Denver's younger, daredevil brother and praying that he was safe.

Mitchell shook his head. "John and Colton are in town, and I think the rest of the hands are accounted for."

"Make sure," the chief insisted. Snapping the bullhorn over his mouth again, he barked, "Okay, we've got four people trapped inside, possibly more. Upstairs and down. Get 'em out!" He glanced back at Tessa and must have read the dread on her face. "Get her out of here," he said to Mitchell. "There's nothing she can do."

"I'm not leaving," she insisted.

"Come on, Tess—"

"Not when Denver and Dad are in there. No way!" She started forward and tripped over a hose.

"You're in the way, lady," the fire chief said.

"Hey, Chief! We got one!" One of the firemen was dragging a coughing, soot-streaked man from the fire. Tessa tried to run forward, but Mitchell's arms tightened around her waist.

"Maybe you don't want to see this," he said.

"Let me go!"

"It might be Denver—"

"Then I have to be with him!" Her heart pounding with dread, she shook him off and started running.

The paramedics reached the rescued man first. They were already working over him, forcing oxygen into his lungs when Tessa recognized her father, his face black, his white hair singed.

"Thank God," she whispered, falling to the ground near him.

"Hey, lady, give us a break! We need a little room," one paramedic snapped, and she backed away on her knees, her eyes glued to her father's face. Gray beneath the streaks of soot, his skin looked slack and old. His thick white hair had been singed yellow and he was coughing so hard he nearly threw up.

But he was alive. Closing her eyes, she prayed silently.

Her father blinked rapidly, still coughing, his eyes unfocused.

"Get him into an ambulance," the fire chief ordered. He glared grimly at her father. "You see anyone else in there?"

"I—I don't know," he mumbled, still coughing.

The paramedic glanced at the fire chief. "He wouldn't know. He's three sheets to the wind."

Tessa swallowed back a hot retort as she leaned over her father and smelled the familiar scent of whiskey on his breath.

A pickup roared down the drive and slammed to a stop. The driver, Denver's younger brother, Colton, jumped out of the cab and started forward, his boots crunching on gravel as he ran faster and faster toward the fire chief. "What the hell's going on here?" he asked, his face white as he stared at the stables. Orange flames shot out of the roof and heat rippled in sickening waves from the inferno.

Curtis coughed loudly and stirred, his red-rimmed eyes focusing on his daughter. "Tessa, gal?" he murmured, cracking a weary smile.

"Thank God, you're all right!" She wrapped her arms around his grimy work shirt, buried her head in his chest. "Did you see Denver?"

"You were with him," Curtis said. He shook his head. "No one—"

"But Denver's in there! So are his parents," she protested, her head snapping up.

"Oh, God!" Colton cried. Without thinking he started for the stables.

"It's too late!" Mitchell yelled. "Colt—stop! Damn him!"

"Stay back!" the chief commanded through the horn. "Christ! Somebody stop him—"

A blast ripped through the stables, and the building exploded in a fiery burst. Glass shattered, spraying out. Timbers groaned and crashed to the ground. Flames crackled and reached to the sky in hellish yellow fingers. The earth shuddered.

Tessa fell to the ground sobbing, knowing in her heart that Denver would never survive.

"Come on, Tess," Mitchell whispered, picking her up and carrying her to his old, battered truck as the firemen and hands recovered and scurried toward the stables.

As if in a dream, Tessa saw her father being loaded into the ambulance, felt the scratchy denim of Mitchell's jacket against her cheek. "There's nothing more we can do here," Mitchell said softly. "I don't think there's anything anyone can."

"But Denver..."

"I know, Tess. I know."

Chapter One

I don't want it!" Denver McLean declared as he dropped into a tufted leather chair close to Ross Anderson's desk.

"We're talking about the entire ranch," the young attorney reminded him. Ross was serious, his watery blue eyes steady behind thick lenses, his narrow features pulling together. He smoked a twisted black cigar.

The old-fashioned Western cheroot smelled foul and seemed completely out of place in this modern chrome-and-glass office building, Denver thought. He rubbed the scar on the back of his left hand. "I guess you didn't hear me. I don't want it. Sell the whole damned thing!"

"We can't do that without your brother's consent," Ross said in that soothing lawyer tone that irritated the hell out of Denver.

"No one knows where Colton is. I haven't heard from him in years."

"Nonetheless, half the ranch is his—half yours. Split fifty-fifty. That's the way your father wanted it, and your uncle saw fit to carry out his wishes."

"I wish John had talked to me first," Denver said flatly. If his uncle weren't already dead, he gladly would have wrung the old meddler's neck.

"Too late now," Ross said succinctly.

Denver's lips twisted at the irony. Though he'd been away from the McLean Ranch for seven years and had ignored his uncle's repeated pleas to visit, the old man had gotten him in the end. "Okay," he decided, flopping back in his chair. "Just sell my half."

"Can't do it. Back taxes."

"Son of a—"

The door opened and Ross's secretary, a willowy woman with pale blond hair, eyes heavy with mascara and a glossy smile, carried in a tray of coffee, cream and sugar.

"Just set it on the desk, Nancy," Ross instructed as he puffed on his cigar, gradually filling the room with bluish smoke.

Nancy did as she was bid, casting Denver an interested glance that made him shift uncomfortably in his chair. Even after three successful operations, he felt as if his burns were as red and harsh as when he was dragged barely alive from the fire.

The fire—always the fire. He had never escaped it. Not really. And he never would.

His guts churned at the memory, and he tried to concentrate on the plastic cup of black coffee Ross handed him.

"So, you think your uncle was getting back at you by leaving you the ranch?"

"Wasn't he?"

"It's over a thousand acres of Montana ranch land," Ross said dryly. "Doesn't seem like such a curse."

"No?" Denver sipped the coffee. It was scalding and bitter. He didn't really much care. "Why weren't the back taxes paid?"

"The ranch has been in the red for the past few years."

"I thought there were supposed to be huge silver deposits on the land," Denver said, thinking back to those years of speculation, before the fire, when both his parents and his uncle had been excited at the prospect of mining silver from the ridge overlooking the ranch—the ridge where he'd lain with Tessa while a smoldering cigarette butt ignited dry straw in the stables far below.

"I guess the silver didn't exist," Ross said.

"Too bad," Denver muttered. "What about the stock?"

"It's holding its own, I think. Your uncle seemed to think that he was on the brink of turning things around."

Denver doubted it. Ross was just giving him the sales pitch that good old Uncle John had peddled him time and time again over the past few years. Denver hadn't bought it then and he wasn't buying it now. "The stables were never rebuilt after the fire, right?"

"The insurance company paid reluctantly—claimed the fire was arson. The fire chief concurred. Unfortunately the building was grossly underinsured. The money only covered cleaning up the mess and adding a few stalls to the barn." Ross squinted through his glasses. "John was hell-bent on suing the insurance company—claimed he'd been misrepresented, that he'd paid higher premiums than he should have for the amount of coverage. But he finally gave it up."

"On your advice?"

Ross nodded and drew on his cigar. "What's your point?"

"The point is that the McLean ranch is little more than a few decrepit buildings, some rangy cattle, a few horses and acres of sagebrush."

"Some people would see it differently."

Denver leaned back in his chair. "Maybe. I call 'em as *I* see 'em. The place isn't worth much. Let's get what we can out of it and call it good."

Ross sighed. "This is a mistake."

"Not my first." Tugging at his collar with two fingers, Denver wished this whole mess were over and done with. He didn't need any reminders of the past.

Shoving a copy of the will across the desk, Ross said flatly, "There's nothing you can do until the taxes are paid."

"I'll pay them."

"Okay, that's the first hurdle. Now, what about Colton?"

"Find him."

"That won't be easy."

"There has to be a way," Denver said wearily. "Last I heard he was still a United States citizen. Start with the State Department, a private investigator, the IRS and the CIA."

"It'll take time."

Denver narrowed his eyes. "Maybe you'll get lucky."

"I tried writing him through that magazine he free-lanced for a couple of years back," Ross explained. "Never received a reply."

"Keep trying." Denver glared angrily at the will. "I can wait." He felt his jaw clench at his next thought. "Is old man Kramer still running the place?"

Shrugging slim shoulders beneath his jacket, Ross said, "Far as I know. But I heard John say once that Kramer's daughter is really in charge. I can't remember her name." He crushed out his cigar.

"Tessa," Denver bit out, her name stinging his tongue. After seven years, he still felt needlelike jabs of regret that had turned bitter with age. If he tried, he could still recall the taste of her skin that hot day. But he wouldn't. No need to dredge up a past based on lies.

"Yeah, that's it. John confided in me that she covers for her old man." Ross leaned back in his chair and regarded Denver carefully. "Apparently Curtis Kramer has a drinking problem."

"Some things haven't changed," Denver observed.

"You can do what you want, of course. But since you're in Montana already, you may as well drive over and check out the place, make sure you really want to sell."

"I do."

"So you've said. I just thought you might want to find out why a ranch that was owned free and clear was losing money hand over fist—at least until recently."

Denver considered. He knew why: poor management. Curtis Kramer knew horses but couldn't handle a ranch. Denver's father had seen it and had been ready to let Curtis go just before the fire...the damned fire. Unfortunately Uncle John had kept Tessa's old man on. No one could prove Curtis had started the blaze, and John had been convinced of the man's innocence. Denver wasn't so sure. He drummed his fingers on the arm of his chair. "Isn't finding out how much the ranch is worth and how much it earns a job for the bank that's probating the estate?"

Ross smiled crookedly. "Are you willing to trust someone from Second Western Bank to understand the ins and outs of ranching?"

Denver snorted.

"Right." Ross tugged on his tie. "Of course it's up to you. It's yours now."

"Great. Just great." Denver shoved his chair back and strode angrily out the door, past the blond receptionist and through the labyrinthine corridors of the law firm—the largest in Helena, Montana. Although small compared to most in Los Angeles, where Denver had lived for the past seven years, the firm of O'Brien, Simmons and Taft was top-notch even by California's high standards, and Ross Anderson, a junior partner, knew his stuff.

Shouldering open the glass door, Denver stalked onto the street. The pace in Helena was much slower than that in Los Angeles and Denver was restless. Ross's advice followed him into the parking lot where his rented car was baking in the late-afternoon sun. Clouds gathered above, but there wasn't a breath of wind, and the humidity was unusually high, the air sticky.

Denver climbed in and switched on the ignition, unwillingly remembering the inferno.

It had all happened so fast. One minute he'd been lying on Tessa, her dew-covered skin fusing with his own, her lips soft and sensuous, her hazel eyes glazed in passion—the next he'd witnessed the horror of the blaze, horses screaming in death throes, hooves crashing in the billowing, lung-burning smoke. He'd felt the explosion, been thrown to the floor.

When he finally awakened, his skin burning, his face and hands unrecognizable, it had been three days later. He'd learned the devastating news: both his parents had been killed.

Colton, eyes red and shadowed, coffee-colored hair falling over his eyes, had been waiting for Denver to wake up.

"It's old man Kramer's fault," Colton insisted as he huddled near Denver's bed, avoiding his eyes and watching the steady drip of an IV tube that ran directly into the back of Denver's right hand.

"How—how could it be?" God, he hurt all over.

"He's been stealing from the ranch. He was up in the office altering the books when the fire started. If you ask me, he did it to destroy the evidence."

"You can't prove it."

"Can't I?" Colton thundered, his gray eyes sizzling like lightning. "Weren't you supposed to go over the books that day? Didn't Tessa insist that you go riding with her instead?" He stood then, the back of his neck dark in anger, his boots muffled on the carpeting.

Denver's dry throat worked in defense.

"What did she do? Seduce you?" Colton must have seen some betraying spark in Denver's eyes. "Of course she did," he muttered in disgust.

"No—"

"Don't you see? It was all part of the plan—Curtis's plan to rip off the ranch! Dad was on to him, and he had to cover his tracks."

"No way!" Denver rasped.

"Whose idea was it to go riding?"

Denver didn't answer.

"Right. And I'll bet Tessa was more than willing."

"Get out of here."

Colton didn't move. "You're a blind man, brother! She and that drunk of an old man of hers have been bleeding us dry. I'd even bet Mitch is in on it with them."

Denver tried to sit up, pushing aside the pain that scorched the length of his body. "I won't believe—"

"Then don't. But think about this. Mom and Dad are dead, Denver. Dead! Dad thought Curtis was embezzling, and he was out to prove it. Doesn't it seem a little too convenient that all the records were destroyed on the day Dad asked you to go over the books?"

"He didn't say a word about Curtis."

"He couldn't, could he?" Colton pointed out. "He wanted an impartial opinion!" Colton's furious gaze skated across the wrinkled sheets and gauze bandages to land on Denver's scarred face. "I know that you and I have never seen eye to eye, but I thought you'd agree with me on this one." His jaw worked for a minute. "They're gone, Denver. And you—look at you." Colton's eyes clouded with pity. "Look at what they did, for Christ's sake."

"Get out!" Denver didn't want to think about the damage to himself. He'd always been proud, and the look on Colton's face twisted his guts. He couldn't think about the pity in Tessa's eyes should she ever see him again.

Colton's gray eyes flashed furiously. "Anyway you cut it, Denver, Curtis Kramer is to blame." He strode out of the room then, leaving Denver alone with his scars and his memories.

Now, shaking his head to clear it of the unpleasant past, Denver rammed the car into gear and backed out of the law firm's parking lot. The car rolled easily onto the street and Denver turned north, toward the airport. Not once since the fire had he returned to the ranch. He'd never seen Tessa again.

At first pride had kept him from her, and eventually Colton had convinced him that she had, intentionally or not, conspired against him. He'd told himself he was doing her one big favor by leaving, and he'd been right. He had been badly scarred, physically and emotionally. Plastic surgery had fixed the exterior, he thought cynically as he glanced in the rearview mirror and saw the same blue eyes he'd been born with. One lid was a mere fraction lower than the other, but his skin was smooth, the result of more skin grafts than he wanted to count. But no surgeon or psychiatrist had been able to remove the bitterness he felt whenever he thought about that day.

"So don't think about it," he muttered aloud, scowling at himself. It was many miles north to the ranch, and the airport was only across town. He could drive to the airport and return to Los Angeles as he'd planned, or he could phone his partner and take time off—the vacation he hadn't allowed himself in years. Jim would understand, and business was unseasonably slow. But if he stayed in Montana, he'd have to face Tessa again.

His lips curved into a crooked, almost wicked smile. Maybe it was time. He saw the flashing neon sign of a local tavern and pulled into the pothole-pocked parking lot. One beer, he decided, then he'd make up his mind.

With one quick stroke of her jackknife, Tessa cut the twine. The bale split open easily. Snapping the knife closed, she shoved it into her pocket, then forked loose hay into the manger. Dust swirled in the air, and the interior of the old barn smelled musty and dry.

Though it was evening, no breeze whispered through the open doors and only faint rays from a cloud-covered sun filtered past the grime and cobwebs of the few circular windows cut high in the hayloft.

The air was still, heavy with the threat of rain. She hoped the summer shower would break quickly and give relief to the parched ranch land. The ground was cracked and hard. And it was only the middle of August.

She was already feeding the horses and cattle hay she'd cut barely a month before.

Frowning, she heard the familiar sound of thudding hooves. Tails up and unfurling like silky flags, several of the younger horses raced into the barn. Behind the colts, the brood mares plodded at a slower pace.

"Hungry?" Tessa asked as several dark heads poked through the far side of the manger. A gray colt bared his teeth and nipped at a rival as the horses shoved for position. "Hey, slow down, there's enough for everybody." She chuckled as she forked more hay, shaking it along the long trough that served all the McLean horses.

Once the McLean horses were fed, she tossed hay into a manger on the other side of the barn and grinned widely as three more horses plunged their heads into the manger. Their warm breath stirred the hay as they nuzzled deep, searching for oats. "In a minute," Tessa said, admiring the stallion and two mares. These were her horses, and her heart swelled with pride at the sight of them. She owned several—six in all—but these three were her pride and joy, the mainstay of her small herd. "Hasn't anyone told you patience is a virtue?" She petted the velvet-soft nose of Brigadier, the stallion. A deep chestnut with a crooked white blaze and liquid eyes, he was spirited and feisty—and one of the best quarter horses in the state. At least in Tessa's opinion.

The two mares were gentler and shorter, one a blood bay, the other black. Both were with foal, and their bellies had started to protrude roundly. These three horses were the center of Tessa's dreams. She'd worked long hours, saved her money and even delayed finishing college to pay for them, one at a time. But the herd was growing, she thought fondly, eyeing Ebony's rounded sides, and finally Tessa was through school. She reached across the manger and patted Brigadier's sleek neck.

His red ears pricked forward then back, and he tossed his head, his mane flying and his dark eyes glinting.

"Okay, okay, I get the message." Grinning, Tessa poured oats for her horses and heard contented nickers and heavy grinding of back teeth.

Rain began to pepper the tin roof, echoing through the barn in a quickening tempo. "At last," Tessa murmured. She jabbed a pitchfork into a nearby bale, tugged off her gloves and tossed them onto the lid of the oat barrel. Stretching, she turned for the house. But she stopped dead in her tracks.

In the doorway, the shoulders of his denim jacket soaked, his wet dark hair plastered to his head, stood a man she barely recognized as Denver McLean. She hadn't seen him for so long—not since that awful day. Though his face was familiar, it had changed, the harsh angles and planes of his features more rugged than ever. His hair was the same coal black, shorter than she remembered, but still thick and wavy as he pushed a wet lock off his forehead.

"Denver?" she whispered, almost disbelieving. Her heart began to slam against her ribs. Her father and Milly, the cook, had both speculated that Denver might return to the ranch after his uncle's death, but Tessa hadn't dared think he would show up.

He crossed his arms and leaned one shoulder in the doorway. Behind him rain spilled from the gutters and showered the ground in sheets. The smell of fresh water meeting dusty earth filled the air. "It's been a long time, Tessa," he finally said.

Swallowing against a hard lump in her throat, she walked forward several steps. The horses snorted behind her and shifted restlessly, as if they, too, could feel the sudden electricity charging the air. "Yes, it has been a long time," she agreed, her voice as dry as the earth had been only a half hour before.

As she met his blue, blue eyes, painful memories crowded her mind. As vivid as the storm clouds hovering over the surrounding mountains, as fresh as the rain pelting the roof, the pain of his rejection flashed through her thoughts.

So many times she'd hoped she might meet him and not even mention the past—pretend total indifference to the wretched nights she'd lain awake, wounded to her very soul. But now that he was here, standing in front of her, she couldn't find one thread of that mantle of pride she'd sworn she'd wear. "I—I never thought I'd see you again."

"No?" His expression was wry, his tone disbelieving. "Haven't you heard? I own the place."

"Yes, I know, but—" Words failed her. Silence stretched heavily between them. "I—I knew it was possible, but it's just been so long." *So damned long.*

"I came back to straighten out a few things," he stated flatly, indifference masking his features. "I'll be here a couple of weeks. I thought I'd better tell someone I was here. I can't find your father or the cook, what's her name?"

"Milly Samms."

"Right. Anyway, you're the first person I've run into."

A little hurt tugged at her heart. Deep inside, she'd hoped he had been searching for her. She forced an even smile, though she couldn't help staring at his face, a face she'd loved so fiercely. Whatever scars had once discolored his skin were gone—faded to invisibility. Though he seemed changed, it was his callousness and age that caused the difference more than any surgery. But he was still handsome and earthy, she had to admit—and sensual in a way she hadn't remembered. "Most of the hands have gone into town," she said, struggling to keep her voice steady. "It's Friday night."

He raised one of his thick eyebrows skeptically. "So who's holding down the fort?"

"You're looking at her."

"You?" He held her gaze for a second before glancing at his watch and frowning. "I figured you might have a date later."

Damn him. "I do," she replied, a little goaded.

If the thought of her going out bothered him at all, he managed to hide it. *What did you expect after seven years?* she asked herself.

"A date with a hot bath and a good book." She found her work jacket on a hook near the door and slid her arms through the sleeves.

"That's not what I meant."

"I know," she admitted, trying to compose herself. Why after all these years did her heart race at the sight of him?

She dusted her hands and thought about the reason he'd come back: his uncle's estate. "I'm sorry about John."

"Me, too."

"He didn't want a funeral—"

Waving off her explanation, he shrugged. "Doesn't matter. I just came back to tie up a few loose ends, that's all. Where's your father? I thought he was running things."

"He is. He, uh, had business in town."

"But he's coming back?"

"Of course."

"When he gets back, tell him I want to see him. I'll be up at the house." He glanced through the rain toward the weathered two-story farmhouse across the yard.

Tessa's gaze followed his.

With its high-pitched roof, dormers and broad front porch, the old house had stood in the same spot for nearly a hundred years. It had been updated since the turn of the century—two bathrooms, central heat and electricity had been added—but it still appeared as it had when it was built by Denver's great-great-grandfather.

Denver cleared his throat then looked at her again, his eyes studying her face. She felt his gaze sliding from her straight red-blond hair past hazel eyes and a freckle-dusted nose to the sharp point of her chin. She wondered how he saw her—if she looked as he'd remembered. If he even cared.

"You know," she whispered, clinging to her rapidly escaping courage and feeling her fists curling into tight balls as she thought about the past, "I've waited all this time to ask you this one question."

His head jerked up. "Shoot."

"Why?" She stood dry-eyed in front of him, her chin tilted upward, her eyes searching his face—a face she'd loved with all her youthful heart. "Why wouldn't you talk to me?"

A muscle jumped angrily in his jaw. "Didn't seem the thing to do."

"But you could have called or something—" She lifted her hands helplessly and hated the gesture. Despite the fact that seeing him again opened old wounds, she couldn't let him see that she was still vulnerable to him in any way.

Shoving his hands into his jacket pockets, he crossed the weathered barn floor, eyeing the munching horses, the hayloft now full of new-mown hay, and the bins and barrels of oats, wheat and corn. "By the time I thought about it, there was no point," he said. Then his gaze softened a little and he studied the rusted bit of an old bridle hanging on the wall. He ran his fingers slowly along the time-hardened leather reins. "I thought by now you'd be married with about five kids."

"So did I."

"What happened?" He regarded her with genuine perplexity, and she felt some of her old anger simmer again.

"The man I wanted to marry left town without saying a word."

He didn't move. The rain beat steadily on the roof, breaking the silence that stretched yawningly between them.

Tessa forced the issue. Though quaking inside, she sensed this might be her only chance to find out what had happened. "You wouldn't see me in the hospital," she accused, her voice surprisingly calm, "wouldn't take my calls and returned all my letters unopened."

His jaw hardened. He dropped the reins but didn't say a word. One horse nickered and Tessa glanced toward the manger.

The way she saw it, Denver's silence was as damning as if he'd said he hadn't cared. She drew on all her courage. "Before I knew what was happening, my dad told me you'd taken off for Los Angeles."

He almost smiled, his eyes narrowing. "I couldn't keep the plastic surgeon waiting."

"Without saying goodbye?" she asked, bewildered and wounded all over again. "After everything we'd planned?"

"We didn't plan anything, Tessa."

The wind shifted. Rain poured through the open door. "But you'd asked me to marry you, move to L.A.—"

"I *never* said a word about marriage," he cut in, his voice harsh. "Think about it. You were the one who wanted to tie me down."

Tessa nearly gasped. "I didn't—"

"Sure you did. You kept trying to convince me that I should stay here, with you, on this damned ranch." Standing at his full height, using its advantage to stare down at her and drill her with his frosty blue gaze, he added, "I had no intention of staying."

"I loved you," she said boldly, the words ringing in the barn. "I might have been naive, but I did love you, Denver."

Denver's muscles tensed, the skin over his features stretching taut. "We were two kids experimenting, Tessa—finding out about our bodies and sex. Love had nothing to do with it."

"You don't believe that!" she cried, feeling as if he'd slapped her. "You couldn't!"

"Time has a way of making the past crystal clear, don't you think?"

Tessa's chin wobbled, but she forced her head up proudly. He wiped the rain from his hair, and she saw his hand, the burns still visible. Suddenly she understood. "You were afraid to see me," she whispered, her eyes widening with realization as they clashed with his again.

His face was unreadable and stony. "Think what you want."

She walked toward him, her steps quickening as she closed the distance. "That's it, isn't it? You were afraid that because of your scars—"

"Has it ever occurred to you that maybe what happened between us just wasn't that important?"

"No!"

"Oh, God, Tessa. You always were a dreamer."

His words hit hard and stung, like the cut of a whip. As if to protect herself, she stumbled backward, wrapped her arms around her waist and leaned against one cobweb-draped wall. "What happened to you, Denver?" she murmured, staring at the bitter man whom she had once treasured. "Just what the hell happened to you?"

"I got burned." Hiking his collar up, he turned and strode through the slanting rain. Ducking his head, he marched across the gravel yard, his boots echoing loudly as he disappeared into the house.

Tessa stared after him, her heart thudding painfully. Dropping onto the hay-strewn floor, she buried her face in her hands. For years she'd imagined running into him again, hoping deep in her heart that there might be some little spark in his eyes—a hint that he still cared. And even if he didn't love her again, she'd told herself, she could be content knowing that he, too, felt a special warmth at the thought that she had been his first love.

She'd been practical, not harboring any fanciful dreams that one day they could fall in love again. But she'd hoped that after an initial strained meeting, she and Denver would eventually become close—not as lovers, but as friends.

It had been a stupid, childish dream. She knew that now. Denver had changed so much.

Surprised that her hands were wet, that she'd actually shed tears for a man who had turned into such a soulless bastard, she sniffed loudly, wiped her eyes and tossed her hair over her shoulder. Never again, she told herself bitterly. These were the last tears she would ever shed for Denver McLean!

Chapter Two

Determined to be as cool and indifferent as Denver, Tessa marched through the rain to the house. The nerve of the man! she thought. He'd waltzed back into her life only to tell her that everything they had shared had been lies. He had twisted the truth to serve his own purposes. Well, he could twist it all he liked!

She wasn't afraid of Denver or his lies. He couldn't possibly hurt her more than he already had.

Seething, she kicked off her boots on the back porch and stalked into the kitchen in her stocking feet. The mingled smells of warm coffee, stale cigarettes and newsprint filled the air. Illuminated by the one remaining low-watt bulb, the room was muted, some of its defects hidden.

Tessa half expected to find Denver at the table, but the kitchen was empty. She knew he had to be in the house—or on the grounds nearby. His rental car was parked near the garage, under the overhanging branches of an ancient oak, and she'd watched him storm into the house just minutes before.

"So who cares?" she asked herself angrily. He'd made himself perfectly clear. She meant nothing to him and so much the better. At least now they could get down to business. She poured herself a cup of coffee from a glass pot still warming on the stove, took a sip and grimaced before tossing the remaining dregs down the drain. She refilled the cup with hot water for instant coffee and placed it in the microwave.

She listened, but didn't hear a sound other than the hum of the refrigerator, the gentle whir of the tiny oven and the drip of the rain outside. Maybe Denver had left through the front door.

Usually after chores, if Tessa found a few minutes to herself, she enjoyed the time, but now, as she stirred decaf crystals into her cup and pretended to read the headlines of the newspaper spread all over the kitchen table, she was tense.

The overhead bulb flickered, strobing the chipped Formica, the yellowed layers of wax on the old linoleum and the nicked cabinets. The entire ranch was falling apart, and the disrepair was glaringly evident. Denver would soon discover just how bad things were. Maybe she should tell him— get everything out in the open.

Still wrestling with that decision, she walked through the corridor leading to the stairs but stopped when she noticed a crack of light glowing under the study door. So Denver had holed up in the office. No doubt he was already poring over the books—searching for flaws. Her fingers curled tightly over the handle of her cup. If it took every ounce of grit within her, she had to find a way to work with him and get through the next few days without antagonizing him. Her father needed this job. Since the fire no one else in Three Falls would hire Curtis Kramer.

She twisted the knob, shoving on the door.

Denver was right where she expected him to be—seated behind John McLean's old walnut desk. Leaning over a stack of ledgers and invoices, his head bent, light from the desk lamp gleaming in his black hair, he worked, finally glancing up. "What?" His shirtsleeves were pushed over his forearms, leaving his dark skin bare.

An old ache settled in Tessa's heart. She stared at him a second, and she had trouble finding her voice. "Making yourself at home?" she asked finally. Though she tried to sound nonchalant, as if she didn't care one whit about him, there was a wistful ring in her words.

Denver leaned so far back in his chair that it creaked against his weight. Impatiently he stretched his arms, then cradled the back of his head in his hands. "I'm only staying a couple of weeks—to iron out a few things."

"Such as?"

"Back taxes for starters." His gaze shifted to a stack of unpaid bills. "Those next. And eventually the accounts with the feed store, hardware store—" He lifted a thick pile of paper. "Whatever it takes."

"To do what?"

His eyes narrowed. "To clean up this mess. According to John's lawyer, there have been all kinds of problems here—repairs that need to be made and haven't, bills unpaid, you name it!"

"Every ranch has . . . cash flow problems," she pointed out.

"What about that stallion that disappeared last spring—the best stallion on the place?"

Tessa cringed inside. She had hoped Denver hadn't heard about that. "Black Magic was lost. But we found him again—"

"He wasn't found. He just showed up."

Her voice was tight. "It doesn't matter. The point is, Black Magic returned and he's fine!"

Denver's lips twisted. "The point is that things are going to hell in a hand basket around here." He thumped his fingers on a stack of past-due bills. "This place is drowning in red ink."

"It's not that bad."

"Isn't it?" His eyes flashed.

She bit back a hot retort. "Things are just beginning to turn around, Denver," she said, ignoring the doubt in his eyes. "Tomorrow, when it's light, I'll take you around the ranch, show you the progress that isn't recorded in the checkbook."

His jaw shifted to the side, but he didn't argue.

"A ranch is more than dollars and cents, debits and credits, you know. A ranch is horses and cattle and machinery and people working together on land that matters."

One corner of his mouth curved up. "You haven't changed, have you?" he said, his voice husky. "Still a dreamer."

"I know what's valuable, Denver. I always have. And sometimes it doesn't show on a checkbook stub." She gazed directly at him, wishing the strain near his eyes would disappear.

"You've been wrong," he reminded her.

"I don't think so—not about the things that really matter."

His jaw clenched and he looked away—through the window to the dark night beyond. The desk lamp was reflected in the rain drizzling down the panes. "I should have talked to you a long time ago, I suppose."

"It would have helped," she replied, feigning indifference.

He looked as if he wanted to say more. For a second she caught a glimpse of him as he had been years before. His blue eyes turned as warm as a July morning. Then, as swiftly as the warmth appeared, it disappeared again. "It doesn't matter now," he said, clearing his throat. "It's all water under the bridge."

"Right," she lied. The entire room seemed filled with him, and, absurdly, she wanted to linger. "Can I get you anything? Make a fresh pot of coffee?"

The corners of his eyes softened a bit. "Don't bother."

"It's no bother."

"Tessa," he said quietly, "don't." Skin tightening over his cheekbones, he added, "If I need anything, I'll get it. I know my way around."

Goaded, she quipped, "You're the boss," and was rewarded with a severe glance.

Reaching for the doorknob, she heard the sound of an engine in the distance and recognized the rumble of her father's pickup. She glanced out the window. Curtis Kramer's dented yellow truck bounced into the yard.

"Company?" Denver asked.

"Just Dad."

His eyes narrowed. "Good. He and I have to talk." He watched the beams of headlights through the rain-speckled windows, and his mouth compressed into a thin, uncompromising line.

The temperature in the room seemed to drop ten degrees. "What about?"

"Everything. We'll start with what he knows about all the money he's managed to lose for this ranch."

"Denver," she whispered. "Don't—"

"Don't what?"

Her eyes sparked. "Don't judge before you have all your facts straight."

"But that's what I'm here to do," he said, turning to her, his voice cold. "Get my facts straight. Curtis can help clear up a few cloudy issues."

"What's that supposed to mean?"

"He's been in charge a long time and things—" he gestured around the shabby room, to the scarred desk, the dingy walls and threadbare drapes "—haven't gotten any better. In fact, this place seems to be on the verge of falling apart."

"And you blame Dad."

"I don't blame anyone. Not yet. But there's got to be a reason, Tessa. I just want to know what it is."

The screen door banged shut and Tessa heard her father call out. "Tessa? You 'round? Milly?"

A satisfied smile crossed Denver's lips as he stood and started for the door. But she clamped her arm around his elbow, her fingers tight over his bare forearm. The feel of his skin shocked her. Hard muscles flexed beneath her hands, soft hair brushed against her fingertips.

Denver stopped, glaring at her fingers as if they were intruders.

"Dad didn't start the fire, Denver," she insisted. "No matter what Colton said. Dad wasn't behind it."

"Who said anything about the fire?"

"You didn't have to," she replied, meeting his seething gaze with her own. "It's written all over your face."

"Is it? How?" He shoved his face close to hers, so close that she saw the pinpoints of fire in his eyes, read his anger in the flare of his nostrils. "What is it you see when you look so closely, Tessa?" he bit out.

The scent of rain lingered in his hair.

Tessa could barely breathe. Though her senses were reeling, she wouldn't back down, not for a second. Her fingers dug into his arms. "What I see," she said evenly, though her heart was hammering out of control, "is a bitter man, hellbent on extracting his own punishment for an imagined crime, a man whose irrational desire for retribution clouds his judgment."

"Is that right?" he mocked.

"And more! I see a man who's taking all his bitterness out on a tired old man and a woman who once thought he was the most important thing in her life!"

A muscle worked in his jaw. "Then you're a blind woman, Tessa."

"I don't think so."

"Maybe you'd better take a harder look."

"Don't worry, I will. You left this ranch and haven't stepped foot on it in seven years. *Seven years*, Denver. So what gives you the right to come back now?"

The cords in his neck tightened. "I own the place. Remember?"

"You and Colton."

"Well, he isn't around, is he?"

"Tessa? That you?" her father called through the study door.

"In here, Dad!" she shouted back.

"What in blazes are you doin' in here at this time of—?" Curtis Kramer shoved open the door and stepped into the dimly lit room. Color seemed to wash out of his weathered face. "Well, I'll be," he muttered, unconsciously smoothing his white hair with the flat of his hand. The scent of stale whiskey and cigarettes followed him as he crossed the room. His pale eyes focused more clearly. "I was wonderin' when you'd show up."

Unspoken accusations hung like cobwebs, dangling between them. Denver's eyes had turned so frigid, Tessa actually shivered.

Through tight lips, Curtis said, "I figured it wouldn't be long before you and Colton would want to check things out."

"I've already started." Denver's jaw was rigid, his eyes blazing with warning, but Curtis, whether bolstered by the whiskey or his own sense of pride, didn't back down.

"Good," he shot back. "About time you took some interest in things." Hooking his thumbs in the loops of his jeans, he turned to Tessa. "I'm gonna make me a sandwich. You want anything?"

"I'm fine," Tessa lied. Beneath her ranch-tough veneer, she was shredding apart bit by bit, and she wouldn't have been able to eat a bite if she tried. She heard her father amble down the hallway to the kitchen as she whirled on Denver. "What was *that* all about?"

"What?"

"You know what! You were baiting him, for God's sake."

"Was I?" He arched an insolent eyebrow. "All I said was that I was going to look things over."

"It wasn't so much what you said as how you said it. You implied something was going on here that wasn't above-board."

"You're overreacting."

"Just don't act like my dad's some kind of criminal, okay? Try and remember who stayed here and held this ranch together while you and your brother took off to God only knows where."

"I went to L.A.," he said, his voice cold. "Just as I'd planned."

She turned away. All these years she'd harbored some crazy little hope that he'd really cared for her, that he'd considered staying with her on the ranch, that she could have convinced him to stay in Montana with her if not for the fire. She hadn't really believed his words that their affair had meant nothing to him.

Her chin trembled, but she met his gaze. His eyes glared back at her without a hint of warmth in their cerulean depths. "So you said." She strode furiously down the hall to the kitchen. Her cheeks were flaming with injustice, and she felt her fists curl as tight as the hard knot in her stomach.

Her father was sitting in one of the beat-up chairs at the table. His cigarette burned in an ashtray, and a cup of coffee sat steaming on the stained oilcloth. "So he's back," Curtis grumbled, eyeing the local newspaper with disinterest.

"For a little while."

"How long?"

"I don't know."

"Humph."

"As long as it takes," Denver said from the hall. Leaning one shoulder against the doorjamb, he crossed his arms over his chest, the cotton weave of his shirt stretching taut over his shoulders.

"As long as it takes to do *what*?" Curtis asked.

Denver's expression was calculating, his features hard. "I'm here to figure out why this ranch has lost money for the past five years."

"That's simple enough," Curtis said. "The silver mines were a bust."

"We made money before the mining."

Curtis took a long drag on his cigarette. "But John took out loans for the equipment. Besides, prices are down and we had two bad winters—lost nearly a third of our herd. It's no mystery, Denver. Ranchin' ain't exactly a bed of roses."

"So I've heard," Denver mocked.

Curtis squinted through the smoke. "Seven years hasn't improved your disposition any, has it?"

One of Denver's dark eyebrows cocked. "Should it have?"

Stubbing out his cigarette, Curtis shook his head. "Probably not. You McLeans are known for your bullheadedness."

Surprisingly, Denver's lips twitched. "Unlike you Kramers."

"Right," Curtis said, but he chuckled briefly as he pulled his jacket from a hook near the back porch. Squaring his stained hat on his head, he shoved open the back door and headed outside.

"You don't have to badger him, you know," Tessa said, keeping her back to Denver's lounging form.

"I thought he was badgering me."

"Maybe he was," Tessa decided. "But you deserved it." Through the window, she saw her father's old truck bounce down the lane. Rain ran down the glass, blurring the glow of the taillights. "Dad's just an old man whose only crime is that he's given his life to this ranch."

"And what's mine, Tessa?" he asked, his voice low.

She turned and caught him staring at her—the same way he'd studied her in the past. His face had lost some of its harsh angles, his expression had softened, and his eyes— Lord, his eyes—had darkened to a seductive midnight blue.

"You left me," she whispered, her throat suddenly thick. "You left us all—without a word of goodbye."

He glanced away. "I regret that," he admitted, shoving a lock of dark hair from his forehead.

"Why, Denver? Why wouldn't you see me in the hospital?"

His eyes narrowed and the line of his jaw grew taut again. "Because it was over. There was no point."

"You could have explained it to me."

"Unfortunately, I wasn't in tip-top shape," he said, his words cutting like a dull knife.

"Neither was I! You were in the hospital—I didn't know if you were going to live or die. My father was being accused of heinous crimes he had no part in, and no one would tell me anything! Good Lord, Denver, can you imagine how I felt?"

The corners of his mouth turned white. "And can you imagine what I was going through?" he said, his voice barely a whisper. "I was told I would never be the same, that I would probably never use my arm again. Both my parents were dead because of the fire, and a woman I trusted had set me up to cover for her old man!"

"No!" Tessa's eyes widened in horror. "You couldn't believe—"

"I didn't know what to believe!" Advancing on her, his eyes boring into her, he said, "I just knew that my entire life had gone to hell!"

He was so close that she could feel the heat radiating from his body, sense the anger simmering within him. "You could have given me a chance to explain before you set yourself up as judge and jury!"

"It was too late for explanations."

"Maybe it's never too late."

He gave a wry smile and some of his anger seemed to melt. Reaching forward, he brushed a strand of hair from her eyes, his fingertips grazing her cheek. "Still the dreamer, aren't you, Tessa?"

She swallowed hard, fighting a losing battle with the raw energy surging between them. "I—I think I've dealt with the past seven years realistically. At least I didn't run away."

Sucking in a swift breath, he dropped his hand. His eyes blazed again. "Is that what you think?"

"That's what happened. And now you're back, sweeping back in here like some sort of avenging angel—accusing

my father of everything from arson to involuntary manslaughter.''

"I haven't accused him of anything.''

"Not in so many words, maybe,'' she said, her temper
flaring wildly. "But it's obvious you blame him for the fire,
just as you blame me.''

"When Curtis was here, we were talking about running
the ranch.''

"Were we?'' She strode across the room, tilting her head
back, forcing her eyes to meet his. "You could have fooled
me.''

"I don't want to talk about the fire,'' he snapped.

"Then leave it alone, Denver. Leave all of it alone. Because, believe it or not, we've been working our tail ends off
around here to save this place—a place you don't give a
damn about!'' She strode out of the room, letting the screen
door slam behind her, then fumbled for the light on the
porch.

"Mule-headed bastard,'' she muttered, tugging her boots
on before running down the back steps. The rain was coming down in sheets, pounding the earth, turning the dust to
mud. Bareheaded, Tessa stalked furiously down the well-
worn path to the paddocks. She leaned against the wet
fence, feeling the wind tease her hair and toss the wet strands
across her face. She didn't care. This summer storm couldn't
match the tempest of emotions raging deep in her soul.

Damn! Damn! Damn! Her fingers flexed and curled.
Why did he have to come back? Why now?

Closing her eyes, she prayed the cool rain would wash
away the pain, dampen the fires of injustice that burned so
brightly in her heart.

"Tessa?'' Denver's voice, so near, made her jump, her
heart still fluttering at the sound.

"Leave me alone!''

"What do you think you're doing out here?'' he asked so
calmly she wanted to scream.

"Trying to put things in perspective.''

Leaning over the top rail, his eyes squinting against the darkness, he stood so close that his shoulder brushed hers. She didn't move. Couldn't. Raindrops, reflecting the blue glow from the single outside lamp, collected in his hair and drizzled down his throat.

He hadn't bothered with a jacket, and his shirttail flapped in the wind. "Aren't you afraid of drowning?" he asked softly.

"In case you haven't heard, we're in the middle of a drought!"

His eyes searched the dark heavens. "Not tonight, we're not."

"The rain feels good." Why did she feel so defensive around him? Slowly counting to ten, she tried to control her temper. "Besides, we need every drop we get. The river's low and the fields are tinder-dry."

As the wind slapped against his face and the rain plastered his hair, Denver said, "This is crazy. Let's go inside where it's dry."

"I'm fine out here."

"Are you?" He tried to smother a smile and failed as he brushed a drip from the tip of her chin. His gaze shifted restlessly over her face. "You look like a drowned rat."

"I bet you say that to all the girls," she snapped, but couldn't help smiling.

"Only when I'm trying to impress them."

"So you're still the charmer you've always been."

He laughed, a low rumbling sound that warmed the cool night. "Low blow, Tessa."

"You deserved it. You haven't been pulling any punches yourself."

"I guess I haven't." The breeze snatched at his hair, ruffling it. "Come on inside. *I'll* pour *you* a cup of coffee." The determined line of his jaw relaxed, and he looked more like the young man she'd loved so fervently. He touched her lightly on the shoulder, his fingertips warm through her wet blouse. "Truce?"

She shook her head. "I don't know if that's possible, Denver." But she let him take her hand and told herself that the tingling sensation she felt in her palm was because of the storm. Hands linked, running stride for stride, they dashed through puddles in the backyard to the house.

In the kitchen he tossed her a towel, and Tessa wiped the rain from her face. As she sat in one of the chairs at the table, she studied him. His face had become lean and angular over the years, his skin dark and tight. But no amount of reconstructive surgery had been able to straighten his nose— a nose that had been broken when he fell from a horse at the age of twelve.

He'd changed. The lines of boyish dimples that had creased his cheeks had deepened into grooves of discontent, and his sensual mouth was knife-blade thin. A webbing of lines near his eyes indicated that he still squinted— but did he laugh and tease and smile as he once had?

After pouring the coffee, he handed her a steaming mug.

She took a sip, nearly burning her tongue. Cradling her mug in her hands, she leaned back in a chair and tossed the wet hair from her eyes. "I didn't really think you'd show up," she said. "I expected you'd sell your half of the place by phone."

He scraped back a chair, straddled it and leaned forward, blowing across his mug. "I wanted to, but it wasn't that easy."

So there it was. He admitted it. This ranch that she and her father had worked their bodies to the bone for meant nothing to him.

"As I said, there's a problem with back taxes," he said. "Seems they've been neglected."

"Money's been tight." A defensive note crept into her voice.

"So I've heard."

"And Colton?" she asked, wondering about Denver's brother. "Does he feel the same about this place?"

"I wish I knew." Denver glanced pensively into the dark depths of his coffee. "Since he owns half the place, I need to know if he wants to buy out my share or put the whole spread on the market."

"So, no matter what happens, you're going to sell."

"Right." He took a swig from his cup, without the slightest indication that he felt one second's regret.

"Just like that?"

"Just like that."

She leaned closer to him, placing her elbows on the table for support, her wet hair falling forward. "What would you say if I told you I wanted to buy you out?"

His features froze. "You?"

"Right. And not just your share, but Colton's, too."

Denver's mouth dropped open before he clamped it shut. "You don't want this ranch, Tessa," he said quietly. "You couldn't."

"Don't you presume anything about me, Denver Mc-Lean," she replied, her eyes serious, her voice surprisingly strong. "I've thought about it a long time. I've worked too hard on this place to have it sold out from under me."

"Tessa, this is crazy—"

"I'm not kidding, Denver. If you're going to sell Mc-Lean Ranch, I intend to buy it." Before he could protest, she added, "I've got some money of my own, livestock I could sell if I need to, and I've already done the preliminary talking to a banker in Three Falls."

"So you've got it all figured out."

"Most of it."

"Tell me," he drawled, "how do you expect to pull a ranch that can't hold its own back on its feet?"

"It can be done."

"With a huge mortgage?" He shook his head and finished his coffee. "I don't see how."

"That's the problem, Denver," she said evenly. "You've got your eyes wide open, but you can't see what's right in front of your nose." Feeling a hot lump forming in her throat, she whispered, "You never could."

Denver's fingers curled over his cup. Tessa was beautiful—*too beautiful*. He kicked back his chair, tossed the

dregs of his coffee into the sink and tried to ignore the firm
thrust of Tessa's jaw, the fire in her hazel eyes, the way her
damp blouse clung to her skin. Her hair, though wet, shone
beneath the dim wattage in the kitchen, and her face was
flushed in fury, touching the forbidden part of his soul he'd
hoped had smoldered to a cold death seven years before. "I
think I'll unpack." He needed time to think, time to put
everything into perspective, time to remind himself that
she'd betrayed him and his family. Distance would help.
Being in the room with her, feeling her accusing gaze still
drilling hot against his back, wasn't good.

What was the old saying? That there was a thin line between love and hate? Convinced he was walking that line,
Denver realized he had to be careful—or he was sure to fall.

"You can have the room at the top of the stairs," she
said.

"*I* can have?" he asked, turning. She was still seated at
the table, her eyes cool and distant, her face more beautiful
than he'd remembered.

"It was John's room."

"*I* know whose room it was. I used to live here. Remember?"

She let out a little strangled sound, then cleared her
throat. "Unfortunately, I could never forget."

To his disgust, he felt his guts wrenching, that same horrid pain that he'd felt when Colton had convinced him that
Tessa was involved with her father in Curtis's scheme to
fleece the ranch. To hide his weakness he leaned his hips
against the counter and curled his fingers around the sharp
edge. "What about my parents' room?"

"I'm using it."

"*You?*" he repeated. "You *live* here?"

"Yes." Standing, she shoved her fingers into the pockets
of her jeans. "You can have any room you want, Denver.
Just let me know, so I can move my things."

"Hold on a minute. Why are you living here?" he demanded, hot, fresh anger searing deep inside. Tessa had
lived under the same roof as John before his death?

"It was more convenient."

"I'll bet," he muttered, imagining her with his uncle. A bachelor for life, John McLean had gained a reputation with the local women. But Tessa? Denver's insides knotted. Repulsed at the image of John and Tessa making love, he closed his mind and gritted his teeth. He wanted to discard the ugly idea, and yet he couldn't. He didn't really know Tessa, not anymore. Maybe he never had.

"What do you mean?" she asked before she caught the message in Denver's stormy eyes. "You're kidding, right?" she whispered, lips twitching. "You don't really think I was John's—"

"Were you?"

Laughter died in Tessa's throat. Denver was serious. Dead serious. And there was a possessive streak of jealousy lighting his eyes. "Think about it, Denver," she taunted, wounded once again. "You tell me." Her back so stiff it ached, she strode out of the room and ran up the stairs to her room.

How could he think that she would sleep with his uncle? The ugly thought made her sick! She threw open the closet and began stripping her clothes off hangers, hurling them onto the bed and kicking shoes into the center of the room.

One thing was certain, she thought furiously, she couldn't stay here at the house with Denver. She yanked her suitcase and an old Army duffel bag from the shelf and heaved both onto the bed. Cheeks burning, she began attacking the drawers of her dresser with fervor.

She slammed the top drawer. It banged hard against its casing, rattling the mirror. "Argumentative, insensitive beast!" she muttered through clenched teeth just as she caught sight of Denver's image, staring at her from the mirror over the dresser.

He surveyed her scattered clothes expressionlessly. "Don't let me stop you," he drawled.

"You won't!" She threw her clothes haphazardly into the suitcase and stuffed the remainder into the duffel bag. "Believe me."

Not everything fit. Corners of blouses and sweater sleeves poked out of the bag and she had trouble closing the lid of the suitcase. Finally it snapped shut. Lifting her head high, she said, "I'll be back for the rest in the morning."

With the suitcase swinging from one arm and the duffel bag tucked under the other, she strode across the bedroom and waited, the toe of one boot tapping impatiently, for him to move. "If you'll excuse me," she mocked.

"No way."

"Move, Denver."

"Not until you explain what you were doing in this room."

Her hazel eyes snapped. "I don't have to explain anything to you, do I? You left me without a word—*not one damn word*! I don't owe you anything."

His mouth tightened, but he was wedged in the doorjamb and she couldn't get around him.

"This is stupid, Denver."

"Maybe."

"Let me by."

"As soon as you tell me why your father lives down at the ranch foreman's house and you live here."

The truth was on the tip of her tongue, but her pride kept her silent. She glared up at him, willing her heart to stop beating like the fluttering wings of a butterfly, praying that he couldn't see the pulse leaping in her throat or notice that her knuckles had clenched white around the handle of her battered old suitcase. "As I said, Denver, it was more convenient. Think what you want, because I don't really care."

She attempted to brush past him then, but as soon as she stepped one foot over the threshold, his arm snaked forward and captured her waist. So swiftly that she gasped, he dragged her against him. Feeling every hard muscle in his chest, watching the fire leap in his eyes, she knew she was trapped—pressed tightly against his hard frame.

Outside thunder cracked. Rain blew through the open window. The curtains billowed into the room. Yet Tessa couldn't do anything but stare into Denver's eyes. "What do you want me to say?'' she rasped, barely able to speak. ''Do you want me to say that your uncle and I were lovers?''

A muscle leaped to life in his jaw, and his lips flattened over his teeth.

''Or do you want me to say that he was just one in a long line—a line you started?''

His arm dropped suddenly, and she nearly fell into the hallway. Disgust contorted his features, but she couldn't tell if he was revolted at her or himself. ''You can stay,'' he said hoarsely. ''I'll take the room at the end of the hall.''

''I don't want to stay.''

He plowed his fingers through his hair and leaned back against the old wainscoting in the corridor. But his face remained drawn, his muscles rigid. ''It doesn't matter what happened. It's none of my business.''

''You're right, but it is your place.'' Wrestling up her bags again, she said, ''I'll go down to Dad's house.'' She dashed down the stairs before she could change her mind.

''Tessa—''

''I'll move back when I own the place.'' Shoving open the back door, she felt the rain and wind lash at her face. She took two steps toward the garage before she remembered she had no car. Her father had the pickup, the station wagon was in the shop, and her brother, Mitchell, had borrowed the old flatbed.

''Wonderful,'' she muttered, soaked to the bone almost before she started walking. If she cut through the fields, the trek was only a quarter of a mile—if she took the road, the distance tripled.

She glanced longingly back at the farmhouse. The windows glowed in the night—warm, yellow squares in the darkness. Setting her jaw, she shoved open the gate and started across the wet fields.

Before she'd gone ten yards, she felt a hand clamp on her shoulder and spin her around. ''You little idiot,'' Denver hissed.

''Let go of me!''

"Not until you're back in the house!" He snatched her bags with one hand.

"I'm warning you—oooh!"

Hauling her off her feet, he threw her, fireman style, over one shoulder, one hand wrapped around her ankles in an iron vise.

"Let me down right now! This is ridiculous!" *Damn the man.* But he didn't heed her muttered oaths or flailing fists as she pummeled his back.

"Denver, put me down! I mean it."

Tightening his grip on her suitcase and bag, he strode purposefully back to the house. Mortified, she had to hang on to the back of his shirt for fear of sliding to the sodden ground. Her hair fell over her eyes, rain drizzled from her chin to her forehead, and she silently swore that when she was back on her feet again, she'd kill him. He hauled her up the steps and into the house.

"There you go," he said, depositing her unceremoniously on the floor, once they were back in the kitchen.

"Of all the mean, despicable, low and dirty tricks—" she sputtered, planting her fists firmly on her hips.

"And what were you planning to do—ford the stream?"

"There hasn't been a drop of water in the creek for over a month!"

"Why were you walking?"

She didn't bother with an answer. Still fuming, she raked her fingers through her wet hair and hoped to hold on to the few shreds of her dignity that were still intact.

He glanced to the floor, where the duffel bag and suitcase sat in a pool of water on the cracked linoleum. As if noticing the Army bag for the first time, he bent on one knee and fingered the tags still tied to the duffel's strap. "Private Mitchell Kramer?" He stared up at her, his brows drawn into a bushy line. "Your brother is back?"

She nodded. The less she said the better.

"I thought he left after the fire."

"He did."

"So when did he show up?"

"Six months ago. You've been gone a long time, Denver. Mitchell's hitch was over last year. He's going back to school in a few weeks."

Frowning, he studied the name tags then straightened. "So where is he?"

She shrugged. "Around. Probably in town tonight. It is Friday."

"Still raising hell?" Denver asked.

Bristling, she snapped, "That was a long time ago, Denver. Mitchell's changed."

"Has he?" Denver asked sarcastically.

Tessa couldn't begin to explain about the mixed emotions she felt for her brother. He'd stood by her after the fire, when Denver had left her aching and raw—lost and alone. It was true that Mitchell had joined the Army soon after the blaze, but he was back, and for the most part, he'd straightened out. The hellion he'd been after high school had all but disappeared. "Mitchell's been through six years in the Army. He's grown up. If you haven't noticed, a lot of things have changed around here!"

"That they have," he said quietly, his gaze lingering in hers. "That they have."

Tessa's heart started thudding so loudly that she was sure he could hear it.

"Look, why don't you go upstairs, put those—" he motioned to the bags "—away. You said something about a hot bath earlier."

Tessa was chilled to the bone. A soak in a tub of warm water sounded like heaven. But she wasn't convinced that staying in the same house with Denver McLean would be smart or safe. "And what about you?" she asked.

"As I said, I'll move into the room down the hall."

"I don't think that would be such a good idea."

"This is my house," he reminded her. "And it's only for a week. Two at the most."

Knowing she was making a mistake, Tessa relented. Wet, dirty and just plain tired of arguing with him, she decided one night wouldn't hurt. In the morning, after the shock of seeing him again had worn off, she'd decide if she should move out.

"Just for tonight," she said, hoisting her bags.

"I can take those," he offered.

"No thanks." She hauled her bags up the stairs, and unpacked her nightgown and robe. Feeling like a stranger in her own home, she hurried to the bathroom, locked the door and stripped off her wet clothes.

Steam rose from the tub as she glanced in the mirror and groaned. Her hair was lank and wet, her face smudged with mud, her skin flushed from the argument. "This is crazy," she told herself as she stepped into the hot water. "Absolutely crazy!"

Denver poured himself a stiff shot. His second. Nervous as a cat, he paced the study, listening as the ceiling creaked. He knew the minute she dashed down the hall to the bathroom, heard the soft metal click of the lock, felt the house shudder a little as she turned on the shower and the old pipes creaked.

Closing his eyes, he imagined Tessa stepping into the bath and wondered if her body had aged, or if it was still as supple and firm as the last time he'd been with her. Groaning, her image as vivid as if their lovemaking had been only yesterday, he gritted his teeth. "Forget it, McLean," he warned himself, tossing back his drink.

Swearing loudly, he dropped into the chair behind the desk and started working on the invoices. But he couldn't concentrate. Aware of the water running, he listened until the old pipes clanged and the hum of the pump stopped suddenly. Gripping his pen so tightly that his knuckles showed white, he leaned back and listened as she unlocked the bathroom door and padded softly to her room—his parents' old room.

Why the devil was she living in the house? He wanted to believe that she'd moved in after John died, to manage the old house and keep it running. But he knew better. She had admitted as much.

Had she been John's mistress? He doubted it. Yet uncertainty gnawed at him. She hadn't denied having an affair with the old man, but Denver wouldn't let himself believe her capable of making love to a man more than twice her age. He couldn't. Though, all things considered, it was none of his damned business. He'd given up any claims on her when he'd accepted the cold truth that she'd betrayed him.

He reached for the neck of the Scotch bottle again, intent on pouring himself another, then twisted on the cap. After shoving the bottle back in the drawer where he'd found it, he stood at the window and stared out at the night.

Lightning slashed across the sky, illuminating the ridge near the silver mine, the ridge where he'd first discovered how exquisite making love to Tessa could be. There had been women before and since, of course, but none of those brief experiences had been as soul-jarring as that one suspended moment in time when he'd made love to Tessa Kramer.

Angry with the turn of his thoughts, he yanked down the blind to blot out the picture, but it snapped back up again and the ridge was there again, knifing upward against the sky. He'd been a fool to return to this damned place; he'd known it and still he'd come back.

Tessa was just upstairs, lying in his parents' wedding bed of all places.

How, he wondered, fire burning hot in his loins, would he get through the night?

Chapter Three

As the first streaks of dawn filtered through her open bedroom window, Tessa tossed back the covers on the old brass bed. She'd barely slept a wink. Because of Denver.

"You're a fool," she muttered to herself as she tugged on a pair of jeans and buttoned her work shirt. Plaiting her red-blond hair away from her face, she caught sight of her reflection in the mirror and grimaced as she snapped a rubber band around the end of her braid. "You don't love him anymore," she tried to convince the hazel-eyed woman in the mirror. "And he never loved you—so just get through the next week and pray that he'll leave."

An old pain spread through her and she set her brush on the bureau. Denver had left before. Without a word. She could remember that night as vividly as if it had been twelve hours before....

"I want to see him!" Tessa demanded, planting herself squarely in front of the information desk of the hospital. For five days she'd been thwarted by the hospital staff, but no more. Though her letter had been returned unopened, her gift of flowers sent back, her visits refused, she wasn't about to be put off. Denver was somewhere in this hospital and she intended to see him.

"I'm sorry, Ms. Kramer, but Mr. McLean is to have no visitors," the nurse said, her mouth compressed firmly, her spine as rigid as the crease in her white uniform.

"I know his brother has seen him!"

"Colton McLean is family."

"But so am I," Tessa lied, persevering despite the woman's uncompromising stare. "I'm going to be his wife. I'm his fiancée!"

The nurse glanced down at Tessa's ringless left hand. "I'm sorry, Ms. Kramer. Doctor's orders."

Desperate, Tessa said, "Then let me talk to the doctor."

The nurse hedged, then picked up the phone at the desk. A few seconds later, Tessa heard the page. "Dr. Williams. Dr. Brandon Williams to the main lobby."

"Thank you," Tessa said, unable to sit on one of the cold plastic couches that lined the reception area. She paced instead, walking a worn path between a potted palm tree and a magazine rack. "Come on, come on," she whispered, glancing at her watch.

The seconds ticked by, and finally a thin man with sharp features, wire-rimmed glasses and thinning gray hair swept into the lobby. Wearing a white doctor's coat and carrying a clipboard, Dr. Brandon Williams was the epitome of authority.

"I'm Tessa Kramer," Tessa said, extending her hand.

He shook it weakly, then crossed his arms over the clipboard. "I understand you want to see Denver McLean."

"I'm his fiancée."

Dr. Williams's expression clouded. "I didn't know he was engaged," he said slowly, obviously doubting her.

"It's, uh, recent."

He shifted uncomfortably from one soft-leather sole to the other. "Listen, Ms. Kramer, you have to understand that Denver has gone through not only physical but emotional trauma," he said patiently.

"I realize that."

"He's very confused right now. Until the surgery—"

"Surgery!" she repeated, gasping.

"Cosmetic surgery," he assured her quickly. "But until he's convalesced completely, he doesn't want to see anyone."

"Anyone?" she asked, willing the horrid words over her tongue, "or just me?"

"This is difficult for him—"

"If I could just see him, talk to him. I know I could help," she insisted, glancing down the hall. She knew Denver was somewhere on the first floor, but had no idea which room.

"His brother and uncle are complying with his wishes— as I am. In a few weeks, after Denver's had time to deal with everything, he'll probably want to see you."

A few weeks. Tessa couldn't wait that long. It was a week since the fire, five days since she'd first tried to see him here, and now the doctor was talking about *weeks?*

Was it possible, as her father and brother had suggested, that Denver didn't want to see her? She swallowed back every ounce of pride she had. "Could you please tell him— right now—that I'm here. That I have to see him."

The doctor sighed, his thin face drawn. "It won't do any good."

"Why not?"

"Because I've spoken with him about you before. He doesn't want to see you."

"I don't believe it!" she said, stricken, her worst fears confirmed. "I won't. Not until I hear it from him!"

"I'm afraid that's impossible."

"Nothing's impossible!" she hissed, and started to half run, the soles of her boots muffled against the brown carpet. The fear that had been with her since the night of the fire gnawed at her, tearing a greater hole in her heart. Something wasn't right—something more than the terrible tragedy of the fire.

"Hey! You can't go down there!" she heard someone behind her yell, but she didn't stop.

"Miss—miss! Stop her! Oh, hell! Someone call security," another man said.

Tessa had been in the hospital only once before, but she tore down the halls, looking into private rooms, scanning the signs at each junction of the corridors. *Where was he? Where?*

She rounded a corner and collided with Colton McLean. She fell against the wall, the wind knocked from her lungs.

Colton's gray eyes were cold as slate. "What're you doing here?" he demanded, catching hold of her arm as she tried to scramble past.

"I have to talk to Denver."

"No way."

"Let go of me," she demanded, jerking on her arm as her eyes peered into the surrounding rooms. "He has to be here. Where is he, Colton?"

"You don't get it, do you?" Colton said, ignoring her question. "He doesn't want to see you."

"I don't believe you! If I could only see him—talk to him—" She wriggled free and started down the hall again, only to be met by two burly security guards.

"I think you'd better leave," the larger man said.

"Not until I see Denver McLean," she insisted. She was so close! She had to see him—tell him how much she loved him!

"If you don't leave on your own volition," the shorter guard added, his kind eyes understanding despite the rigid set of his shoulders, "we've been told to call the police."

"That wouldn't be a good idea," Colton added. "Your family's in enough hot water as it is."

"My family had nothing to do with the fire!" She glanced yearningly past the shorter guard's shoulder, down the hall to a wing labeled ICU. Intensive care! Of course! Desperate to see Denver again, she turned to Colton. "Please," she begged, "please tell him to call me!"

Colton's gray eyes flickered with sympathy before turning stone cold. "I'll tell him you were here," he said tautly as the heavier guard clamped a beefy hand over her upper arm and dragged her toward the doors.

The next day, she'd gone back to the hospital only to be told that Denver had been flown to a hospital in Los Angeles. All her cards and letters had been returned and even John McLean had kept Denver's whereabouts a secret. If it hadn't been for her brother, Mitchell, she wondered if she would have gotten through those first long, lonely weeks.

Now, as she thought of those seven lost years and the fact that Denver was back for the sole purpose of selling the ranch, her blood boiled. He had a hell of a lot of nerve, she decided, hurrying downstairs.

The house was quiet as a tomb, aside from the ticking of the grandfather clock in the hallway.

Tessa assumed that Denver, wherever he'd spent the night, was still sleeping. Relieved that she didn't have to face him, she poured water into the coffeepot.

Last night she'd reacted to him much too violently. His appearance had surprised her, but now that she knew where she stood, she'd be able to face him more calmly. Somehow, some way, she'd have to keep a cool head.

She'd just poured herself a cup of coffee and was prodding strips of bacon with a fork when she heard a creak on the stairs. Her heartbeat instantly went wild. She tried to concentrate on the meat sizzling in the frying pan, but she knew the moment he walked into the kitchen.

"Hungry?" she asked, without turning around.

"Starved."

Dear God, he sounded so close, and she was reacting to him as stupidly as she had the night before. With an effort she asked, "Will bacon, eggs and toast do?"

"Sounds great." She heard him pour coffee from the glass carafe on the counter then listened as a chair scraped against the floor.

Carefully, she forked sizzling bacon onto a platter, pushed down the button on the toaster, then cracked eggs into the frying pan. She felt his gaze boring into her back. When she turned to place plates on the table, she met his eyes briefly and her heart thundered.

Sleep still hovered in his eyes. Startlingly blue, they touched a vital part of her she had hoped was long dead. His hair was rumpled, falling over his forehead in a thick black thatch that matched the shadow covering his jaw.

"Rough night?" she asked, unable to resist baiting him.

"Rough enough. How about you?"

"I slept like a baby."

The corners of his mouth twisted a bit. "Don't tell me you woke up crying every two hours."

She couldn't help but smile. The fleeting glimpse of tenderness she'd seen in his eyes lifted her spirits. She slid into a cane-backed chair at the table.

He took a sip from his cup and motioned toward the food. "I didn't expect this sort of hospitality."

"I guess you got lucky."

His lips twitched. "No arsenic in the jelly?"

She smothered a grin. "Not yet. But you'd better be on your best behavior."

"Always am."

"Hah! Last night you came charging in here like a bloodthirsty pack of wolves! Arsenic would've been too good for you."

His gaze touched hers, remaining for a second before it shifted back to his plate. "You weren't exactly all cordiality yourself."

"I get that way when my character is assassinated."

Pretending that he didn't affect her, that she didn't notice the seductive glint in his eyes, that her heart wasn't slamming against her ribs, she buttered a slice of toast.

"I guess I deserved that."

"And more," she said, remembering his remarks about his uncle. A bite of toast stuck in her throat.

"I'll try to keep that in mind."

"Do."

He watched her closely, studying her movements before finishing his meal and shoving his plate aside. "I thought you had a cook."

"Milly usually gets here around nine-thirty. She makes lunch and supper for the hands, then leaves about seven. I may as well warn you now, you'd better not tangle with her. You might own this place, but she definitely considers the kitchen her turf."

"I'll remember that." He stared at her again with that same stripping gaze that stole the breath from her lungs. "There's something else I wanted to say."

Here it comes. "Oh?"

"Last night got a little bloody."

"You noticed," she said dryly.

"I said some things I didn't mean."

She lifted a skeptical eyebrow, but let him continue, hoping he didn't notice that her pulse was doing somersaults in the hollow of her throat.

"I was out of line."

"Way out of line."

He grimaced. "Right."

"Forget it," she said, trying to sound casual, as if nothing he said had wounded her so deeply that she hadn't slept a wink.

"Then we can start over?"

Her heart skipped a beat and her hands trembled. *Start over.* If he only guessed that for years she had prayed for just that—to start all over—from the beginning. Before the fire, before the lies, before he had turned away from her forever. She couldn't answer, but nodded quickly, hoping to find her voice as she cleared the table.

Denver set his cup on the counter and Tessa saw his hand. A few dark scars webbed across from his wrist to his fingers, the difference in skin tone barely discernible.

He, too, noticed the ugly reminder of the tragedy and shoved the disfiguring palm into his pocket. "It never lets me forget," he said, his jaw growing taut.

Instantly she pitied him, and the hard look in his eyes told her he must have recognized her pity for what it was. "Maybe we can't start over—not completely over," she said uncomfortably, avoiding his gaze. "But at least we can back up a little and ignore what happened last night."

"I doubt it," he ground out, shoving his hand under her face. "This—" he shook his palm under her nose "—won't let us." His eyes blazed, and any trace of tenderness had left his features. "I don't want your pity, Tessa. I don't want anything from you!" He shoved his hand back into his pocket and strode out of the room, his footsteps ringing up the stairs.

Stunned, Tessa decided to put as much distance as she could between herself and Denver. She slammed the back door as she strode through the porch and down the steps, away from that man and his mercurial temper. One minute he'd been kind and caring, the man she'd once loved—the next he'd once again become a bitter stranger.

Outside, the air was clean and clear. There wasn't a trace of the storm, not one solitary cloud to wisp across the blue Montana sky. The hills seemed to gleam, and the grass smelled fresh with the earthy scent of dewdrops clinging to the dry blades.

In the pastures, spindly-legged foals frolicked near their mothers, kicking up their heels and nickering noisily. In the larger fields, cattle grazed, moving lazily across the lower slopes of the surrounding hills. Tessa breathed deeply, slowly counting to ten, willing her emotions under control.

She paused near the barn and leaned against the fence. Brigadier whistled at the sight of her. His eyes ablaze with mischief, he tore from one end of his paddock to the other, his fiery red tail unfurling like a banner behind him.

"Show-off," Tessa whispered. She watched as the sleek chestnut trotted to the fence and shoved his head into her empty hand. "I'm sorry, boy, nothing today."

Disgusted, Brigadier snorted against her palm, tossed his head and raced to the far end of the paddock.

"You'd sell you soul for an apple," she called after him.

Boots crunched against the gravel.

Denver!

"And what would you sell yours for?" he asked.

"That," she said through clenched teeth, "is my secret."

He touched her shoulder and she moved quickly away. "I'm sorry."

"For what?" She faced him then, saw the remorse etched across his features.

His jaw slid to the side. "I can't stand pity."

"Then you won't get any from me."

"Good."

She stared into his eyes, then forced her gaze back to the paddock. To change the course of the conversation, she pointed to Brigadier. "He's my pride and joy. And he's not part of your ranch. I bought him and paid for his upkeep here out of my own pocket."

"I'll remember that," Denver said tightly.

"He's part of a herd of six. Brigadier and two of the mares, Ebony and Red Wing, are special."

"Where did you get them?"

"At auction. From one of the neighboring ranchers. You remember Ivan Aldridge?"

"Ivan the Terrible—that's what Colton used to call him."

"Right." Tessa frowned and ran the tip of one finger along the dusty fence rail. "Ivan's had a few rough years himself. Most every rancher in this valley has. Anyway, he had to sell Brigadier. Two years later, I found Red Wing. Ebony and the rest came later."

Denver's eyes narrowed on the small herd of pregnant mares. "Were they Aldridge's, too?"

Shaking her head, Tessa said, "All the horses came from different ranches."

Denver's gaze shifted back to her. "How could you afford to pay for them?"

"I don't see that it matters."

"Just curious."

"Sure." Denver McLean always had an angle. "Not that it's any of your business," she finally said, "but I'd saved some of the money and I borrowed the rest." Gathering her courage, she met his eyes and decided to go for broke and tell him the truth. "Of course no bank would loan me any money. I was still going to school and working here."

"Of course."

"Fortunately, John saw Brigadier's potential. He loaned me the money to buy the stallion."

"And how," he drawled, eyeing her suspiciously, "did you pay him back?"

"Stud fees."

Blue lightning flashed in his eyes and a muscle jumped in his jaw. But before he could ask any more questions, a green station wagon rattled up the drive.

Mitchell climbed from behind the wheel. Squaring his hat on his head, he approached Tessa and Denver. "So you really did show up," he said, his eyes narrowing on Denver McLean for the first time in seven years. He wedged himself between Denver and Tessa.

Denver returned Mitchell's cold smile. "Thought I'd better check on my investment."

"Investment?" Mitchell snorted. "I wouldn't be counting on retiring from this place if I were you."

"I'm going to sell it."

If this information surprised Mitchell, he hid it. His thin mouth didn't move beneath the gold-colored stubble covering his jaw. His gaze didn't flicker. He shoved a wayward strand of straw-blond hair from his face. "I figured you would."

"Your sister wants to buy me out."

"Does she?" Mitchell's brows shot up. He cast Tessa a questioning glance.

"Where's your father?" Denver asked. "I'd like to talk to him."

"He'll be here. He had to pick up some feed in town."

Tessa threw her brother a worried look. That was a lie. They both knew it. Tessa was going into town later for supplies, not Dad. She was about to correct Mitchell, but the look in his eyes warned her to stop, before she said something that would embarrass him or Dad.

Mitchell said, "When he shows up, I'll tell him you're looking for him."

"Do that." Denver shot a hard glance at Mitchell then strode into the house.

Tessa whirled on her brother. "Why did you lie?" she demanded.

"Because it's none of his business what Dad's doing." Mitchell started for the barn.

"He owns the place," she reminded him.

"How could I forget?" Mitchell threw open the barn door and walked swiftly to the medicine cabinet. He grabbed a bottle of pills. "I'll be working with the calves—"

"Dad works for Denver," Tessa cut in. "We all do."

"Don't I know it," Mitchell grumbled, jamming the bottle into the pocket of his jacket. For years he'd felt it his duty to protect Tessa, and obviously he still did. "Don't tell me you're on McLean's side!"

"Of course not."

"He's not interested in the ranch, you know."

"He doesn't claim to be."

"Look, Tessa," Mitchell said gently. "From what I hear, McLean's had plenty of women—so don't get any ideas—"

"I don't have any 'ideas,'" Tessa protested. "Denver doesn't interest me in the least!"

"Tell that to someone who'll buy it," Mitchell murmured.

"You think I'm lying?"

"Nope. I think you're deluding yourself. Just like you always do with Denver McLean."

Tessa wanted to throttle her brother. Instead, she decided to change the subject before things really heated up. "What was all that baloney about Dad being in town? Where is he?"

"At the house. Sleeping."

"Hung over?"

Mitchell shrugged. "I suppose. When I came in last night, I found him on the couch, passed out."

"Wonderful," Tessa said on a sigh. She slit the twine on a bale of hay and forked yellowed grass into the manger. "Denver won't be as understanding as John was."

Mitchell asked, "What's all this nonsense about you buying the place?"

"It's not nonsense."

"Just impossible," Mitchell decided.

"And why's that?"

"Financing, for one thing. Who's gonna back you now that old John's gone?"

"I've already talked to Rob Morrison at the bank."

Mitchell let out a hoot. "That guy? He's still wet behind the ears. How old is he, twenty-two? Twenty-three maybe?"

"At least he was willing to listen to me," Tessa grumbled.

"Big deal. He was probably hoping to put the make on you."

"No way—he was interested in what I had to say."

"Or sneaking a peek down your blouse when you were signing the papers."

"Knock it off!"

Yanking the pitchfork from her hands, Mitchell gave her a knowing look. "He's been after you for the past six months."

"That has nothing to do with it."

"Of course it doesn't," he mocked, shaking some hay into the manger as he winked at his sister. A crooked smile slashed across his jaw. "But it just might work, you know. His old man does own the bank."

"That's enough!" she said, ripping the pitchfork from his fingers. "I don't have to take this abuse from you." *Or Denver McLean,* she added silently. She was tired of inquisitions. "Don't you have something more important to do than snipe at me? Maybe you could muck out the barn."

"Touchy this morning, aren't we?" he teased. "I don't suppose that has anything to do with the fact that Denver's here."

"Out!" she muttered, aiming the pitchfork at his chest and jabbing playfully.

Mitchell took off his hat in a sweeping gesture and bowed. She poked at him again.

"I'm leaving already," he said, hands raised, backing toward the door. But as he reached the doorway, he added, "Just be careful, Sis. Denver's back. Don't let him walk all over you."

"I won't," she swore, lowering the pitchfork a little as he turned on his heel, opened the door and disappeared.

Denver snapped the file closed and rubbed his eyes. It was late afternoon, and he'd been studying tax forms, income projections, profit and loss statements and invoices for nearly six hours. The sandwich Milly had left him on the corner of the desk was still there, the bread dry, the filling oozing a little.

His stomach rumbled and he took one bite before tossing the rest back on his plate.

Tessa hadn't shown up at the house. He'd seen some of the crew assemble for lunch, staying only long enough to catch their names and tell a disappointed Milly that he couldn't join them.

Driven to check the figures and get out of this place with its painful memories, he'd worked until he saw several of the hands drive away. Though he listened all afternoon, he hadn't once heard Tessa's voice nor seen her through the window.

Also, Curtis Kramer hadn't bothered showing up at all. Not only had the old man avoided the den, but as far as Denver could tell, Curtis hadn't set foot on the ranch. Curtis could be anywhere, Denver told himself; the ranch was huge, and much of the spread wasn't visible from the house or this one solitary window. But still he felt uneasy. Something wasn't right, and it gnawed at him. He twisted his

pencil between his fingers and glowered at the stack of unpaid bills lying haphazardly on the desk.

Frowning, he stretched, hearing his back crack. For the
hundredth time he looked through the window. Where was
Tessa and what the hell was going on here?

Tessa climbed a back fence. She ran through the fields to
her father's house. He hadn't bothered showing his face all
day, and his absence was glaringly obvious.

She opened the gate and sprinted along a weed-choked
path to the back door of a small, rustic cabin. Originally this
house had been built as a temporary shelter for the first
homesteading McLeans. Little more than three rooms, the
cabin had quickly been replaced by the main house on the
knoll for the McLean family. Afterward, the cabin had become quarters for the foreman and his family.

Tessa had grown up here. She'd shared a room with her
brother, Mitchell, until the age of seven, when Curtis had
converted the back porch into a private room for his son.

She glanced around the yard. The grass was yellow and
dry, but the old tire swing still hung from a low branch on
the gnarled maple tree near the front porch. The screen door
sagged, and the hinges were so rusty they creaked as she
pushed open the door. "Dad?" she called as she strode into
the living room. "Dad—are you here?"

"Back here," he growled.

She followed the sound of her father's raspy voice to the
kitchen alcove where Curtis was scrambling eggs over a
wood stove. A cigarette burned unattended in an ashtray on
the windowsill and an open bottle of beer rested near the
back burners.

"Milly's expecting you for supper," Tessa said softly.

"Guess I won't make it."

"You have to."

He shook his head. His face had become lined with the
years, and the veins across his nose had broken. His hair,
snowy white, had thinned, but he was far from bald.
"Why?"

"You know why. Denver's back."

"Humph." Curtis snorted in disgust and drained his bottle.

Tessa noticed that the alcove reeked with the smell of stale beer. Empty bottles were stacked neatly back in their cases near the old refrigerator.

"What difference does that make?"

"A lot. He owns the place."

"Bah." Curtis scraped his eggs onto a plate and held up the pan, offering some of his haphazard meal to his daughter. She shook her head and watched as he lowered himself into the same chair he'd used for thirty years.

"Dad, listen, Denver wants to talk to you; he expects you to run the ranch—"

Curtis reached for his beer and took a long draft. "So what's he gonna do? Fire me?"

"Maybe," she said, panicked.

"Doesn't matter. He's plannin' on sellin' the place anyway, isn't he?"

"Yes, but—"

"But nothing. The new owner isn't going to want a man pushin' seventy to run the place, not even if his daughter is the best horsewoman in the state." He smiled a little then, his faded eyes shining with pride.

"*I* wouldn't fire you."

He glanced up sharply.

"I'm planning to buy the place."

"You?" He held his fork between his mouth and plate. "How're you going to manage that?"

"I've already talked to the bank, and if I have to I'll sell part of my stock—Brigadier, Red Wing and Ebony."

Her father snorted. "That's the craziest thing I've heard yet," he muttered. "The reason you want the ranch is to breed horses, so if you have to sell Brigadier and the mares what would be the point?" He shoved a forkful of eggs into his mouth and swallowed.

"I'll still have the other mares," she said. "Besides, when I buy the ranch, I'll own the McLean stock. Including Black Magic."

"Magic doesn't mean half to you what Brigadier does."

"I know. But he's a great horse."

"I don't know, Tessa," her father said, leaning back in his chair to study her. "You love those horses you plan on sellin'. Seems to me you aren't thinkin' straight. But then maybe you can't when Denver McLean's around."

"What's that supposed to mean?"

"Just what I said. You seem to lose all your common sense when that man looks your way." Disgusted, he took another bite.

"So do you," she pointed out. "Denver won't like it that you're not working. Mitchell and I can't cover for you all the time."

"Don't bother," Curtis grumbled as he scraped his plate into the trash. "Denver McLean's no fan of mine. He wasn't before the fire and he sure as hell hasn't changed his mind in the past seven years." He found his now-dead cigarette, frowned and lit another. "Take my advice and stay away from him."

"He'll only be around a week or two."

"Long enough." Blue smoke curled to the ceiling. "Maybe you should move back here while he's at the ranch. I don't trust him."

Tessa laughed. "You don't trust him, he doesn't trust you—this is insane." Shaking her head, she walked to the back door. "Don't worry about me."

"Just be careful," he warned, his pale lips thinning. "Denver's not the man he was."

"None of us are the same."

"You know what I mean."

"Yeah," she said, yanking open the Dutch door and stepping onto the front porch. "I know. Try and show up tomorrow, okay?"

"Don't know why," Curtis said, coughing.

He was right about one thing, Tessa mused. Denver had changed. Gone was any sign of the soft-spoken young man with that special wit and genuine smile. In his stead was a cynical man, hard-featured and grim, who didn't trust anyone.

The wind, warm and moist, pushed the straggling strands of hair from her eyes. She squinted against the lowering sun, staring at the tall ranch house silhouetted against a blaze of lavender and pink. The house had been owned by generation after generation of McLeans, and now she intended to buy it.

If she could.

Gazing across the golden meadows of stubble, she watched the ruddy-hided Herefords, heads bent as they plucked at the dry grass. Calves mimicked their mothers, trying in vain to eat the tiniest scrap of straw. Maybe Denver was right. Maybe she couldn't handle this much land alone.

But she didn't like being beaten; especially not by Denver McLean. Pride thrust her jaw forward mutinously.

Halfway across the field, she saw him. Her heart somersaulted. Backdropped by the fields and dusky hills, Denver looked again like the man she'd fallen in love with. He was still lean and trim, and his hips moved with the fluid grace of an athlete as he walked with quick, sure steps. His chest was broad, shoulders wide and he held his head high. The wind tossed his black hair away from his face, and his features, growing more distinct, weren't as hard-edged as they had seemed the night before.

"Where've you been?" he asked as he met her.

"I thought I'd check on Dad."

"He didn't show up today." It wasn't a question.

"No, he, er, wasn't feeling well." Nervously, she avoided his eyes.

"Mitch said he went into town."

She couldn't lie. He'd find out the truth soon enough. "No. Mitchell thought he had, but I took the truck in and picked up the feed."

"I could have come with you," he said softly, and stupidly her pulse leaped.

"You were busy."

"Not *that* busy."

They were closer to the house now, near a thicket of oaks at the corner of one field. The last rays of sun filtered through the branches, dappling the ground and casting luminous splotches on the few standing puddles that hadn't dried from the storm.

She glanced at him from the corner of her eye. "So, have you solved all the ranch's financial problems yet?"

"Hardly," he admitted, scowling.

"You could start by selling the place to me," she pointed out, placing herself squarely in his path. Overhead, leaves shifted restlessly in the wind.

"Not without Colton's consent."

"So get it."

"I will. Just as soon as I figure out where he is."

"Don't you have any idea?" she asked skeptically.

"Your guess is as good as mine. He's been undercover so long he's probably forgotten who he is." Denver felt the muscles in his jaw tighten, just as they always did when he considered his younger, reckless brother and his passion for danger. Since graduating from college, Colton had been traveling as a free-lance photojournalist, assuming fake identities to gain the most spectacular, honest camera shots of men fighting wars throughout the world. "Last I heard he was in Afghanistan. But that was a few years back."

"John never heard from him," Tessa said on a sigh. She reached up and grabbed one of the lowest branches of a small oak, and Denver took in the way that her upstretched arms pulled the cotton of her blouse taut over her breasts, showing all too clearly the pattern of lace on her bra and the dark peaks of her nipples.

Denver noticed everything about her. The way her hair shimmered gold in the fading light, the dusting of perspiration across her brow, the pensive pout of her lips and the provocative swell of her breasts. Beneath her tan, he noticed the small freckles swept across her nose and the flush to her cheeks.

Swallowing hard, he glanced away from her, concentrating instead on the cattle moving restlessly over the arid hills. "Why do you want this place?" he asked, his voice uncomfortably tight. The fragrance of her perfume caught in the breeze and swirled around him in a delicious cloud. "And don't give me some baloney about how hard you and your family have worked here. There's got to be more."

"There is. A lot more." She let go of the branch. The limb snapped up, leaves rustling. "I've never wanted to live anywhere else."

"You haven't been anywhere else," he reminded her, hoping to chase away her girlish fantasies, fantasies that could trap him as easily as they had her.

"I've been to Seattle, Dallas and Phoenix." Glancing over her shoulder, she added, "John thought I should see a little more of the world."

Denver's mouth thinned. "Did he?"

"Um-hmm. He liked showing me cities I hadn't seen."

"I'll bet."

"And of course, I went to college—not away to a campus, but I drove into Three Falls three times a week."

"Three Falls isn't much in the grand scheme of things."

"And L.A. is?" she taunted.

"Yes."

She arched one beautiful brow, saying more clearly than words that she didn't believe him.

"If you had ever gone there, you would have seen that Southern California is more than cars, smog, beach and Disneyland."

"I didn't get a chance, did I?" she said.

He moved quickly. One hand wrapped around her wrist and he pulled, yanking her to him. Her breasts crushed against his chest, her eyes were level with the determined line of his mouth, and she could barely breathe. "I thought we were going to put all that behind us," he growled.

She watched a muscle tighten in his jaw, smelled soap mingled with musk and wondered at the beads of sweat on his lip. "You're right. I shouldn't have said anything." He was too close—the pressure of his arms around her too possessive. Forbidden flames licked through her blood as she shifted her gaze to those blue, blue eyes.

"Why do you insist on taunting me?"

"Me, taunt *you*?" Her mouth dropped open, and in that second he groaned.

"It's more than that," he rasped. "It's as if you're deliberately fighting me."

"I only offered to buy the ranch. Nothing more."

"And you haven't meant to torture me?"

"What in the world are you talking about?" she asked, but her blood was already on fire, pulsing through her veins.

"This!" He covered her lips with his. They molded perfectly against hers, moving gently, the pressure bittersweet and familiar. Her knees buckled and she couldn't think, didn't let herself. His tongue was hard and wet and warm, pressing insistently against her lips.

She moaned softly, her mouth opening of its own accord. His tongue slid enticingly between her teeth to plunder the soft recess of her mouth. Her traitorous body wanted more. Seven years she'd waited for just this moment!

She drank in the smell of him, drowned in the power of his arms, felt the warm river of desire flow from deep within. She savored everything about him, tasting the salt on his lips, feeling as if she'd sampled a long-forbidden wine.

"Tessa," he whispered, barely lifting his head, his eyes glazed. "Don't do this to me."

"I—I haven't done anything."

He groaned and kissed her again, his lips stealing down the length of her throat, past her collar, to the V where her blouse met over her breasts.

He still cares, she thought for a wondrous moment, ignoring the part of her that thought he might be using her. Her fingers laced through the coarse strands of his hair and she let her head loll back.

Nuzzling lower, he pressed wet kisses to the hollow between her breasts, and she arched closer to him, her braid nearly dragging to the ground, her arms twined around his neck.

Her breasts strained upward, through two thin layers of cloth, and his mouth closed over one rounded mound.

Tessa's mind whispered a thousand warnings. She refused to hear any. Eyes closed, feeling the coming night shroud them, she was conscious only of the play of his lips across her breast.

She felt her blouse open, knew tiny buttons were sliding free of their bonds. Fresh air touched her skin, and then his tongue, quick and sure, stroked against the lace of her bra, torturing her so that she pressed her hips urgently upward.

"Sweet Jesus," he murmured just as his mouth closed over her breast, suckling gently, teasing with his teeth, leaving a wet brand against the patterned lace.

Tessa's fingers dug into his shoulders, past his shirt, deep into the corded muscles hidden by rough cotton. "Denver, please—" she cried, trying to tame the desire running like a swollen river out of control. A small needle of pride pierced the rapturous splendor fogging her mind. *Don't let him hurt you again! This time you may never get over him.*

"Please—what?"

She struggled with the words clogging her throat. "Please, stop," she begged, her voice hoarse and rough. "For God's sake, don't do this to me!"

His head snapped up, and the hand at her back dropped so quickly that she landed on her rear near a puddle. His face was white and lined, his eyes smoldering hot and blue. "Don't do this to *you*?" he choked out, wiping a shaking hand across his mouth as if her kiss revolted him. "Don't do this to you? Oh, Tessa, if you only knew!"

Without another word, he vaulted the fence, landed on his feet on the other side and, hands thrust deep in his pockets, strode toward the house.

"Bastard," she hissed, though the delicious salty taste of him lingered provocatively against her lips. A small part of her had hoped that he couldn't stop, that he had been as caught in that roiling river of passion as she had been. But she'd been wrong. She was just a distraction for him. Whatever he'd felt for her had died long ago, and she had no recourse but to face it.

She buttoned her blouse, and her fingers grazed the tender skin of her breasts, still moist where he had so recently suckled. Tears sprang to her eyes, but she pushed them back. Standing, she dusted off her rump, squared her shoulders and shoved aside any trace of sadness. *It won't happen again,* she told herself. She wouldn't let Denver McLean tromp all over her pride again!

Denver shoved the back door open so hard that it banged against the wall.

"What in the world?" Milly asked, nearly jumping out of her skin. She was pulling a chocolate cake from the oven. "Mr. McLean, is everything all right?"

"Just fine," he snapped, his black brows pulled together in a single line of frustration. "And call me Denver."

"All right," she said nervously. "Will you be eating with us in the dining room?"

"I don't think so."

"But you didn't take time off for lunch," she pointed out, her lips pursing.

"I had a big breakfast."

"Did you, now?"

He didn't bother to answer her. With long strides he headed straight for the den and closed the door behind him. The sooner he dug through the mounds of paperwork on this damned ranch, the sooner he could take off for Los Angeles and the sooner he would leave Tessa to rot here if she wanted to!

Furious with himself and his stupid impulse to kiss her, he shoved his hand through his rumpled hair and was disgusted to find that his fingers were trembling. So that's how he reacted to her!

"Bah!" Grimacing, he dropped into the chair and stared at that damned, traitorous hand. He noticed the scars running across his skin, remnants from the fire.

"Damn it all to hell," he swore, thinking of the bottle of Scotch in the desk. He reached for the handle of the second drawer and pulled hard. There it was—half full, amber liquid sloshing against the clear glass.

But he slammed the door shut again. Alcohol was no answer to what ailed him. He needed a woman. And not just any woman. His blood ran hot, desire burning feverishly for just one woman—Tessa.

No, Scotch would dull his mind, but it wouldn't stop the burning ache that scorched through his brain and settled uncomfortably in his loins.

He shifted, painfully aware of the bulge straining against his jeans. His only relief would come from lying with Tessa again and making love to her. But he wouldn't succumb. Making love to Tessa was the one pleasure he would deny himself, no matter what the cost!

Chapter Four

The next four days were torture. Tessa avoided Denver like the proverbial plague, and fortunately he left her alone. The kiss they'd shared beneath the oaks had charged the air between them—changed the complexion of their relationship, igniting old emotions that should have long ago smoldered into ash.

"You're a coward," she told herself, glancing into the rearview mirror as the old Ford bounced down the lane. She and Denver had studiously avoided crossing paths, even missing each other at dinner. Most of the time he was holed up in the study, and Tessa kept herself busy outside. At night, she found excuses to go into town, only to return late and wonder where Denver was.

Not that she cared, she told herself as she parked the truck near the barn and flipped off the ignition. She glanced at the house and sighed. Sooner or later, she'd have to face Denver again. If only he'd just pack up and leave, she thought angrily as she climbed out of the cab and glanced at the hazy sky. Tattered clouds floated high above the valley, and insects thrummed in the lazy afternoon. Overhead, swallows cried and vied for positions under the eaves of the barn.

Tonight, Tessa decided as she yanked open the barn door, she would talk to Denver and make a formal offer on the ranch.

She snapped on the lights then marched to the oat bin. Running her fingers through the grain, she didn't hear the door open again.

"Looks like the rats are havin' themselves a feast," her father said. He surveyed the bin with a practiced eye. "Maybe we should get another cat. Marsha doesn't seem to be doin' her job."

"Marsha's busy with four kittens," Tessa replied. The old calico had delivered her litter three weeks before. Hidden beneath the floorboards of the barn, the little kittens mewed softly. Even now, Tessa could hear their worried cries.

"Still—a good mouser is a good mouser."

"Tell Marsha that the next time you see her."

"Don't think I won't." He sat heavily down on an overturned barrel. "Denver cornered me today."

"Did he?" Tessa didn't look up. As if she had no interest in Denver whatsoever, she fixed her gaze on the dusty seeds running through her fingers. "What did he want?"

"The same old thing. I swear that man's a broken record." He shook out a cigarette and thumped it on the barrelhead. "He seems to think there's some reason this place has lost money—something more than what we've told him or what he can see in plain black and white."

"Meaning?" Tessa asked. Her hand stopped moving restlessly through the grain.

"He suspects me of mismanagement." Curtis's lips twisted cynically in the gloomy interior.

"He'll find out differently," she said.

"I doubt it. It really doesn't matter how hard we talk or what the figures say on paper, the man has it in his mind. It's that simple."

"So he's already convicted us." A heavy weight settled upon her shoulders.

"That's about the size of it. I guess we should be glad that he's only talking mismanagement rather than embezzling."

"Embezzling!"

"He claims some of the figures don't add up."

"Hogwash," she snapped, furious again. Ever since Denver had returned, her emotions had been riding a roller-coaster that was climbing steep hills and plunging down deep valleys, running completely out of control. "He's wrong."

"He's also the boss."

Damn Denver! Embezzling? That was the craziest notion he'd come up with yet!

"Calm down. Like I said, he hasn't really accused anyone yet—"

"He wouldn't!" Tessa cried. "He—he couldn't! No one's taken a dime."

Curtis's old eyes warmed fondly at his spirited daughter. "Just remember, Tessa, that man's got a chip on his shoulder—a chip that's grown to the size of a California redwood in the past seven years." He straightened slowly, his old muscles tight from sitting too long in one position. "Stay away from him," Curtis advised.

"I have."

"Smart girl."

I wish, she thought ruefully, not wanting to count how many sleepless hours she'd spent thinking about that one, earth-shattering kiss she'd shared with Denver.

Curtis clicked his lighter over the tip of his cigarette as he left the barn. Tessa heard him shuffle down the ramp leading to the main field. A few minutes later an engine caught, and through the open door she saw his old yellow truck rumble down the drive.

She had no excuse to leave the ranch, no errand to run, no friend's home where she could escape. Tonight she was stuck at the house. With Denver. And later, once she'd thought through exactly what she was going to say, he was going to get a piece of her mind!

Determined not to make the same mistake as she had under the oak trees, she walked into the tack room and took down a bridle. The leather was soft in her hands and the bit jangled as she hurried to the paddock where Brigadier, his nostrils flared, glared at her from the far corner.

"Come on, boy," she whispered, digging in the pocket of her jeans for the small apple hidden there.

The chestnut snorted, his eyes rolling suspiciously as she approached. He pawed the dusty ground, but couldn't resist the tantalizing morsel she held in her palm. As he reached for the tidbit, Tessa slipped the bridle over his ears.

"Serves you right for being such a pig," she teased as he tossed his head and stomped, one hoof barely missing the toe of her boot. "Careful," she said, laughing as she climbed onto his broad back and swung her leg over his rump just as he sidestepped. "Come on." Leaning forward, she pressed her heels into his ribs.

He stopped at the gate and waited nervously as she leaned over and pushed it open. Then, just as she caught her balance again, Brigadier bolted.

He took the bit in his teeth and raced across the dry earth, his hooves pounding, dust clouding in his wake. Wind screamed past Tessa's face, tangling her hair and tearing the breath from her lungs. Her fingers clutched the reins and wrapped in his silky mane as they tore across the fields.

She rode as she had as a girl, bareback and carefree. She didn't think about the ranch, about the unpaid taxes, the low supply of feed or the painful fact that she might have to sell this magnificent creature running so wild and free beneath her. Tessa hadn't felt this rush of joy in years. Seven years.

Denver had forced her to grow up before she was ready.

"And you were more than willing to," she muttered angrily as Brigadier slowed near the creek—or what had been the creek. Now just a winding ditch with a bare trickle of water threading through smooth, dusty stones, the stream cut through the fields on its path to the Sage River.

Near an old apple tree, she slid off Brigadier's back, tethered him and stretched out on the dry ground. The sun was just setting over the hills in the west. Fiery streaks of magenta and amber blazed across the wide Montana sky.

Leaning her head against the tree's rough bark, Tessa studied the shadows lengthening across the valley floor. Insects buzzed near the water, and somewhere in the distance a night bird cried plaintively.

The bird's call echoed the loneliness in her heart—loneliness she'd denied until she'd seen Denver standing in the barn door, the sheeting rain his backdrop.

Her heart squeezed at the memory.

Clouds gathered over the hills, clinging in wisps to the highest peaks. She heard hoofbeats and dragged her gaze away from the dusky sky.

Denver was riding toward her. Astride a rangy gray gelding, his hair tossed back from the wind, he reminded her of the last time she'd seen him upon a horse, the afternoon of the fire. Tessa's insides tightened and her heart did a stupid little flip. Though she'd wanted to avoid him, she couldn't stop the rush of adrenaline that flowed eagerly through her veins.

The gray slid to a stop at the edge of the creek. Denver swung his leg over the gelding's back and landed on the ground not ten feet in front of Tessa.

"What're you doing here?" she demanded, trying to ignore the sensual way his jeans stretched over his buttocks as he slid from the gray.

"Looking for you."

Her stomach knotted and her pulse jumped crazily. "Why? So you can accuse me of mismanagement and embezzlement?"

He grinned, that cynical slash of white she found so disarming. "You've talked to your father."

"Why don't you just leave him alone, Denver?"

"I will—soon." He stretched out beneath a tree opposite her, his legs so long, they nearly brushed her boots. "You've been avoiding me."

She shrugged. "I thought it was better this way."

He considered that. "Maybe," he allowed, his gaze drifting to the shadowy hills as he took a handful of dust and let it drift to the ground. "But I can't very well accomplish everything I need to without your help."

He needed her? Her heart constricted, but she ignored her leaping pulse. Wanting her help on the business end of running the ranch didn't mean he needed her. "What do you want?"

"Just some cooperation. Your father isn't too helpful."

"Do you blame him?" she asked.

"Maybe I did come on a little strong."

"The way I hear it, you practically accused him of embezzling."

"It didn't go that far."

"Didn't it?" she snapped. "Since the minute you set foot on this place, you've been insinuating that Dad's the sole cause for the cash flow problems here."

"I'm not blaming your father, Tessa."

"Sure. Just like you don't blame him for the fire!"

His lips tightened. "I thought we'd settled that."

"Far from it, Denver. Even though we're supposed to forget about the fire, none of us can because you never bothered to come back until you had to. We can try to ignore the fire, but it happened, Denver."

"Don't you think I know that?"

"Of course you do, but you don't have to wear your scars like war wounds, for crying out loud!"

He moved quickly. With the speed of a lightning flash, he rolled forward and caught her shoulders in his hands. She tried to scoot backward, but the apple tree wouldn't budge. Rough bark dug through the thin fabric of her blouse and into her skin.

"If you want to know the truth, Tessa," he growled, "I wish I could erase that ungodly night from my mind forever."

"Do you?" Lifting her chin, she met the fire in his eyes with her own blazing gaze. "I don't believe you. I think you've been waiting to come back, savoring the day when you could point your finger at all of us. All the stories that you heard, all the lies, have built up in your mind. And now you, in all your self-righteous fury, have the power to destroy everyone!"

His eyes glittered fiercely. "Is that what you think?"

When she didn't answer, his fingers curled over her shoulders, pressing deep into her muscles. "Maybe you're wrong."

"No, Denver. I heard the rumors, the gossip. It ran like wildfire through town. Dad was to blame—your parents were dead and you were nearly killed because of his carelessness." She blinked hard, battling wretched tears of shame. "The fact that you wouldn't talk to me, to any of us, only made it worse. And you—you believed Colton's lies! You wouldn't even talk to me—hear what really happened!"

"My parents were dead!" he retorted.

"It was an accident!"

As their furious gazes locked Tessa felt his anger. Raw and wild it surged through his muscles until the grip of his scarred fingers hurt her shoulder. "You tried and convicted my family without a trial," she insisted, still not backing down. "That's why Mitchell left for the Army—to get away. Dad tried to get me to leave too, to go away to college."

His eyes searched her face, his fingers relaxed a little. "Why didn't you?"

"Because someone had to stay! I love this place, Denver, and Dad couldn't face all the gossip, the speculation, the interrogation from the insurance company and the sheriff's department by himself."

"Noble of you," he mocked.

She felt as if she'd been kicked. Struggling against the lump in her throat, she whispered, "John believed in us."

"Good old Uncle John."

"That's right!" she shot back, tears drizzling from her eyes. "He was good!"

Denver saw her anguish. Guilt pricked his conscience, but his doubts, fueled by her tears over his uncle, tore at him. "How good?" he asked, eyes narrowing.

Gasping, she reacted—slapping him across his stubble-dark cheek. The sound of skin meeting flesh clapped loudly, startling birds overhead.

He sucked in his breath, then moved with lightning speed. Shoving her shoulders to the ground, he pinned her against the dry grass. His blue eyes flamed jealously as he straddled her. "How good?" he repeated. "Tell me about your relationship with John."

"Get off me, Denver," she said through clenched teeth, ignoring the warmth charging through her veins—the dizziness in her head. She couldn't feel like this, with him, not now. He'd insulted her so horridly, and yet a coiling desire deep within warned her that all too soon she'd lose her will and body to him again. All he had to do was kiss her—show her some trace of tenderness.

"I asked a question."

Was it her imagination, or was he rubbing suggestively against her, his taut jeans shifting slowly over her abdomen? He was on his knees, his weight evenly distributed so that he didn't rest on her, and yet she couldn't move. He placed the flat of one hand between her breasts, on the V of flesh exposed by the open collar of her blouse. His fingers spread lazily over her skin, grazing her bra. She began to ache inside and wanted to move with him. But she couldn't let him win, not this way.

Closing her eyes, she wounded him the only way she could. "John was the best."

Denver froze. He tried to tell himself that she was baiting him, but his fists balled and he saw red. Looking down at her, he shuddered. He wanted her as violently as ever, more with each passing day. He'd followed her to the creek with the express purpose of laying his cards on the table—telling her that he couldn't get her out of his mind, admitting that each and every moment without her had been torture. Just the night before he had opened the door to her room, had seen the moonlight playing on her rumpled hair, turning the blond streaks to silver, had watched in fascination as she'd groaned and turned over, her face innocent and unwary.

He'd used every bit of his energy to walk quickly back down the hall and stand for twenty minutes under the sharp needles of a cold shower.

Now, his legs holding her prisoner, her body warm against his thighs, his cheek still smarting, he shuddered, fighting the urge to undress her, make love to her—and suffer the consequences if she scorned him. Slowly he withdrew his hand.

Tessa willed her eyes open. Staring up at him, she caught a glimmer of pain in his eyes—or was it only her imagination? His face was in shadow and she tried to convince herself that he appeared sinister. But she knew better. Deep in her heart, she believed there was still some tenderness in Denver McLean. Buried beneath a charred layer of cynicism, this was the same man she'd loved with every breath in her body.

"Is this why you came out here, Denver?" she asked, her voice hoarse. "To prove that you're stronger than I am, to show me that you could have your way with me if you wanted to? To humiliate me?"

"What do you think?" he asked, but all the sarcasm had left his voice, and his jaw slackened.

"I hope to God that you didn't follow me to degrade me. I hope there's some shred of decency left in you."

He laughed hollowly. "Not much." But he swung his leg off of her and stretched out beside her on the grass.

She didn't move away. She didn't want to give him the satisfaction of thinking she was afraid of him. "That was a childish thing to do."

"And this wasn't?" he asked, rubbing the red mark on the side of his chin.

She sighed. "You deserved it."

"So did you."

"It wasn't the same thing. I just reacted."

"So did I."

"You tried to frighten me," she said. "But it didn't work. I'm not afraid of you, Denver, and you can growl and bluster and try to humiliate me all you want. I still won't be afraid of you!"

With a groan, he rolled onto his back and stared at the sky. The first winking stars blinked high in the heavens. "I don't want you afraid of me, Tessa," he conceded.

"You have a strange way of showing it."

Closing his eyes, he whispered, "I wasn't even going to come back, you know. John's attorney talked me into it." He shifted his gaze back to her face. "Then I thought I'd show up here, stay a couple of days and take off for L.A. again."

Tessa's heart began to pound so loudly it drowned the tiny gurgle of water in the stream. "And now?"

"God only knows," he muttered, staring at her as if he were memorizing her every feature. "Why aren't you afraid of me?"

"Because I know you, Denver."

"I've changed."

"Not as much as you'd like me to believe."

He eyed her skeptically, one dark brow arched.

"Okay, you've changed a lot," she admitted, "but basically you're the same man you were that afternoon on the ridge."

He sighed. "If you only knew," he muttered, picking at a dry blade of grass and watching it float on the breeze. "Nothing's the same, Tessa. Nothing will ever be." He sat up then, dusting his knees. "We both better face it."

But she wasn't through. She had to settle things with him. Reaching forward, she caught the front of his shirt, crushing the fabric in her fingers. "I'll never be afraid of you. You could have stripped off all my clothes and forced yourself on me, and I wouldn't have been scared."

His head snapped around quickly, his eyes filled with self-loathing. "Don't you know what just happened, Tess? Couldn't you feel it?" Trembling, he held up his hand, his

finger and thumb close together. "I was this far from rap-
ing you."

"No!" She shook her head violently. "You would *never*
force me."

His jaw set in revulsion, he muttered, "I guess we'll never
know, will we?" Rolling to his feet, he reached for the reins
dangling from his horse's bridle, then climbed into the saddle.

Digging his heels mercilessly into the gelding's sides, he
leaned forward. The gray leaped away, leaving a plume of
dust that sparkled in the moonlight as horse and rider disappeared.

Tessa wrapped her arms around her knees and refused to
cry. What had happened to her? Why couldn't she tell Denver the truth about her relationship with John, that she'd
only been his nurse after his heart condition had been diag-
nosed?

"Because he wouldn't believe you anyway," she whispered, kicking disgustedly at a clod of dirt with the toe of
her boot. Denver didn't trust her. He wanted to believe the
worst of her, and her pride had held her tongue.

She could argue her virtue until she was blue in the face
and Denver wouldn't listen. "Think what you want," she
muttered, as if he could still hear her. She grabbed the reins
and swung onto Brigadier's broad back. "Go right ahead!"

By the time she'd ridden back to the ranch and cooled
Brigadier, Denver was gone. His rental car wasn't parked
near the garage and the house was empty. She should have
been relieved, but she wasn't. There were still a few things
she'd like to set straight with him, one of which was that she
intended to buy the ranch. She'd already started the wheels
in motion. She had an appointment with the loan officer at
the bank the following morning, and she planned to stop by
the Edwards ranch. Nate Edwards, the owner, had always
been interested in Brigadier, and he'd once told her to contact him first if she ever wanted to sell the stallion. Tomorrow, she thought sadly as she climbed the stairs to the
second floor, she'd take Nate up on his offer.

Once in her bedroom, she stripped out of her clothes and tossed her blouse and jeans into a hamper near the bureau. She caught sight of her reflection in the mirror, her lean, strong limbs, slender hips and waist, small, high breasts. Her hair was a wild cloud of untamed strawberry-blond curls that fell past her shoulders.

How did she compare to the women Denver usually saw, the sophisticated women in Los Angeles? she wondered.

"Who cares?" she muttered, angry at herself. She found her robe and dashed toward the bathroom. Intending to sit in a hot bath until the water turned tepid, she turned on the spigots and started brushing the tangles from her hair. With swift strokes, she tugged the brush through the twisted strands and tried not to think about Denver and how much she'd wanted him to kiss her—to make love to her. The urge had been undeniable, and even though he'd intended to degrade her, she'd wanted him.

"You don't love him," she told her hazel-eyed reflection. "You can't!"

Still arguing with herself, she lowered herself into the tub, sucking in her breath as her rear touched the hot water. Closing her eyes, she sank even deeper, still trying to convince herself that her feelings for Denver had died with the years.

Three Falls, Montana wasn't much of a town in comparison with the cities and towns fanning out from Los Angeles. Denver drove down the main street, past a small college campus and into the business district. Most of the buildings were one or two stories, with neon lights blazing against the darkness.

The town had grown, he decided, noting a bank, motel, strip mall and two fast food restaurants that hadn't been around when he'd live at the ranch.

He pulled into the rutted parking lot of a tavern on the south end of town. The weathered plank building looked the same as it had years before. Once a livery stable, it was now the local watering hole and boasted a live band on the weekends.

The interior was dark. A smoky haze lingered over the crowd despite the noisy attempts of an old air conditioner to recirculate and freshen the air.

"What'll it be?" the bartender asked. A burly man with a ruddy complexion, flat nose and world-weary expression, he stared straight at Denver, then grinned. "McLean?" he asked, his sandy brows lifting. "Well, I'll be damned!"

Denver recognized him as soon as he spoke. He'd gone to school with Ben Haley. "How're you?"

"Can't complain. And yourself?" Ben's gaze narrowed, as if he were looking for the scars from the fire.

"I'm all right."

"What'll it be?"

"A draft."

Ben poured quickly and slid the mug over to Denver. "On the house. I own the place these days." He swiped at the scratched bar with a white towel. "I heard you were back at the ranch."

"Just for a week or two."

"Rumor has it that you intend to sell."

"Soon as I can," Denver admitted, sipping from his glass. "Know anyone who's interested?"

"Just Tessa Kramer," Ben replied as he caught a shapely redhead's eye at the end of the bar. She signaled and he poured her another drink. When he'd finished refilling her glass, Ben returned.

Denver twisted his glass in his hands. "Did Tessa tell you she wanted to buy me out?"

"No," Ben said, pouring another drink. "Tessa's brother, Mitch, he comes in here quite a bit. He mentioned something about it."

"What did he say?"

"Nothing much," Ben hedged. "Just that John was gonna make some provision for Tessa in his will—make sure she could buy the place." He frowned and looked away, almost guiltily. "She was awfully good to him."

"Was she?"

Ben shrugged his big shoulders. "Maybe he changed his mind."

"Maybe," Denver agreed as Ben was called into the kitchen. Denver studied the foam dispersing from his drink. He felt the familiar coil of jealousy tighten in his gut and told himself it didn't matter. What Tessa and John had meant to each other was none of his business. Still the idea of his uncle and Tessa together struck in Denver's craw. And no amount of beer could wash it away.

Chapter Five

She heard Denver return. Lying on her bed, ears straining, Tessa heard the scrape of his boots on the stairs and listened as he stumbled at the top step, swearing loudly.

He started down the hall, but paused at her door.

Tessa sucked in her breath, her every nerve end tingling. *What now?* The knob turned, the door opened. Denver stood on the threshold. Light from the hall threw the lean lines of his body into stark relief. His broad shoulders nearly touched each side of the frame. His hair fell over his eyes and the smell of liquor wafted into the room. "Tessa?"

"I'm awake." Her nerves were stretched tight as bowstrings. Sitting up, she clutched the sheet to her breasts and shoved a handful of thick hair from her eyes. "What do you want?"

"I wish I knew, Tessa. I wish to God Almighty I knew." Rubbing one tanned hand tiredly over his shoulders, he expelled a long breath. "I made a mistake today at the creek."

"Is this an apology?"

"Of sorts." He frowned and leaned one shoulder against the molding. "This afternoon—I just wanted to talk to you. You'd been avoiding me, and I really didn't blame you, but I figured it was time we got a few things straight. I saw you ride to the creek, so I followed."

"To talk."

"Right. But I blew it."

As her eyes adjusted to the darkness, she could see that one side of his mouth had curved in self-mockery.

"What 'things' did you want to get straight?" she asked, wishing she had the nerve to throw him out.

His eyes bored into hers. "Us."

"There was no 'us.' Remember?" She couldn't help wanting to hurt him—just as he'd wounded her.

"I guess that's what I said."

"And you were right."

"Of course I was." Still, he didn't leave.

Her teeth bit into her bottom lip. Here he was in her bedroom, for crying out loud, in the middle of the night, trying to apologize. Her mind was spinning and she was caught in the trap between trusting him and knowing that he was lying. "Then why are you here? Have you changed your mind?" she whispered, dreading the answer. "I mean, about 'us.'"

"I don't know." His jaw tensed. "I've never been so damned indecisive in my life. I hate it."

"And that's what you wanted to tell me?" Convinced that he was holding something back, she arched an eyebrow skeptically.

"There was another reason," he admitted, his eyes narrowing on the bed.

Tessa's throat constricted. "And that is?"

"Because I want you, damn it!" he admitted angrily. His fingers curled into a tight, impotent fist. "God knows I've tried to fight it, but the truth of the matter is, I've wanted you from the first time I saw you in the barn."

"Because I'm here. Because I'm convenient," she bit out, angry with herself and with him.

"Because you're *you*," he said heavily.

If she'd expected anything, it wasn't this kind of confession, and though a part of her longed desperately to hear just those words, the more rational side of her mind told her it was the liquor talking—not the man.

Dropping the sheet, she slid to the side of the bed. His eyes followed her every move as she grabbed her robe and shoved her arms down the sleeves.

"Don't," he said, when she tried to tie the belt at her waist. "Leave it open."

Jaw taut, she cinched the belt as hard as she could and swept across the room. "What do you really want from me, Denver?" she demanded, wishing he were stone-cold sober. "An affair? A quick roll in the hay? A little more 'experimenting'—isn't that what you called it—like we did when we were younger?"

He winced. "Of course not." His gaze drilled into hers. "I just want you."

Tessa's heart beat a quick double time, but she didn't trust him—couldn't. Not after her humiliation at the creek. Not after seven years of being treated as if she didn't exist. "The way you wanted me earlier?" she asked, feeling a hot flush of indignation steal up her neck.

"I said I was sorry—"

"I heard you." She inched her chin upward. "But I don't trust you, Denver. You've come back here practically accusing every member of my family of trying to rob or steal from you. You think we're all a pack of arsonists, embezzlers and liars. And you think I was your uncle's mistress." She could feel the flames leaping to her eyes, the anger burning brightly in her soul. Just because he wanted her was no reason to believe that he had ever loved her. So furious that her breasts were heaving, she placed her palms firmly on his chest and pushed. "I think you'd better leave."

His hands flew from his sides, capturing each of her wrists. They tightened possessively and his nostrils flared. "If you're through destroying my character—"

"Not quite," she retorted. "And now you have the audacity—the unmitigated *gall*—to think you can waltz into my bedroom, claim that you want me and think I'll fall into bed with you just because you're *sorry*?"

"Oh, no, Tessa. I've never thought you could be pressured into doing anything you didn't want to do." A furious muscle worked in his jaw, but his thumbs rubbed in slow circles along the insides of her wrists, and his smoldering gaze never left hers.

"Then what?" she demanded, trying to ignore the erotic feel of his gentle fingers.

"You've always given me a fight—a run for my money. But always before you've been honest with yourself."

"I am," she insisted, though her voice faltered a bit. If he'd only quit touching her, then maybe she could think!

"I don't think so."

"And what about you? Have you been honest with yourself?" she threw back, but his arms surrounded her and he kissed her fiercely. His lips were hard and sensual, and she could taste the liquor lingering on them. Her heart pounded erratically, beating like the wings of a frightened bird, thudding wildly against her ribs. All the taunts forming on her tongue disappeared into the shadowy corners of the room.

Though she tried to push away, he held her close, hands splayed across her back, forcing her to curve against him, hips and thighs pressed tight, the thrust of his desire hard against her abdomen.

"Get out," she commanded, but even as the words passed her lips, she'd circled his neck with her arms, her mouth returning all too eagerly to him. Heat, liquid and dangerous, began to curl within her, and she had trouble breathing, couldn't think. "Don't—"

"Don't what?" he whispered across her ear, and she shivered with the ache that was building out of control.

"D-don't touch me—oohh." She felt his hand move forward along her belt, untying the knot. The terry fabric parted and his hands delved inside, long fingers searching.

"You want me to stop?"

"Y-yes. Oh, Denver, *please*!" She shuddered when he touched the firm point of one hard nipple and could barely hold back a cry when he bent his head and took that hard little button, hidden in the folds of soft cotton, in his warm mouth.

Her fingers tangled in his hair, she held him close, and her legs seemed to turn to water. She felt each tiny button of her nightgown as it slipped through its hole, knew when the yoke had parted and the cool night air touched her breast. Still he toyed with her through the cloth, the fabric wet and hot as his tongue searched for and laved her nipple.

"Please?" he repeated, his voice hoarse.

Moaning softly, she tried to fight the tide of desire that kept pulling her under its warm, liquid depths. Her head was swimming, her breath trapped deep in her lungs, but one tiny scrap of her pride surfaced. "Please, *don't*—don't—try to humiliate me again. Don't use me."

He stopped then, his muscles instantly rigid. "Never," he whispered, straightening, his hands moving swiftly to her chin, forcing her to look deep into his eyes. "I *am* sorry, Tessa," he vowed, his voice filled with regret. "I've never meant to hurt you."

And yet he had. She'd died a thousand deaths all those years ago, just thinking that he'd used her—that she'd meant nothing to him. And again, when he'd seen her in the barn and denied loving her at all. Her throat was hot, her eyes luminous with unshed tears.

He brushed one solitary drop from her lashes and cursed under his breath. "What the hell am I going to do with you?" His thumb caressed the curve of her cheekbone and she felt him tremble.

"I—I can handle myself," she murmured.

"I know you can, Tess." With a sigh, he swept her off her feet and carried her back to the bed. She buried her face in his neck, drinking in the clean scent of him, the powerful feel of his muscles. She kissed the warm crook of his neck.

"Stop it!" he rasped. "I'm trying to be noble here."

"Noble?"

Before she could say another word, he tucked her robe around her and drew the covers to her neck.

"You're leaving?"

"If and when we make love again—"

"Don't flatter yourself," she snapped, lashing back. He was rejecting her again!

His night-darkened eyes searched her face. "Next time, there will be no regrets."

She shoved the covers aside and sat up in the bed. "There won't be a next time!"

The cords in his neck protruded. "Stop pushing, Tessa. You're lucky I still have some self-control."

"Sure," she taunted, thrusting her chin forward defiantly. "Now just leave!"

His jaw worked and his eyes clashed with hers. Then, as if afraid he might change his mind, he turned on his heel and strode quickly out of the room. A few minutes later she heard the shower running.

The next morning Tessa didn't waste a minute. She'd spent most of the night laying plans, and today she intended to put them into action. If the night had proved anything, it was that she was still just as susceptible to Denver's charms as she'd ever been. Ignoring the traitorous part of her heart that had argued long and hard with her, she reasoned the sooner she sent him packing to L.A., the better.

She showered, then dressed in a wheat-colored linen suit and magenta blouse. Curling her hair, she twisted it into a thick braid at the back of her head before stepping into tan heels and adding color to her lips, cheeks and eyes. With a satisfied glance at her reflection, she decided that she was ready to face Rob Morrison at Second Western Bank. He'd indicated that he would loan her the money to buy the ranch. Now she had to make sure he was as good as his word.

Downstairs, Milly was already bustling around in the kitchen. Apple pies were cooling on racks by the windows and she was poking at the corners of the floor with her broom.

"I won't be around for lunch today," Tessa said.

"You skip too many meals, if you ask me." Straightening, Milly set the broom in the corner, then eyed Tessa up and down. "My, don't you look nice."

"Nice?" Tessa repeated, rolling her eyes. "I don't want to look nice. How about professional or sophisticated or chic?"

"All of the above," Denver said as he opened the door from the back porch. Unshaved, hair mussed, he was squinting, as if the morning light were much too bright.

Smothering a smile, Tessa realized he was suffering from a hangover. Good, she thought wickedly. Serves him right!

Milly took pity on him. "How about a cup of coffee?"

"And about two dozen aspirin," he said, forcing a smile as he fell into one of the table chairs and studied Tessa. "Where are you going?"

"To the bank." Placing the cup on the table in front of him, she offered him an emphatic smile. "I have an appointment with Rob Morrison."

"Isn't he a teenager?"

"He was, Denver. Not only has he graduated from high school, but college, and now he works for his dad as a loan officer."

"I remember when he was still stealing hubcaps and shooting the hell out of mailboxes," Denver grumbled.

"No more," Milly said. "Rob's become a real straight arrow. Belongs to the city council and all. Time didn't just stand still, you know."

"So I've been told," Denver admitted, his gaze catching in Tessa's. Lord, she was beautiful. "Over and over again."

"Guess you're a slow learner," Milly observed as she shoved the broom in a cupboard on the back porch.

"I guess so." Denver couldn't take his eyes off Tessa. Seeing her dressed as a lady—no, as a businesswoman—did strange things to him. She was fascinating enough in her jeans and work shirts, her attractive ranch-tough veneer. But dressed elegantly, in an expensively tailored skirt and jacket, she made him face the fact that she was truly the most captivating woman he'd ever met. The fire in her stormy hazel eyes, the proud lift of her chin and the confident set of her shoulders were potent and evocative.

Seven years ago he'd been attracted to her, maybe even loved her, but her innocence and spunk had been childishly intriguing. Now, he was faced with a full-fledged woman, a mature woman who knew her own mind, a woman he'd tried to humiliate the day before, a woman he'd nearly made love to last night.

The phone rang and he realized he'd been staring.

"I'll get it," Milly called out as she reached around the corner and picked up the receiver. "McLean Ranch," she answered brightly, then glanced sharply at Denver. "Yeah, he's here. Just a minute." She held the receiver toward Denver. "Long distance," she whispered. "Jim somebody."

"Van Stern," Denver said, placing his cup on the table. "My partner. I'll take it in the den." With a quick glance at Tessa, he strode out of the room. A few seconds later Milly replaced the receiver.

"I wonder what that was all about?" the housekeeper muttered.

"He does have a business in L.A., you know." Tessa finished her coffee. "Maybe Van Stern wants him to go back to Los Angeles. Denver only intended to stay a few days." That particular thought should have been uplifting, but Tessa's spirits didn't soar. Quite the opposite. After she'd avoided him for days, swearing to herself that she didn't care for him, not one little bit, that her attraction to him was just chemistry, the thought that he would suddenly be out of her life was difficult to accept. Frowning, she reached for her purse and said, "I'll be at Second Western Bank this morning, then I'll stop over at Nate Edwards's place. I should be back in time to feed the stock, but if I'm not, tell Mitchell he can handle it.''

Milly snorted sarcastically. ''He'll like that a lot.''

''I know, but he can just bloody well do it.'' With a wave she walked out the back door.

Second Western Bank was a two-story concrete structure on the corner of Main and First streets. With its narrow, black-framed windows, the square gray building looked more like a jail than a financial institution. Only a few trees and shrubs planted between the bank and parking lot softened the sharp angles.

A security guard was posted in the front entrance, and inside, the main lobby floor was brick, shined to a glossy finish. If only there had been bars on the windows, the penitentiary decor would have been complete.

Rob Morrison was waiting for her in his office on the second floor. Less austere than the rest of the bank, his corner suite was decorated with a few oil paintings of rugged coastlines and high mountains, cream-colored furniture and thick burgundy carpet.

Rob rose from his chair when she arrived. A thin man with rust-colored hair, freckles and narrow features, he extended his hand. ''Tessa! What a pleasure,'' he said, smiling and waving her into one of the side chairs near his desk. ''What can I do for you?''

''Guess.''

''The McLean ranch, right?'' He twisted his pen in his fingers.

''Right. I'd like to take out a loan and buy the ranch.''

Still twisting his pen, Rob leaned back in his chair. ''All of it?''

She nodded. ''Unfortunately, no one's been able to find Colton, and he owns half the place.''

''You don't think he'll want to buy out Denver's share?''

''Do you?'' she asked.

Rob laughed. ''It's doubtful. The last I heard, Colton was in Afghanistan or somewhere.''

"Even if he can't be found, I still want to buy out Denver's share."

"He wants to sell?"

"In a hurry," she said, smiling dryly. The one trait that hadn't changed in Denver was his need to escape. He intended to leave Montana as quickly as he could, and though she tried to tell herself that his departure was for the best—that she'd lived well enough without him—she couldn't forget his words, loosed by liquor. *If and when we make love again, there will be no regrets.*

"Have you settled on a price?" Rob asked.

"Not yet."

"That's the first step. As soon as you and Denver and Colton work out an agreement, I'll go to work. I'll give you the loan application forms and you can take them with you. The land will be mortgaged, of course, but the bank will require a down payment. You can work that out with Denver."

Tessa wasn't sure she could work anything out with Denver, but didn't say so. A few minutes later, she was back in her car, driving south.

Nate Edwards's ranch was all that the McLean ranch wasn't. The main house looked as if it were more suited to a Southern plantation than the windy hills of Montana. Rising three full stories, the shiny white exterior was punctuated with huge bow windows and cobalt-blue shutters. A porch, complete with an old-fashioned swing and wicker furniture, ran the length of the building, as did an upper balcony.

The ranch buildings and fences were all of gleaming white. A lake fitted with huge irrigation pipes forced water across the dry acres. Even in late August, the grass on Nate Edwards's property was healthy and green.

Tessa parked her car at the curve of a circular drive and mounted brick steps. She rang the bell and waited until Nate's wife, Paula, opened the door. Red-haired and younger than her husband by fifteen years, Paula grinned widely.

"Tessa! This is a surprise. Come in, come in," she invited. "It's about time you stopped by. Sherrie's been asking about you."

"I've been busy," Tessa explained, feeling a little guilty. She and Paula had been friends since high school, and Paula's daughter, Sherrie, was a child after Tessa's own heart.

"Who is it, Mommy?" a small voice called as Tessa stepped inside the cool interior.

Glancing up, she spied a dark-haired imp on the landing of the stairs. "Don't tell me you don't remember me," Tessa said.

The child squealed in recognition. "Tessie!" she cried, hurrying down the sweeping staircase and running into Tessa's outstretched arms. "You promised to take me riding!"

"That I did."

"Over my dead body!" Paula interrupted, wagging a finger in front of Sherrie's pert little face. "You can't ride until you're five, remember."

Sherrie crossed her plump little arms over her chest. "I won't *ever* be five."

"Sure you will," her mother teased, touching the tip of Sherrie's nose with her finger and winking at Tessa. "Come out to the back porch. I've got a pitcher of iced tea in the refrigerator, and Sherrie and I baked cookies this morning."

"Apple squares!" Sherrie chimed in, scrambling from her mother's arms and making a beeline for the kitchen. "I'll show you."

The kitchen was as formal as the rest of the house. Gleaming pans hung from the ceiling, marble counters stretched around the room and every appliance sparkled. On the center island were two huge platters of warm cookies. Sherrie picked out the largest square in her plump little fingers and handed it to Tessa. "Try it," she commanded, her eyes bright, her pink cheeks flushed.

"Delicious," Tessa pronounced as she bit into the gooey confection.

"I know," the girl said proudly.

Paula promptly lectured her daughter on the virtues of being humble.

Hiding a grin, Tessa strolled outside. Paula joined her a few minutes later on the back porch. While Sherrie picked flowers in the garden, Paula and Tessa sat beneath a table umbrella and sipped from frosty glasses of iced tea.

"So where've you been this morning?" Paula asked, eyeing Tessa's suit.

"The bank. I'm trying to buy the ranch. That's why I'm here." Tessa shoved her hair from her eyes and watched Sherrie pick the petals off a budding rose. "I wanted to talk to Nate about Brigadier and a couple of mares. He was interested in buying them once."

"Still is," Paula said. "He's never forgiven you for buying that stallion right out from under his nose at the auction.

"I guess he has a chance to get even."

Paula studied the ice cubes dancing in her drink. "I hear Denver's back."

"For a while," Tessa replied, her eyes squinting against the sun.

"How's it going?"

"So far, so good," she said, knowing she was evading the truth. Paula was a trusted friend, but Tessa doubted she could understand the tangle of emotions that linked Denver and Tessa as well as drove them apart.

"You don't think you can convince him to stay?"

Tessa shook her head. "I couldn't before the fire, and now...a lot has happened. Besides, we have separate lives now. He loves L.A. I like it here."

"You've never been to L.A.," Paula reminded her gently.

"I know."

"Aren't you just a little curious?"

"About what?"

"The city. The beach. Why Denver lives there?"

Tessa blew a wayward strand of hair from her eyes. "A little," she admitted. In truth, she wanted to know everything about Denver. What he'd done the past seven years. Where he'd lived. With whom he'd shared his life.

"You loved him once," Paula reminded her.

"I was young—and foolish."

Paula, always the matchmaker, lifted a lofty red eyebrow. "So, if you're not still hung up on Denver, why haven't you married?"

One corner of Tessa's lips curved upward. "Maybe I haven't met the right man."

"Oh, you've met him, all right. And you're living under the same roof with him. If I were you, I'd use that to your advantage."

"It's not that simple."

"I don't know," Paula mused, her eyes crinkling at the corners. "Seems to me, life's as simple as you make it. You're not married. Denver's still single, and you used to be so in love with him that you couldn't think of anything else. Some thing's just don't change."

"I'll remember that," Tessa said, finishing her drink and finally turning the conversation away from Denver to Paula and her plans for Sherrie.

Two hours later, as she drove back to the ranch, the interior of her car so hot she had begun to perspire, Tessa considered Paula's advice then promptly discarded it. Denver had come back to the ranch to sell it. Period. His return had nothing to do with her—he'd admitted as much that first night when he found her in the barn. Any tenderness he'd felt for her had died in the fire. Even the night before, the gentle way he'd touched her had been because of the alcohol he'd consumed—nothing more.

Hands shoved deep in his pockets, Denver walked through the gloomy machine shed, eyeing each battered piece of equipment and remembering some of the older rigs. The combine, mower and drill were the same he'd used himself. Trailing his finger along the dented seat of the old

John Deere tractor, he frowned. He'd spent more hours than he wanted to count chugging through the fields, dragging a harrow or hay baler behind. From the time he could first remember, he'd wanted out—a chance at another life. Years ago, before the fire, he'd thought he would claim that life, make a name for himself as an engineer, study for an M.B.A. and marry Tessa Kramer.

But, of course, things hadn't turned out as he'd planned. And now, he wasn't so sure that he was ready to leave.

Scowling darkly, he dusted his hands, as if in so doing he could brush aside any ties that bound him to this land.

Though ranching wasn't what he'd dreamed of all his life, he'd found a quiet peacefulness here that he hadn't felt in years; the slower pace was a welcome relief from the tension and stress in L.A. Even his condominium on the beach in Venice didn't interest him. Not without Tessa.

He hadn't really acknowledged his growing attachment to the ranch—or was it his fascination with Tessa?—until his partner had called, reassuring him that things were slow in the engineering firm and that he could handle everything for a few more weeks. Oddly, Denver found the extra time soothing.

He shouldered open the door and stopped suddenly. There, only forty yards directly in front of him were the charred ruins of the stables. The debris had been hauled away years before, but a few blackened timbers, now overgrown with berry vines, were piled near what had once been the concrete foundation.

Though the wind was hot, he shuddered as memories of the blaze burned before his very eyes. Once again, he was seven years younger....

Fire crackled high in the air. Smoke scorched his lungs as he ran to the stables. Horses screamed in terror, and fear thudded in his heart. Inside the heat was so intense, the roar of the flames so deafening, he couldn't see or hear. Throwing one arm over his mouth, he held his breath and moved by instinct, fumbling with locks on the stalls, hoping to set free a few of the scrambling, terrified animals. Stallions and mares squealed. Kicking madly, they bolted as soon as Denver tore open the gates.

He heard a cough, then a tortured cry, and he whirled toward the tack room. God, were his parents trapped inside? *Hold on,* he thought, *I'm coming. Just hold on!*

As he stepped forward, a blast ripped through the stables, throwing him off his feet. His hands scrabbled in the air, catching on the bit of a bridle still dangling from the wall. The scorched leather snapped and he fell to the floor. In his last few seconds of consciousness he knew he would die....

"Denver?"

He whirled, the old memories fading as he stared into Tessa's worried eyes. Standing only inches from him, her golden hair catching in the breeze, a small smile quivering on her lips, she whispered, "Are you all right?"

"Fine," he muttered, praying silently that he would become immune to the fragrance of her perfume and the tenderness in her perfect features. The vision had been so real—so ghastly—that once again he remembered how she'd betrayed him. He swiped at his forehead with a shaking hand and noticed the beads of sweat lingering at his hairline.

"You...seem..."

"I said I'm fine!" he growled. If she would only go away so that he wouldn't notice the way the hem of her skirt flirted around her knees or the shapely length of her calf. Right now, when his emotions were still raw, he couldn't talk to her objectively, couldn't slow the thundering rush of adrenaline in his blood. As much from her nearness as from the horrifying memory, his heart was hammering crazily, pumping blood in a rush that echoed through his brain.

She glanced at the ruins of what had been one of the grandest stables in the county. "It's not easy," she said softly—her voice as gentle as a lazy summer breeze. "I know. But it's over. It was over a long time ago."

"I only wish to God it were," he said through clenched teeth. The memory of his parents seared through his mind until he willfully shut the agonizing thoughts aside.

Tessa swallowed hard. "I never said I was sorry," she said quietly. "About what happened. But I am. You know that I cared for your father and mo—"

"It wasn't your fault, remember?" His voice was like a whip cracking with sarcasm.

"Empathy has nothing to do with blame!" Her eyes blazed with gray-green fire and her small chin wobbled. "Hide it from everyone else and hide it from yourself, damn you, but don't try to hide it from me! I know you too well."

His eyes narrowed maliciously. "*Knew* me. Past tense. You don't know me at all anymore."

"You think not? You think I can't see past that hard shell you've covered yourself with? Think again, Denver. Think back to what we meant to each other!"

"I already told you what we meant."

Flushing furiously, she jabbed a finger at his chest. "So you did. You tried to hurt me, Denver, and you did one hell of a job at it. But I knew you then, and I can't believe—no matter what's happened—that you don't have one shred of the decency, one ounce of the kindness and moral fiber you once did. I won't accept that you have become a callous, jaded cynic who wants nothing more from life than enough money to keep him comfortable!"

His skin tightened menacingly. "You're deluding yourself, Tess."

"Am I? Then what about last night? Was that all my imagination, my *delusions*, or was that you?"

"I was drunk."

"Not *that* drunk."

"It was the booze talking."

"I don't think so," she said fiercely. "Tell me, is it just me or the world in general that infuriates you?" Tossing her head proudly, she turned and strode back to the house.

Denver's fists coiled. He watched her stomp up the steps to the back porch and heard the door bang shut. Swearing angrily under his breath, he slammed one clenched hand into the side of the machinery shed, sending splinters of siding flying through the dry air.

Flinging her skirt onto the bed, Tessa wondered why she bothered dealing with Denver. "...insufferable, arrogant bastard!" She kicked her shoes into the closet. Why had she even bothered trying to reach him? The man was the most temperamental, moody beast on the ranch!

One minute she thought he wanted to make love to her, the next strangle her. "Just the way you feel about him," she reminded herself angrily.

She'd found him standing near the ruins of the stables, his face drawn with pain, his eyes focused on some private horror that only he could see, and she'd been foolish enough to try to comfort him.

"That's what you get," she muttered, flinging herself on the bed, staring up at the ceiling and feeling like an utter fool. If only he would leave, end the turmoil, let her life return to its normal state.

But the thought of his actually packing his bags and walking out of her life again settled like a rock in her stomach. She threw one arm over her eyes and whispered, "You're out of your mind, Tessa!"

How much more humiliation would she let him inflict? "None," she promised herself, reaching for her jeans and tugging them over her hips. When Denver McLean left Montana again, she vowed silently to herself, she would wish him good luck, then pray that she never set eyes on him again.

Chapter Six

The phone rang. Without looking up from the papers strewn across the desk, Denver reached for the receiver. "McLean Ranch," he muttered.

"Denver?" Ross Anderson's voice boomed over the wires. "How's it going?"

"As well as can be expected, I suppose." He hadn't talked to Ross since he'd left the attorney's office nearly two weeks before.

"I thought you were heading back to L.A."

"I got side-tracked. Your advice." He leaned back in his chair and waited. Ross wouldn't be calling without a reason.

"I thought you'd like to know I may have a lead on your brother."

Denver sucked in his breath. *Finally!* "You're sure?"

"Nothing's sure until we see him," Ross replied. "But a private detective in New York contacted one of the magazines he works for, and I think we may have gotten lucky. Just three weeks ago, Colton was in Belfast."

"I'll be damned," Denver said, wondering if his luck were changing.

"You and me both," Ross said with a laugh. "The investigator is flying to Ireland tonight. We should know something in the next couple of days."

Denver sighed. "I guess I'll owe you one, Ross."

"Let's wait and see. But the editor seems to think Colton is still working undercover, posing as a member of the IRA."

Denver's stomach knotted. "He's lucky to be alive."

"If he still is."

"Let me know."

"Oh, I will. The minute I hear."

Denver hung up and wondered how Colton would take the news that he'd inherited half of the ranch and Tessa Kramer wanted to buy it. A slow smile spread over Denver's features. If nothing else could entice Colton back to Montana, the threat of selling out to Curtis Kramer's daughter just might.

Nate Edwards was a big, burly man whose dark hair was shot with gray. He'd been a horseman all his life, and his eyes gleamed as he leaned on the fence and watched Tessa lead Brigadier around the paddock.

"A fine-looking animal," he said, eyeing the stallion.

Brigadier's muscles quivered as Nate reached across the top rail and rubbed the stallion's muscular shoulder.

"I think he's the best in the state."

Nate smiled, exposing one gold-capped tooth. "I don't know if I'd go that far. What about Black Magic?"

Tessa considered the gleaming black stallion—John McLean's pride. "It's hard to compare," she said grudgingly. "But I'd still put my money on Brigadier."

Nate's gaze swung to the two mares, both pregnant, standing head to tail, and switching flies in the next paddock. "You're sure you want to sell all three?"

No, she wasn't, but she had no choice. For the past few years, she'd pinned her dreams on these animals, and the thought of selling the two mares and Brigadier hurt. But it was worth it, she told herself, for the ranch. "If I get the right price," she whispered, as her fingers caressed Brigadier's sleek neck. It seemed sacrilege to sell this horse. Aside from his value in dollars and cents, Brigadier had become a big part of her life. She enjoyed his feisty spirit and ornery streak. Now, Brigadier minced nervously, rolling his eyes until they showed white, as Nate opened the gate and slipped through.

"Careful," Tessa warned.

Running his hands over Brigadier's back, Nate moved slowly around the horse and had to jump out of the way when one back hoof lashed out, nearly connecting with Nate's shin. "Friendly, isn't he?"

"He can be," Tessa said wistfully and offered Brigadier a piece of carrot. "But he can be trouble, too."

"I'll remember that," Nate replied, giving the horse's rear end a wide berth as he eased back through the gate.

Tessa unsnapped the lead rope and gave Brigadier a slap on the rump. The horse whirled, then took off, his long, red legs flashing as he raced to the far end of the paddock, his ears pricked forward to the next field where Red Wing, Ebony and Tessa's other three mares grazed. The horses nipped grass and switched flies with their tails.

Tessa's stomach tightened and her heart grew heavy. Selling her favorite horses felt like selling a vital part of her family. She felt a traitor to her own kin. A hot lump formed in her throat as she watched the three horses, ears still flicking nervously, standing quietly in the shade of a solitary pine.

"Tessa?" Nate asked gently. "If this is gonna bother you—"

"I'll get over it," she said, though her eyes burned with unshed tears. She hurried through the gate and managed a wan smile.

"Okay. But if you change your mind, let me know." Nate turned toward his Jeep. "I'll call you in the next couple of days with an offer."

"I'll look forward to it," Tessa lied, her heart tearing a little. "And tell Sherrie I'm ready to give her riding lessons whenever she can convince Paula she's old enough to handle a horse."

"Don't hold your breath." Nate chuckled, his eyes bright at the thought of his daughter. "If Paula has her way, Sherrie never will get into a saddle."

Tessa nodded. "I'll bet Sherrie convinces her otherwise."

"We'll see. That chestnut mare—" he hitched his thumb toward the barn.

"Red Wing?"

Nate nodded and climbed into his Jeep. "I think Red Wing or that foal of hers will be perfect for Sherrie. Just give me a couple of days to convince my wife." He slammed the door and started the engine.

Well, Tessa thought unhappily as she watched Nate's Jeep disappear, the wheels were in motion. As soon as Nate bought the horses, she could make Denver a formal offer on the ranch. Kicking at a clod of dirt with the toe of her boot, she wondered why she didn't feel happy at the prospect. She glanced again at the paddock. Ebony was playfully nipping Red Wing's neck and was rewarded with a disgruntled kick. Tessa's eyes filled with tears. *Dear Lord, I'll miss them,* she thought, this small herd that had been the focus of her life until Denver returned.

Denver. He was behind all this. She squeezed her eyes shut and fought the urge to sag against the fence. Could she ever really trust him?

Two days later, Tessa was working with the most temperamental colt on the ranch. "Easy, now," she cooed, straining against the lead rope. An ornery roan yearling, appropriately named Frenzy, was on the other end of the leather strap, pulling and bucking and being a real pain in the backside. As usual. The high-strung roan seemed to enjoy giving Tessa fits.

It didn't help that Tessa had been in a foul mood herself ever since seeing Nate. And her nerves had been on edge since she noticed Denver watching her every move. She'd seen him staring through the study window, known he was in the barn, felt his eyes on her when she was going about her chores. Though they hadn't said a word, the charged tension between them had been stretched as tight as piano string, ready to break.

Frenzy yanked hard on the rope, tossing his red head and whistling. The leather slid through Tessa's hands. "Calm down," she said, soothing the colt with her voice. She inched forward and Frenzy, wild-eyed, reared and bolted. The rope snapped taut and pulled her off her feet. She flew through the air and landed with a smack on the dry ground.

"Oof!" Her bones jarred. Lifting her head, she spied Frenzy at the far end of the paddock. "Ingrate!" Tessa whispered, standing slowly and dusting her jeans. "Stupid, miserable beast!"

Still muttering under her breath, she turned and found Denver standing in the shade of the barn. One shoulder propped against the weathered boards, his arms folded over his chest, he tried unsuccessfully to smother a smile. "I thought you saved all those endearments for me," he said, chuckling.

Tessa's temper, already worn thin, snapped. "No," she said, "I've got special names for you."

"I guess I should be honored."

She shot him a warning glance. "I wouldn't be so sure of that!"

"You're just mad because he—" Denver cocked his head toward Frenzy, who was standing in a corner of the paddock, the lead rope dangling from his bridle "—got the better of you."

"This time." She winced and rubbed her shoulder.

"Are you all right?" Denver walked quickly through the gate and touched her upper arm.

She flinched, gritting her teeth.

"Maybe I should look at that."

His touch was already playing havoc with her mind. "I'm fine," Tessa said, shifting away. "The only thing that's bruised is my pride."

"He didn't look so tough to me." Denver surveyed the feisty colt.

"No?" she said. "You think you could do better?"

Denver rubbed his chin thoughtfully. "Probably."

"Good. Have at it."

Denver's gaze returned to hers and his eyes had darkened. "Okay. But maybe we should make this more interesting," he drawled suggestively.

"It'll be plenty interesting. I guarantee it." She climbed onto the top rail of the fence for a better view.

"I was thinking in terms of a small wager—"

"I don't gamble."

One corner of Denver's mouth lifted provocatively. "Sure you do, Tess. Unless you've changed."

Her throat constricted for a second, and she looked away. "What's the bet?" she asked, hating the breathless tone to her voice.

"Simple. If I get him to accept the saddle and walk calmly, I win."

"And what's at stake?"

"Name it." His eyes glinted magnetic blue.

Tessa had trouble finding her voice. The heat in Denver's gaze was equal to that of the late-afternoon sun still warming the valley floor. "Okay," she finally said. "If you can get him to take the saddle and walk docilely around the ring, you win. But if he won't take the saddle, you lose."

"And my punishment?" he asked, squinting up at her, his sensuous mouth curving suggestively.

Tessa could barely breathe. "If you lose, I—I'll expect you to work on the ranch the next week—shoulder to shoulder with the hands."

"And if I win," Denver said slowly, touching the side of her jaw with his finger, letting his hand slide slowly along it, "I'll expect you to spend a weekend with me in California!"

"That's impossible," she said quickly. The thought of spending a weekend completely alone with him caused her heart to hammer. "I—I can't be gone that long and—"

"And you're afraid of what you'll find out about me and maybe yourself," he suggested, leaning lazily over the top rail of the fence, his elbow nearly touching her thigh.

"That's not it! I have work here! Who'll run the ranch if I leave?"

His face turned hard. "Your father," he bit out. "After all, Curtis *is* the ranch foreman. That's what I pay him for."

"Dad can't do it alone."

"He'll have Mitch and Len and the rest of the hands."

"*If* you win."

"Oh, I'll win all right." A slow smile spread over his face, and with the grace of an athlete, he strode across the paddock and started talking softly to the horse.

Tessa bit her lip and crossed her fingers. She couldn't lose—not after she'd promised to go with him to L.A. *Come on, Frenzy,* she silently pleaded, *don't let me down. Show him who's boss!*

As if he'd heard her, Frenzy reared and shrieked. Head high, nostrils flared, he galloped past Denver at breakneck speed. The ground shook.

Tessa wanted to whoop, but Denver, his eyes steady on the colt, kept after him, talking low, moving slowly. The lathered roan pawed the ground nervously and sprinted past Denver in the opposite direction.

"That's it—" Tessa said.

"Not yet." With the patience of a lion stalking prey, Denver kept walking, gradually making his way until he reached the dangling lead rope and slowly picked it up. Then, each move deliberate, he wrapped the leather around his hands, approached the horse and placed a calming hand on Frenzy's quivering coat.

To Tessa's mortification, he managed to lead the yearling to the fence where a blanket was folded over the top rail. Denver placed the blanket on Frenzy's quivering, lathered hide.

The colt shied. He minced away from Denver, but Denver persisted and finally placed the saddle gently on Frenzy's strong back. He tightened the cinch. The yearling, squealing, took off like a rocket!

Denver braced himself. The lead rope stretched tight, yanking hard on Denver's arms. "Damn you," Denver muttered as the colt dragged him forward a few feet.

Tessa grinned.

But Denver dug his heels into the ground. His shoulders flexed and strained. Frenzy bucked and reared, his hooves slashing as he tried to shake the horrid leather beast from his back, but he couldn't rip the strap from Denver's hands.

"You're only going to wear yourself out," Denver told the horse. Frenzy reared again, shrieking. Denver moved closer. "Come on, boy. Let's see what you've got." Clucking his tongue, Denver urged the colt forward.

To Tessa's mortification, Frenzy began trotting around Denver. The colt was far from calm, his steps were nervous, his eyes rimmed in white, but he did, in fact, run at the end of the lead in a tight circle.

"How about that?" Denver said, gloating.

Tessa, grudgingly, conceded. "I didn't think it was possible."

Denver's face was covered with dust, but he was grinning from one ear to the other. When he finally pulled the saddle from Frenzy's back and unsnapped the lead, he couldn't help rubbing his victory in. "Easy as pie—if you know what you're doing," he said.

Tessa felt the perverse urge to ram Frenzy's bridle down Denver's throat, but she said instead, "Good job."

"So, how soon can you get packed?"

Her eyes rounded. "You're not serious."

"We had a bet," he reminded her.

"But I can't leave!"

"I thought we already discussed this." He wiped the sweat from his forehead and shoved a jet-black lock of hair away from his face. "I have some things I've got to take care of here, too," he said, "but then, you and I are going to L.A."

She fought back the urge to scream at him. For years she'd been able to hate the city where he'd run. It was easy to blame California for the pain he'd caused. But she'd never reneged on a bet in her life, and now, as she stared at his dust-streaked face, she found herself wanting to go to Los Angeles, to find out more about him, to know every tiny detail of his life.... "Give me a few days," she said, hopping to the ground beside him.

"Okay. But since I have to wait, I think you owe me something."

"I don't owe you anything—"

He placed a finger to her lips. "Before you go flying off the handle, just listen. All I want is to spend a little time with you."

Her heart fluttered expectantly. "We're together all the time—"

"You've been avoiding me."

That much was true. "I thought you wanted it that way."

"Maybe I did," he admitted. "But since we're stuck here together, we should try to get along."

She laughed. "Impossible."

"Is it, Tess?" His voice was suddenly serious, his gaze far off, as he stared at the hills.

She swallowed against a lump in her throat. The tender side of Denver had always broken through her resistance. As she stared at him, his face grimy, his hair windblown, the hard edge to his features temporarily erased, she couldn't say no. "What do you want to do?"

"Come on," he said, taking her hand. "I'll show you."

"Wait— Denver—" But he was running across the yard, past the house. She had trouble keeping up with him, taking two strides to his one. "Where are we going?" she asked, gasping for breath, as they wound down a seldom used path to the small lake nestled in a thicket of oak and maple.

Blackberry vines crept through the underbrush and high overhead, beneath the tattered clouds, geese flew, their V formation seeming to float over the sun-dappled water. The old dock was gray and beginning to rot. It listed as it stretched into the lake.

"I haven't been here since I've been back," Denver said, eyeing the lake's smooth surface.

"It's low this year," Tessa remarked, conscious that her hand was still linked with Denver's.

Glancing down at her, he smiled, then led her to the small stretch of sandy beach. Taking a clean handkerchief from his pocket, he dipped it in the water, then gently wiped her face. "Evidence of Frenzy's victory," he chuckled, exposing her freckles and tracing the slope of her cheek.

Shivering expectantly, she took the handkerchief from him. "You, too." Though her hands shook a little, she pressed the wet cloth to his forehead and cleaned the dirt from his smooth brow. "That's better."

She tried to pull her hand away, but his fingers curled possessively around her wrist. His eyes turned dark blue. "You're a fascinating woman, Tessa," he said quietly, "the most fascinating woman I've ever met."

Slowly, using his weight, he tugged on her arm, pulling her down to the dry grass and half-lying beside her. She knew she should get up, stop this madness before it started, but she couldn't. Her heart thudded over the quiet lapping of the lake.

"You're not what I expected." His gaze delved deep into hers, so deep she was sure he could see her soul, that her love for him was painfully obvious. His fingertips moved leisurely over her wrist, as if they had all the time in the world to get to know each other again. The earth was warm against her back, the sky turning a soft shade of lavender.

"I thought you'd be the same as when I left."

Her lips twisted wryly. "I grew up."

"I noticed." His eyes drifted down her body, his gaze scraping against her curves.

"Sorry to disappoint you."

He traced her eyebrows with one finger and she had trouble concentrating on anything but the warmth in his touch.

"That's the problem, Tessa," he admitted, his eyes searching her face. "I'm not disappointed. I wish I was. Things would have been so much simpler." He pulled her into the circle of his arms and held her close, his lips brushing her crown, his breath stirring her hair. She shouldn't be this close to him, Tessa thought. She shouldn't let his kind words in.

"I didn't think you'd become so...determined. You always had a mind of your own but I thought you would change. That after the fire—" His breath fanned her ear and warning bells rang in her mind.

She couldn't let him do this to her! Not now. Not when so many things were unsettled. Not when his scars on the inside were more visible than those across the back of his hand.

She pushed against his chest. Half of her wanted to stay curled in the security of his arms, the other half knew that lying with him near the deserted lake was dangerous. "If you taught me anything, Denver, it was that I had to stand on my own two feet." The old bitterness returned, and she struggled and failed to get away from him. "Fortunately Mitchell was around," she added, remembering those first excruciating weeks.

"Mitch?"

"He helped me pull myself together!"

"I thought he went into the Army."

"Not until he knew that I was okay," she said quietly, remembering back to the pain of Denver's rejection. It still hurt—that burning, gaping hole in her heart. "He was here when you weren't."

"And now he's back—hanging around, doing nothing."

"You just don't understand, do you?" she scoffed. "He came back here after the Army because he had a few months to kill before he started school. He's—he's been a big help."

"Doing what?" Denver asked skeptically.

"Making fence, feeding the stock, repairing the machinery. Just generally helping out."

"And all this time I thought he was just sponging off you."

Tessa's temper flared. "That's what happens when you live in California and make rash judgments!"

"Is that what I've done?" he mocked, refusing to release her.

Was he laughing at her? "Of course it is!"

"Tell me about life in L.A. As you see it," he goaded.

She rose to the bait. "I'd be glad to." Struggling up to one elbow, she shoved her hair from her eyes. "My guess is that you live in your chrome-and-glass apartment with a security guard at the door. Drive a sports car thirty miles an hour in bumper to bumper traffic. Spend vacations in Hawaii or Mexico or Catalina and for God's sake wear an imported Italian suit!"

He smiled, then, a secret, caring smile. "I live in a house near the ocean, Tessa, in Venice—and a lot of my work can be done at home. I drive an old Jeep and avoid the freeways when I can. This is the first vacation I've had in years, and I wouldn't know an Italian suit if it reached up and said, *'Lasciate ogni speranza, voi ch'entrate.'*"

One of her blond eyebrows raised quizzically. "It said what?"

"Literally translated, 'Abandon hope all ye who are foolish enough to plunge your arms down the sleeves of this over-priced imported jacket."

"No!" she whispered, but laughed.

"Well, not really. It means 'Abandon hope all ye who enter here,' but it's the only Italian phrase I know."

"So what's your point?"

"That I'm the same man no matter where I live. And you're the same woman whether you live in Three Falls, Montana, L.A. or New York City. You'll find out soon," he said, grinning. "And I can't wait."

"Why?"

"I think you'll love Rodeo Drive, Melrose Avenue and Wilshire Boulevard. I'll get you on one of those buses that tours through Beverly Hills and shows you the homes of the stars, and then we'll check out the movie studios—''

"Oh, save me," she whispered, groaning and trying to hide a smile.

"You'll love it. I promise."

She shook her head. "Maybe for you it works," she said.

"It does."

"But for me—" she glanced to the lake, where a wood duck was landing on the glasslike surface "—this is where I belong."

"I can change your mind," he whispered, his mouth pressing against her parted lips.

"Never," she replied, her voice caught somewhere between her throat and lungs. A voice inside her mind nagged at her, reminding her that Denver believed that she'd had an affair with his uncle—that her family had been involved in the fire. That the last time he'd been with her at the creek, he'd humiliated her. His words were as false as his love had been all those years before.

With all the strength she could scrape together, Tessa shoved him away and scrambled hastily to her feet. "It won't work, Denver," she said, breathing hard, seeing his expression turning from surprise to anger.

"What are you talking about?" he rasped.

Her eyes narrowed, though her heart was still beating traitorously. "I'm not about to give you the opportunity to humiliate me again."

"I wouldn't," he said slowly, standing.

"You're right," she said quickly. "Because I won't let you!" Then, before she could change her mind, she ran back to the house and took the steps two at a time.

Chapter Seven

She didn't see Denver until the next day at dinner. Seated across the table from Tessa and wedged between her father and Len Derricks, a ranch hand who had stayed with John after the fire, Denver did his best to appear amiable and relaxed. He complimented Milly on the meal and made small talk as if he'd never set one foot off the ranch—as if he'd never accused Tessa or her father of starting the blaze in which his parents had died.

His shirt was open at the throat, his jeans faded but clean, the worn denim hugging his hips. Black hair curled enticingly from beneath his collar. A dark shadow covered his jaw, making his smile, a rakish slash of white, brighter in contrast. His clear blue eyes had lost their hostile shadows, and his thick eyebrows moved expressively as he spoke.

Tessa felt foolish and cowardly. She should never have run from him, and she vowed that she wouldn't again. Unfortunately, she could barely drag her gaze away from the sensual curve of his lips, or the arch of a skeptical eyebrow.

"Delicious," Denver pronounced to a beaming Milly.

"It's only stew," she replied, blushing in pleasure.

"The best stew I've ever eaten."

Tessa's eyes narrowed on him as he placed his elbows on the table and turned to Len, asking his advice on purchasing more cattle for the ranch.

"If we add more head, we'll have to buy extra feed. We're already goin' through the hay we cut just two months ago."

"Can we get it?"

"Don't know," Len said, rubbing his chin thoughtfully. "Everyone around here is in the same fix. Except for Nate Edwards. He's been irrigatin' like mad, and from what I hear, he harvested more bales than he expected."

"Then maybe we can buy from him."

"Maybe," Len agreed, grinning at the prospect of adding to the herd.

"I'll give him a call. Now, tell me what kind of cattle you'd like to see on the ranch. We've got Herefords, right?"

"Ever since I can remember."

"So what about a new breed? Angus or Charolais?"

Len launched into his favorite topic, and to Tessa's horror, even her father and Mitchell added their two cents worth. Eventually everyone at the table was weighing the pros and cons of adding more beef to the stock. Why did Denver care? Tessa wondered. What was his angle? Wasn't he going to sell the ranch to her—or had he lied again?

"So when did you get so interested in ranching?" she asked, finally unable to hold her tongue. She felt her father stiffen beside her, but she glared at Denver. "I thought you were leaving."

Denver leaned forward, pushing his face across the table. "Until I actually sign on the dotted line," he said slowly, "I intend to take part in *all* the decisions that affect this ranch."

"From L.A.?"

"If need be." His eyes glinted wickedly at the mention of California.

"Tessa—" Mitchell warned.

"Do we understand each other?" Denver asked.

"Perfectly," she said, meeting the fire in his gaze with her own.

With a smile, Denver turned back to Len as if Tessa hadn't even interrupted.

Her temper soaring to the stratosphere, Tessa could barely listen. Though she pretended interest in the conversation around her, she couldn't concentrate. Not the way she should have. Not with Denver watching her through hard, calculating eyes. He wasn't actually staring—he feigned interest in the entire group of hands and household helpers seated around the table—but Tessa could feel his gaze follow her. When she reached for the biscuits, as she laughed over a joke Mitchell whispered to her, or even while she helped Milly clear the table, she could feel the weight of Denver's gaze.

"I'd add about fifty head of each," Len was saying, leaning back in his chair as Milly offered thick slabs of apple pie around the table.

"That's an increase of a hundred and fifty. I don't know," Curtis whispered thoughtfully.

Tessa couldn't stand the easy camaraderie, false as it was, a minute longer. "I thought you were going to sell the ranch lock, stock and barrel," she cut in, her eyes trained on Denver's face.

"I am. But not until the ranch is in better shape."

"And you think by spending money on cattle and feed that things will improve?"

"Couldn't hurt," he drawled, one corner of his mouth lifting.

He was actually enjoying her show of temper! "Then maybe it's my turn to make something clear. As I said before, I intend to buy this ranch, and I don't want the added expense of extra stock. Not yet."

Denver's eyes flashed. "And I told you I couldn't sell until the books were straightened out and I found my brother."

"That could take years!"

He did smile then, an infuriating grin that curved his lips lazily and caused her heart to throb. "I've got all the time in the world. Don't you?"

Her jaw fell open. "I thought you couldn't wait to get to L.A."

"I can't," he drawled, and Tessa felt a telling flush creep up her neck. She knew in an instant that he was baiting her again—seeing just how far he could push. "I'm looking forward to California," he said, and for a minute she was afraid he'd tell everyone about their bet. His gaze flicked around the table. "Unfortunately, I might not be able to wait until the place is sold, so I've got to make some plans to get it back on its feet before I leave."

"And do what?" she asked, standing. "Run the ranch from a cellular phone while you're getting a tan at Malibu Beach?"

Denver didn't react. "If that's what it takes," he responded calmly.

Tessa felt everyone's gaze on her, but she didn't flinch. Leaning over the table, she smiled sweetly and said, "Don't bother. I've already talked to the bank for the mortgage, and I can come up with the down payment. Now, all that has to happen is for you and me to come to some sort of an agreement. You won't have to worry about this place once you're back in L.A.!"

"You and I already came to an agreement," he reminded her. "About California."

Her jaw dropped, and she silently pleaded with him to keep their wager to himself.

"But do you honestly think it's possible for us to agree on anything?" he asked, returning to the question of the ranch.

Relieved, she said, "If we're both willing to cooperate."

"And what about the back taxes on this place?"

"Pay them—or make a provision for that payment in the sales agreement. Lower the price of the ranch by the amount of taxes owed, and I'll take care of them."

"And Colton?"

"Find him."

"Seems as if you've got it all figured out," he drawled, lifting his coffee cup and scrutinizing her carefully over the rim. His eyes became slits.

"Almost. Just as soon as you come up with a reasonable price." She felt the tension in the air. Everyone at the table had fallen silent. Not one fork scraped a plate. As if to break the charged silence, Milly coughed. Mitchell scooted his chair back, and Curtis fished nervously in his breast pocket for his cigarettes.

"You prove you're serious. Make a formal offer," Denver said deliberately. "Then, if you can come up with the money and I can find Colton, we'll have a deal."

Tessa couldn't believe her ears. "That's all?" she asked, waiting for the hitch—the strings that had to be attached.

"That—and a certain payoff."

"Payoff?" Mitch repeated.

"It's nothing," Tessa said quickly. She wondered if Denver were lying again—tricking her into believing he would sell. She had no option but to call his bluff. "I'll have everything ready as soon as possible," she said, her throat suddenly dry at the prospect of buying the place and thereby allowing him to leave. Now that he'd returned, the prospect of living without him again loomed in her future like a gaping black abyss.

Denver grinned, that easy, crooked smile that Tessa found wickedly irresistible. "I'm looking forward to it. Then maybe you could take a break from this place. Find some sun and sand and relaxation."

Tessa wanted to drop through the floor.

Denver shoved his chair from the table. "Thanks for the meal," he said to Milly, then he strode, whistling—*whistling* for crying out loud—down the hall.

Tessa snatched several plates from the table and carried them into the kitchen. Her entire body was shaking, and the china rattled in her hands.

"Careful now," Milly warned, eyeing Tessa's flushed features. "You're letting that man get to you."

"He's *not* getting to me!"

Smothering a knowing smile, Milly snapped an apron from a hook near the stove and tied it around her thick waist. "Whatever you say, Tess," she said, turning on the tap. Hot water began to fill the sink, steam rising to Milly's face.

"He's as changeable as a chameleon," Tessa sputtered. "One minute he's nasty as can be, the next he's sweet as pie, praising everyone, asking their opinions, when all he wants to do is get the hell out of here!"

"I wouldn't be so sure of that," Milly said, sliding a knowing glance Tessa's way as she began to stack rinsed plates into the dishwasher.

"What's that supposed to mean?" Tessa had been placing leftover stew into a bowl, but she paused.

"I just happened to walk by the den this morning—you remember, when he took that phone call from Jim what's-his-name, his partner."

"Van Stern."

"That's the one. Anyway, Denver was convincing this Van Stern character that he needed more time here; maybe another couple of weeks." Milly dried her hands on the edge of her apron and grinned. "The way he was talking, barking orders, trying to convince his partner that he didn't need to return to L.A. until certain things were just right, made me think he *wanted* to hang around here."

Tessa couldn't dare believe, not for a second, that Denver actually wanted to stay in Montana. All his life he'd never been interested in the land or the livestock. He'd been restless at the ranch. He was just waiting until she could break away and pay off her debt. *Damn him! Damn her stupid pride for taking that bet!* "He probably just wants the extra time to tie things up and get rid of the place."

"His lawyer could do that," Milly pointed out. "No, if you ask me, that man has another reason for staying here." Her kind eyes met Tessa's and she winked.

"His decision has nothing to do with me."

"Oh no?" Milly's lower lip protruded thoughtfully. "Maybe not. But you'll never know until you take down your armor, now will you?"

"Meaning?"

"If the two of you could ever quit fighting long enough to talk sensibly, you might surprise yourselves."

"I don't think so. Denver made it very clear how he feels about me the first night he was back." But she couldn't forget yesterday at the lake. He'd seemed so sincere. So honest.

Milly's lips pursed pensively. "Well, maybe he was lying to save his pride. Did you ever think of that?"

Remembering how callously he'd told her he'd never loved her on the first night he returned to Montana, Tessa shook her head. "I don't think so."

"We'll see," Milly said. "We've got a couple more weeks of Mr. McLean. A lot can happen." She hung her apron on a hook near the door and reached for her old, plaid jacket. "I'll see you in the morning."

As Milly left with the few remaining ranch hands, Tessa decided to check on the horses and try to get her mind off Denver. She couldn't for a minute think Denver still cared for her. Though she wanted to believe that Milly was right, that Denver still felt something for her, she knew those hopes were only foolish fantasies. And even if Denver had loved her before the fire, too much had happened since for that love to rekindle. Never once had he suggested he loved her. *Wanted* her, yes, but love? Never. Even the other night, when his tongue had been loosened with liquor, he'd never mentioned love.

"Don't even think about it," she muttered to herself, shoving open the door of the barn and snapping on the lights. Though the only sounds she heard were the snorting of horses and rustling of hooves, she sensed someone else was inside. "Who's in here?" she called through the musty, dark interior.

"I am," her father's voice boomed.

"Dad?" Turning, she found him sitting on a bale of hay, a half-empty bottle dangling from his hands. "What're you doing here? I thought you were still in the house."

"I was. But I thought I'd better wait for you."

"Give me that," she said, afraid Denver might show up. She reached for the bottle, but her father yanked it away, twisted on the cap and stuck the flask behind the very bale on which he was seated.

"Don't trust him," he said flatly.

"Who? Denver?"

"Right."

"Hey! Whoa!" She pointed an accusing finger at her father. "Aren't you talking out of both sides of your mouth?"

"What do ya mean?"

"Was I mistaken, or were you the guy hanging on his every word at the dinner table? Weren't you chatting with him about the merits of an Angus over a Hereford?"

"He's the boss, damn it."

"I know, but the last I heard you weren't even planning to show up for work. You thought he'd fire you."

"He didn't," Curtis grumbled. "After that one lecture, he never brought up the fire again. I figured the least I could do was help out."

"So now you're telling me not to trust him? I don't get it, Dad." She leaned one hip against the manger, felt a soft nose nuzzle the side of her jeans and absently patted Brigadier's muzzle. "What's it going to be? Is Denver friend or foe?"

"That's a tough one," Curtis admitted, rubbing a trembling hand over his stubbled jaw. "Just remember that he's different from you and me. He's only here to sell this place. He doesn't give one good goddamn about it, and when it goes, we go."

"Not if I buy it."

Her father snorted, reached behind him and, as the hay stirred and dust motes swirled, extracted the bottle again. "I already told you what I thought of that fool notion—I'm not goin' to waste my breath again.'' He opened the bottle and took a long swallow.

"Stop it," she whispered harshly. "You just said you're getting along with Denver. Don't blow it with this!" She grabbed for the bottle again, grazing it. Spinning crazily out of Curtis's hands, the flask dropped onto the floor, crashing into a thousand pieces and spraying alcohol on the dry hay and old floorboards.

Tessa couldn't move. She stared at the glittering glass and pooling liquid and her stomach turned over. This is how it could have happened! Carelessly spilled alcohol, a dropped match that was still smoldering, combustible hay... Oh God! She remembered the horrid black smoke, the crackling flames, her desperate, haunting fear for Denver's life and her father's body being dragged from the inferno.

"You see anyone else in there?"

"I—I don't know," he mumbled, still coughing.

The paramedic glanced at the fire chief. "He wouldn't know. He's three sheets to the wind."

Tessa stood frozen, scared. The smell of alcohol and smoke had clung to her father that day and she hadn't cared. She had just been thankful that he was alive.

Now, as she saw the amber drops staining the floor, she said angrily, "Let's clean this up before Denver sees it."

"Too late." Denver's voice rang through the barn.

Tessa jumped and her father flinched.

Standing in the open door, his dark eyebrows drawn into an angry black line, Denver glared at the pitiful scene in front of him. "Accident?" he mocked.

"You could say that," Tessa said. She was shaking inside, her stomach quivering. *Please God, not Dad,* she silently prayed. *He couldn't have been responsible for the fire!*

"It's my fault," her father cut in, before realizing the irony in his words.

"Is it?" Denver's eyes narrowed on the old man and his jaw slid to one side. Every muscle in his body tensed. The back of his neck was flaming, his teeth clenched tight. "Go home and sleep it off," he advised slowly. "I'll take care of this mess."

Curtis hesitated.

"Have Mitch drive you," Tessa said softly, her insides wrenching. Was it possible? Could her father really have started the fire accidentally and lied about it to everyone? Everything she'd believed in had somehow crashed with that bottle shattering against the floor.

His arthritic shoulders stiff with pride, Curtis stood and walked tightly to the door. Denver moved enough to let him pass, but the coiled tension in his every muscle was as condemning as a public flogging.

"Don't you ever speak to my father like that again!" Tessa hissed, once Curtis was out of earshot.

"Open your eyes, Tessa, the man has a problem."

"Don't we all?" she snapped back, seeing him flinch a little. She found some towels and a broom and began cleaning up the spilled whiskey. Denver reached for a whisk broom.

"I can handle this," Tessa said coldly. "Don't you have something better to do?"

"Not at the moment, no." His eyes held hers for a second. Filled with accusations, they drilled deep. Tessa swallowed with difficulty.

"You can't keep covering for him, Tessa."

"I'm not covering for anyone!" Fury caused her heart to pound. She swiped at the floor with a towel and sucked in a swift breath when her fingers scraped over an invisible shard. "Damn." The prick was small but deep, and blood dripped from her hand.

"Let me take a look at that," Denver insisted, wrapping firm arms over her wrist.

"I'm fine. Just leave me alone!" She tried to yank back her hand, but his fingers were an unbending manacle.

"Hold it up," he commanded, reaching with his free hand into his pocket for a clean handkerchief.

"It's no big deal—"

"Not yet," he admitted.

"Really, just a small cut . . ."

"That could get infected. This place isn't exactly sterile, you know."

"I'd noticed," she said dryly, her gaze sweeping the long, hanging cobwebs, the dust collecting on the beams and the loose straw scattered in corners on the floor.

"Then you won't argue about going into the house to clean it up. I'll finish here."

"I'm not a cripple," she muttered, but saw the determined gleam in his gaze.

His fingers tightened over her wrist. "For once in your life, Tessa, just do as I say."

"Yes, sir!" she shot back, offering a mock salute with her free hand.

His lips, despite the hard set of his jaw, twitched upward, and he released her arm.

Marching stiffly out of the barn, she tried to calm down—count to ten—do anything to cling to her fleeing patience. She'd never considered herself irrational or quick to anger, but with Denver around, her temper flared as instantly as a match struck against tinder-dry kindling. Every time she attempted to be reasonable, he said or did something that pushed her world out of kilter—like clamping his hand over her wrist and barking an order at her while her stupid pulse raced crazily. Or like tenderly swiping her hair from her eyes and telling her that when he made love to her again, there would be no regrets. . . .

"He's just a man," she reminded herself when she turned on the water in the bathroom a few minutes later. But as the warm water dripped over her hand, she caught sight of her reflection in the mirror and saw the color in her cheeks, the still-pounding pulse at the base of her throat, the fire in her hazel eyes. "Why do you let him get to you?" she demanded of her silly reflection and knew the answer. *Because, damn it, you've never stopped loving him!*

Sick at the thought, she wrenched the faucet closed, rubbed her finger with an antibacterial cream and wrapped her wound quickly with a small Band-Aid.

Walking out of the bathroom, she found Denver sitting on the banister overlooking the entry far below. His hands beside him for balance, he hopped off the polished rail as she entered the hall.

"Are you okay?" he asked gently.

That stupid part of her heart warmed at the concern in his eyes. "I told you I was fine."

"You don't need stitches?"

"Nor neurosurgery either, thank you very much!" She heard the bite in her words the minute they passed her tongue and regretted speaking so harshly. "Look, I didn't mean to snap, it's just—"

"Just what?" he asked.

She felt her shoulders slump a bit, but she looked him squarely in the eye. "It just seems that I can't do anything right when you're around. You're always trying to prove that you're the boss or that you know more than I do, or that—" She thought back to the day by the creek and cringed inside. "Or that you have some sort of power over me."

One corner of his mouth lifted. "I don't think anyone has any power over you, Tessa." His voice was tender, endearing. If she were to close her eyes, she could almost imagine that he was seven years younger and they were in love again. That same gentle tone she'd found so special still brought shivers to her skin.

When he touched her lightly on the shoulder, she wanted to lean against him, beg him to call back the hateful words he'd spoken when he first returned, plead with him to forgive her and her father for inadvertently causing him so great a tragedy.

"You were hard on Dad."

Denver was standing behind her, his hands on her shoulders. "He can't hide in a bottle forever."

"It's difficult for him, too."

His fingers gently pulled her backward until her shoulders met the firm wall of his chest and his breath fanned across her crown. Closing her eyes, she willed the waves of tenderness forming in her heart to recede. Although she yearned to tell him she loved him still, that deep in her heart her feelings had never wavered, she couldn't. He would only laugh at her confession, chide her for being the same silly romantic she'd been years before.

With all the effort she could muster, she tried to think clearly, to fight the magic of his nearness. Her fingers curled around the cool wood banister, her nails digging into the polished surface.

"It doesn't have to be this way," he said softly. "We don't have to keep lunging for each other's throats."

She could hear it then, the hard beat of his heart. Pounding in counterpoint to her own, it seemed to echo through the long, carpeted hall.

"Do you know you've been driving me crazy?"

"Is that what's doing it? It's my fault you've been acting like a madman from the minute you stepped onto the ranch?" she asked, wishing she could add some venom to her words, but her voice sounded breathless and hoarse—as if it belonged to a frightened young virgin.

He chuckled, gripping her tighter, forcing her against him until her spine pressed tight to his chest and abdomen. His hands slid the length of her arms, to her wrists, then closed over her stomach, holding her so close that she felt the hard bulge in his jeans.

Bending a little, he placed his chin over her shoulder. His cheek was warm against hers, and she felt like moaning. Her fingers dug deeper, knuckles white, rigid in their grip of the railing as his lips, warm and inviting, soft and gentle, touched her neck, sweeping slowly from her shoulder to her earlobe.

"Denver, please," she said, trying to think. "Don't."

"You don't like it?" he teased, his fingers lacing under her breasts.

Was he crazy? "I-I just don't think it's wise.... Oh!" His teeth nibbled on the shell of her ear and it was all she could do to hold on to the balustrade. Her knees went weak, her heart beating a wanton cadence. "Denver—" Turning in his arms, hoping to convince him that what they were doing was insane, she caught one glimpse of the passion smoldering in his eyes before his lips captured hers in a kiss that cut off any further protest.

His mouth molded against her skin, covering her parted lips anxiously. His tongue darted and flicked between her teeth. Bittersweet sensations raced through her body. Like wildfire through prairie grass, passion seared through her, until she couldn't think, and didn't want to.

Her arms lifted, circling his neck, holding him closer still as she returned his fever. Pulsing white-hot between them, the smoldering ashes of desire ignited.

His hand stole upward, strong fingers surrounding one breast. Tessa moaned softly, weak inside as he kneaded her flesh, causing her nipple to harden and protrude against the lacy confines of her bra.

Still he kissed her, his hips thrust hard against hers, her back now supported by the railing.

The front door banged open. "Tessa?" Mitchell's voice shattered their intimacy.

Tessa froze in Denver's arms and reluctantly dragged her mouth from his.

"Hey, Tess? Where are you" her brother said, his voice booming up the stairs.

"Up here," she choked out. "I'll be down in a second."

"Good! I'll be in the kitchen. We need to talk." His footsteps echoed through the house and Tessa, forcing her unsteady legs and arms to work, pushed away from Denver.

"We're not finished," he insisted in a hoarse whisper that hissed through the upstairs hallway.

"I think we are."

His arm reached forward, jerking her around. "We're not finished by a long shot, Tessa," he said, his eyes glinting like newly forged steel. "Get rid of him."

"Just like that?" she mocked.

"Just like that."

She yanked her arm away and started for the stairs. "Don't hold your breath!"

He was leaning over the rail, watching her descend. "It's not *my* breath I intend to hold on to," he said suggestively.

Denver McLean had to be the most despicable man on earth!

And you love him.

"Fool!" she ground out, stalking toward the kitchen, her steps echoing through the old house with the same ring as Denver's amused laughter.

Chapter Eight

Mitchell was waiting. The heels of his boots propped on one chair, he leaned back in another and cradled a cup of coffee between his hands.

"Where's McLean?" he asked when Tessa entered.

Much as she wanted to, she couldn't lie. "He's here," she replied, keeping her voice low.

"In the house?"

"I think so."

Mitchell swore roundly, twisting so that he could see his sister.

Hoping beyond hope that Mitchell wouldn't notice her swollen lips or flushed cheeks, Tessa poured herself a cup of coffee with unsteady hands. "How's Dad?"

"How do you think he is? He told me what happened in the barn." Mitchell's green eyes darkened dangerously and deep lines grooved his forehead.

"Dad shouldn't drink so much," Tessa said, taking the chair across from her brother. Placing her elbows on the table, she sipped from her cup, but didn't taste the coffee.

"Who's gonna tell him? You?"

"Maybe."

"Why? You've tried before. Nothing changed."

"I know, but tonight was different. He dropped the bottle, the whiskey sprayed all over the floor. If he'd been smoking, God only knows what would've happened."

"Dad doesn't smoke in the barn."

Tessa gritted her teeth. "What if he forgets? If he's had one drink too many?"

"When has that ever happened?"

Tessa swallowed back the cold lump of betrayal that formed in her throat. "Maybe seven years ago."

Mitchell's feet dropped to the floor. "No way." His green eyes squinted indignantly as he scanned her face and his jaw became granite-hard. "Don't tell me McLean's got your thinking all turned around," he whispered. Shoving a lock of wheat-blond hair off his forehead, he let out a long, low whistle and shook his head. "Well, I'll be," he murmured sadly. "You're falling for him again, aren't you?"

"I am not."

"Oh, no?" His gaze dropped to her lips, so recently kissed, then traveled a knowing path to the scarlet creeping steadily up her neck. His jaw slackened. "Come on, Tessa, don't do this. Not again. McLean's no good. You and I both know it. I was there to pick up the pieces, remember?"

Tessa would never forget how good Mitchell had been, how he'd helped her battle the numbing cold that had settled upon her when she'd finally accepted the fact that Denver had left her. "If Denver's so bad," she asked, her spine stiffening, "why all the friendly talk at the table tonight?"

"He's the boss," Mitchell said simply. "I don't like it, but there it is."

Sighing, she leaned against the wall. "You sound just like Dad."

"I'm just trying to get through the next few weeks, then I'm out of here," he reminded her. "School starts the end of September. I may not like McLean, but I'm trying not to

ruffle his feathers—which, by the way, was your advice."
His lips tightened and sadness stole into his gaze. "Besides,
I'm just trying to get along with the bastard—you're on the
verge of having an affair with him."

"Don't be ridiculous." She wanted to slap him and shout
that a love affair with Denver McLean was the last thing on
her mind, but Mitchell had already guessed the truth. She
cleared her throat. "Not that it's any of your business."

"I saw enough of his kind in the Army. A different girl in
every city." She started to protest but he held up one hand,
palm out. "Sure, you're here and available. So he's interested."

"I am not 'available.'"

Mitchell's face grew taut, as if he could read something
new in her gaze. "Oh, God, Tess, don't tell me you've been
saving yourself for him."

"I'm not telling you anything! What happens between
Denver and me is between us."

Mitchell looked sick. "I just don't want to see you make
a fool of yourself again. Don't you remember how much he
hurt you? How he left without one word? How he and Colton accused Dad of murder? *Murder!*"

"No one actually said—"

"If it hadn't been for John McLean, Dad would have
been strung up by his heels. Colton and Denver would have
seen to it."

"But it didn't happen, did it? John gave Dad a chance."

"And now you're giving Denver one." Mitchell's hands
were actually shaking when he shoved his hair from his eyes.
"I can't tell you what to do, Tessa. I never could. But for
God's sake, be careful. I wouldn't trust Denver McLean any
more than I would a nest of rattlesnakes."

"I'll remember that."

Mitchell scraped his chair back. "While you're remembering, don't forget that McLean's been in L.A. a long time.
You think he's been without a woman all that time?"

"I don't really care."

One golden eyebrow arched as Mitchell said, "No? Well, think about it, Tessa. All of a sudden, he's interested in you. So what happened to the past seven years? Why hasn't he called, written or stopped by? All that time while his uncle was dying, he didn't so much as write one goddamn note."

"He didn't know about John."

"He wasn't too interested, was he?"

Tessa wanted to defend Denver but didn't. What was the point? Mitchell's mind was set. He couldn't believe Denver capable of any kind of compassion or feelings. In Mitchell's opinion, Denver had abandoned his uncle. But John had kept the secret of his heart condition to himself and a few close friends, all of whom were sworn not to tell Denver or Colton. Keeping that secret vow had been easy. Colton seemed to have fallen off the face of the earth, and Denver hadn't been interested in anything or anyone on the ranch. So John had died alone. And Mitchell was condemning Denver.

"As I said, I can deal with Denver."

"I hope so, Tess. I hope to God you can!" He found his hat and jammed it onto his head. Turning on his heel, he was through the back door before she had a chance to argue.

Denver twisted a pencil between his fingers. Through the open study window, he heard the back door slam shut and Mitchell's boots stomping across the yard. A few seconds later an engine sputtered, caught and roared to life. Gears ground and gravel sprayed as Mitchell tore down the drive.

Denver knew that Tessa and Mitch had been arguing, probably over him. Snatches of their conversation had filtered through the old house, and he could guess the rest. Mitchell didn't trust him—didn't like him involved with Tessa.

Denver didn't blame Mitch. Hell, he didn't want to be involved with Tessa himself. But ever since setting eyes on

her again in the barn that first night, he'd been compelled
to be as near her as possible.

Night after night, he had told himself to forget that she
was only a short walk down the hall, that if he played his
cards right, she would eventually make love to him and that,
if he could control his emotions, he'd be able to satisfy
himself with her and walk away again.

His pencil snapped in two. Guilt tore a hole in his heart.
He'd felt her respond, knew that it was only a matter of time
before he could seduce her. And now, when he was certain
of victory, he didn't want it, couldn't bear to see the hurt in
her eyes when he left her again.

The other evening at the creek had been telling. He could
have made love to her and been done with it, except that he
couldn't hurt her. And now, he was looking forward to taking her back to Venice. For what? A day? A week? A lifetime? He didn't know. But he was sure of one thing. Tessa
hadn't betrayed him all those years before—she couldn't
have. She wasn't involved in her father's scheme to ruin the
McLeans. Or else she was one hell of an actress. Her indignation and pain seemed real enough, and he believed her.

He wasn't so sure about Mitch or Curtis. But Tessa, he
felt, hadn't been involved, even innocently, in the fire.

So now he wanted her—more fiercely even than he had
seven years ago. Desire was running at a fever pitch, and he
wasn't sure how much longer he could keep it in check.

Clenching his jaw so hard it ached, he reached for a new
pen and stared down at the figures on the profit and loss
statement lying open on the desk. But the typed pages
couldn't hold his attention, and he wondered how he'd get
through another long night just three doors down the hall
from the only woman who could stir his blood to a fever
pitch.

He heard her walking overhead, knew she was probably
undressing for her bath. When the old pipes groaned loudly,
he closed his eyes, envisioning her naked, her strawberry-
blond hair spilling down her back, her skin pink from the
hot water, her eyes glassy in relaxation. Her breasts would

swell gently at the waterline, her nipples erect little buttons pointing proudly above the lapping water.

He could imagine his tongue stroking those proud little peaks, the hot water touching his lips as he suckled. Her fingers would twine in his hair and with one hand slowly dipping through the waves of warm liquid, sliding past the silky skin covering her ribs and the tight muscles of her abdomen, he'd ravish her slowly. Touching that private nest of fine reddish hair at the apex of her legs, he'd tell her of the nights he'd lain awake wanting her, the years he'd wished she had warmed his bed.

Smiling, Tessa would toss her head back, moaning softly, her hair floating around her as he gently parted her thighs, teasing that special little bud until she was writhing and wrapping her arms around his neck, dragging him into the water with her, begging him to make love to her and never stop.

A quiet rap on the door startled him. He had to stretch his legs and shift on his buttocks to ease the swelling that pressed hard against his jeans. "What?" Damn, but his voice sounded unnatural and husky.

Tessa pushed the door open and poked her head inside. Her fingers were wrapped around the edge of the wood, but she didn't enter. Denver used every ounce of control he possessed not to fly out of the chair and tear that silky pink wrapper off her body. Seeing the wet strands of her hair, knowing how soft and yielding her flesh was beneath the quickly donned robe, he could think of nothing more than giving in to the sweet temptation she was so innocently offering.

"I just wanted to warn you that we're out of hot water—I'll have the element on the tank checked in the morning."

"Thanks," he said, hoping to appear busy as he leaned over the desk. Then, unable to resist, he flashed her a lazy smile as he glanced up at her. "I think if I take a shower tonight, it should be cold, don't you?"

"Whatever you want." But she smiled.

He propped both elbows on the desk and rotated his pen between his hands. "What I want has nothing to do with the temperature of the water around here."

"Oh." She bit her lower lip and seemed about to leave when a mischievous light sparkled in her eyes. "Does this mean I should lock my door tonight?"

"Don't tease me, Tessa," he warned with a wicked grin.

"Wouldn't dream of it," she said, chuckling, her lips curving softly.

Denver's throat tightened and the heat in his loins grew. What was she doing here, flirting so outrageously with him? "It's a good thing I'm a gentleman," he said gruffly, and she had the audacity and lack of common sense to laugh, a merry tinkling sound in the old, creaky house.

"You? A gentleman? You couldn't prove it by me," she quipped before ducking back through the doorway.

Denver couldn't stop himself. Feeling as if he were seven years younger, he was on his feet in an instant. He fairly flew across the room, yanking open the door so hard it crashed against the wall and hearing Tessa's laughter ring through the house. He saw just the hem of her wrapper as she hurried up the stairs.

Knowing he was going to hate himself later, he took the steps two at a time and landed on the second floor just in time to hear a door close and a lock click soundly. So she thought she could tease him and get away with it, did she? he thought, smiling inwardly.

At the door to his parents' room, he knocked softly.

"Go away," Tessa said, but she couldn't stop the giggles that erupted from her throat.

"Open up."

"No way." She backed across the room.

"Do I have to break it down?"

"Don't be silly—"

His foot crashed into the door and she laughed. "Denver, don't—this is crazy. Be reasonable—"

Bang! The door wobbled, and he gave it one last shot, the wood splintering away from the casing as his boot crashed against it. His eyes gleamed, and a smile tugged at the corner of his lips. "Reasonable?" he repeated. "The original, 'insufferable, arrogant bastard'—wasn't that what you called me?"

"You deserved it."

"That and more, I suspect," he admitted, still smiling. Surveying the damage to the door, he asked, "Did you really think you could lock me out?" His voice was low and seductive, but his eyes crinkled at the corners.

Tessa swallowed hard. The backs of her calves met the mattress. "I—I didn't think I'd have to." He was teasing, she could see the amusement in his gaze. But, despite the playful glimmer in his eyes, his jaw was rock hard, the cords in his neck visible.

He took a step into the room, his silhouette dark against the light in the hall. His gaze slid slowly from her face to her throat and the wet ringlets that coiled at her neck, then to the delicate circle of bones at the base of her throat, and lower still.

Tessa's nipples hardened, thrusting against the thin wrapper, visible in the half-light. The lighthearted playfulness seeped out of the room, replaced by an electricity that seemed to crackle between them.

"What kind of game are you playing, Tessa?" he whispered hoarsely, moving slowly toward her.

Tessa's heart thundered, and she licked her lips nervously. "I'm not—"

"Like hell." He stopped mere inches in front of her. "Here we are alone, and you come down to tell me something stupid like we're out of hot water—"

"We are!"

"For God's sake, you could have worn something more than this!" He flipped two fingers under the lapel of her wrapper, his skin grazing hers. She sucked in her breath. The fun-loving light in his eyes had fled, but his hands didn't move. The seductive warmth of his fingertips pressed lightly against her skin. "Don't you have any idea what you're doing to me?" he rasped.

"Probably about the same as you're doing to me."

His fingers wound around her lapel. "Don't tease me, Tessa," he repeated.

"I'm not," she vowed.

His hand slid along the lapel, between her breasts to rest at the belt cinched around her waist. She melted inside. Liquid heat swirled deep at her center as his fingers rested feather-light against her abdomen. "You want me?" he asked.

Closing her eyes, she leaned against him. "Yes."

A muscle throbbed in his forehead, but his fingers worked against the knot.

"I—I—only wish I didn't," she admitted as the robe parted. His gaze wandered recklessly down the gap.

"Why?" His hand caressed her abdomen.

"Because it complicates things—ooh!"

He slid his hand around her waist, pulling her against him as he lowered his head and his lips slanted over hers. His tongue slid easily between her teeth, touching lightly, exploring and plundering sweetly as she wound her arms around his neck.

"Sometimes the best things in life are complicated," he whispered, his breath as ragged as her own as he pushed against her. Tessa lost her balance and together they tumbled onto the bed. "Oh, Tessa," he murmured, kissing her lightly from her forehead to her lips, "why couldn't I forget you? Why the hell couldn't I forget you?"

Tears of happiness filled her eyes. "I—I don't know," she murmured.

His hands tangled in her hair and his lips brushed slowly against her throat, softly stroking her sensitive skin. Aching inside, she quivered beneath him as he pushed the robe from her shoulders and stared for a minute at her breasts, straining upward, inviting him with their rosy-crested peaks.

He stroked one gently. It puckered, and he groaned, moving his hand in sensual circles, staring down at her in fascination.

"Touch me," he whispered, shaping her mouth with his again.

She fumbled with the buttons of his shirt and quickly shoved the soft cotton down his arms to bunch at his wrists. He flung the unwanted garment across the room and lay over her, his bare chest rigid.

Swallowing against a desert-dry throat, she reached upward. Her fingers moved gently along the length of his ribs, tracing a path so slowly through his sworling black hair that he groaned and closed his eyes.

She hesitated at the waistband of his jeans, and he pulled her to him, slashing his mouth over hers, his hands splaying against her bare back as she fumbled with the zipper. Once the zipper was down, he kicked off his jeans and, naked at last, rubbed gently against her. He kissed her face, her cheeks, her throat, moving slowly downward, his lips teasing as he played with her nipple.

Her blood pumped furiously in her veins, and she writhed against him as he took one breast into his mouth, laving it with his tongue.

Heat roiled deep inside her. She kissed his shoulders and chest, tasted the salt from the sheen of perspiration coating his body. He kissed her again and again, whispering her name as his tongue touched and stroked.

I love you, she thought, aching with want.

He groaned and moved over her. "Is it safe?" he whispered into her ear.

"S-safe?" she murmured, not understanding.

"You know—safe." He took in a deep shuddering breath and levered himself up on one elbow. "Protected?"

"Protected?" she rasped. "As in against pregnancy?"

A muscle throbbed near his temple.

Tears filled her eyes. Hot little drops of shame. How could he think she'd been with other men? "There's never been anyone but you."

"No one?" His blue eyes stared down at her in disbelief.

Dying inside, crumbling apart bit by bit, she choked out, "And especially not John." Mortified, she tried to roll away from him, but he pressed her firmly back onto the mattress. His hands clamped over her wrists, holding her close.

"It doesn't matter," he vowed.

"Of course it does, Denver," she cried. "It matters a lot. To you. To me. Ever since you got here, you've been insinuating I slept with your uncle, for God's sake. Your *uncle*! How could you think, even for a second, that I'd—I'd—" She shuddered.

Denver wanted to believe her. She could see it in his eyes. Staring up at him from the tangled cloud of red-gold framing her face, her hazel eyes leveled on him, she knew he wanted to believe her.

"I think you'd better leave," she said slowly, trying to deny the want that still caused her limbs to tingle, her eyes to shine.

"It's too late for that, Tessa," he whispered, kissing her neck, letting his lips linger against her sensitive skin. "I can't go now."

"Then, please, Denver. Please trust me. There's never been anyone but you."

"You don't have to—"

"I would never lie! Not about this!"

"I believe you, Tess," he whispered hoarsely, releasing her wrists. His fingers slid up her arms, across her back, tracing the curve of her spine before he cupped her buttocks.

"I—I've only been with you."

He groaned, a deep, primal sound of pain and pleasure as he kissed her again, his lips crashing down on hers with a need so urgent she couldn't resist. Her hands moved across his shoulders, feeling each firm muscle before slowly sliding down his arms.

When Denver guided her fingers lower still, she didn't resist, and her feather-light touches stoked fires already raging deep in his loins as he moved easily over her and parted her legs.

"No regrets?" he whispered, poised over her.

She swallowed but shook her head and held his gaze. "No regrets," she vowed.

Slowly he plunged deep into the warmest part of her, sheathing himself in her womanhood.

Gasping, Tessa twined her arms around his neck. Her body moved in a magic rhythm with his and she couldn't stop. Not in her dreams had she felt this rapture, this soaring of her spirit. "Denver, oh, Denver," she whispered until she could no longer speak—could only feel. He pushed her higher and higher, upward to a sky as blue as his eyes.

"Denver!" she cried hoarsely as the sky seemed to splinter and her body jolted. He fell against her, breathing raggedly, drenched in sweat and whispering her name.

Tessa welcomed his weight. Her arms encircled his chest, and she pressed light kisses to his cheek. Unbidden tears formed in her eyes, hot little pools that drizzled down her cheeks.

Denver touched her lashes, wiping the silent drops away with his thumb. "Tears?" he asked.

"Tears, yes," she whispered, sniffing, "but no regrets."

He chuckled—a deep, rumbling sound—as he gathered her into his arms and held her. "Sleep," he murmured into her hair.

Closing her eyes, she nestled closer to him, listening to the breath moving in his lungs and the muffled beat of his heart. Tonight she would stay with him. Tomorrow she would face whatever the morning might bring. Even if it meant following him to Los Angeles.

Chapter Nine

Morning shadows played across the room. Tessa opened one eye and found Denver staring at her. His eyes were as blue as a clear mountain stream, his hair rumpled and black, the lines in his face less severe than they had been. He'd kicked himself free of the sheet, and he lay completely naked across the bed. Sunlight streaked his skin, gilding the firm ripple of his muscles.

"About time you woke up."

"Mmm." She stretched. "What time is it?"

"Early."

"And you're awake?" she teased, glancing at the clock.

"I wasn't. But this ravishing blonde kept kicking me and trying to push me out of bed."

She grinned impishly. "Maybe you didn't satisfy her."

White teeth flashed against his dark jaw. "Maybe I didn't," he growled, rolling over so quickly, she didn't have time to escape. "Maybe I should try again."

She giggled as his mouth descended on hers. "Denver, stop," she cried, gasping for air and laughing all at once.

"No way. You threw down the gauntlet, and I'm accepting the challenge."

Wiggling, she tried to squirm away from him, but the task proved impossible. Just when she slid one of her legs out from under him, he captured her again, pinning her against the sheets and grinning wickedly.

"Let me up!"

"Give?" he taunted.

"No—never," she gasped.

"Glad you haven't changed, Tess." With her wrists bound over her head by his hands, and her legs immobile under his weight, he touched the tip of his tongue to her lips, rimming her mouth leisurely.

"You're—"

"What?"

"Incorrigible!" she said, for lack of another word. Her mind was spinning and her blood had already turned molten. His tongue flicked in and out of her mouth quickly, darting and parrying, touching but not lingering. "We— we've got to get up," she whispered, but already her traitorous body was arching closer to his, her hips thrusting upward, demanding more of this delicious torment.

"Why?"

"Dad—and Mitchell. They'll be here any minute—"

"So you give, right?"

"No!"

His eyes darkened seductively. "Good."

She could see the cords highlighting his shoulder muscles, the washboard of his flat abdomen, the soft hair clinging to his legs. He touched first his tongue and then his lips to the tip of one breast and she groaned low in her throat.

Tessa writhed beneath him, but her struggle was not to break free, but to close the gap that separated their bodies. He rubbed against her, molding his hips to hers, letting her feel how much he wanted her.

Her throat was hot and swollen, desire a living thing, stalking through her blood, hungry and wild. Only this one man could satisfy her. She realized with sudden, time-stopping clarity that she loved him more than she had all those years ago.

His lips found hers again and she knew that he'd lost all self-control. His hands slid down her arms, caressing her skin. The game of wills was over.

She sucked in her breath as he thrust into her. The lava within her roiled, spreading through her limbs, moving faster and faster, hot and liquid at her very center. Her soul seemed to burst in a glorious explosion of passion that rocked the earth.

"Don't leave me," she cried, arching upward to be closer to him, her fingers digging into the firm muscles of his shoulders.

"Right here, love," he vowed, his hands on her hips as he spilled himself in her. "Tessa, oh, God, Tessa." His arms surrounded her. His breath was ragged against her skin, his lips still moving as he murmured her name over and over.

If only nothing would ever change, she thought dreamily. If only Denver and I could stay here, entwined, bound as man and woman forever. If only we could shut out the rest of the world.

Slowly, as the minutes ticked by, Tessa shed her cloak of afterglow and the passion-dusted dreams of a woman desperately in love. "I have to get up," she said reluctantly.

Denver's arms tightened around her, but she slid quickly form his grasp.

"Why?" He glanced up at her from the bed, and she almost changed her mind. The rumpled sheets, the scent of lovemaking lingering in the air and the misty light of dawn stealing into the room were hard to push aside.

"One of us has to keep up appearances," she decided.

"We're adults—"

"I know." She was already braiding her hair. "And I'm not ashamed. But let's not announce the fact that we spent the night together—at least not yet."

"You'd rather hide like a teenager caught in the backseat?"

"I'd rather keep my private life private." She snapped the braid into place and pulled on a clean denim skirt and cotton sweater. "I'll deal with Dad and Mitch when I'm ready." Besides, she thought to herself, what would she tell them—that she'd fallen into bed with Denver McLean? That she was in the middle of an affair—a one-night stand—what? How could she explain that despite all the accusations and lies, regardless of the fact that he'd left her without a word, she loved him so desperately that she would rather have one night alone with him than salvage her pride?

"I wouldn't mind breakfast in bed," he said, watching as she tugged on her boots.

"In your dreams." But she laughed.

"Eggs Benedict, fresh grapefruit, sectioned of course—"

"Of course," she mocked.

"Toast with honey, coffee and—"

"And this!" Snatching a pillow that had fallen to the floor, she hurled it across the room and smack into Denver's chest. Before he could exact any retribution, she slipped into the hall. "Fresh grapefruit!" she repeated, laughing as she clambered down the stairs. "You wish!" She knew her cheeks were flushed and her eyes were sparkling outrageously as she entered the kitchen, but she didn't care. Though she half expected her father to be seated at the table with the newspaper spread in front of him, she squared her shoulders.

Luckily no one had arrived yet. She managed to put on the coffee, snap some toast into the toaster and melt butter in the frying pan by the time Denver sauntered down the stairs.

"I guess I should've waited," he said, standing behind her and slipping his arms around her waist.

"For what?"

"To be served, of course."

She cracked an egg in the pan and grinned. "And you would've waited till hell freezes over."

Chuckling, he drew her close, his hands familiar and warm as they spread across her denim-draped abdomen. "I suppose I would have."

"Right!" Dear God, she sounded as breathless as a sultry summer night. "Unless you have something better to do, you can pour the coffee and butter the toast."

"I do have something better to do." He kissed her throat and ear. "Something much more important."

Her chest constricted. "I think it'll wait."

"Slave driver," he grumbled, but unwillingly released her to search in the cupboard for coffee cups.

"Second shelf," she said, catching his glance. In that one heart-stopping moment, she read the love deep in his eyes.

"Thanks."

Swallowing a thick lump forming in her throat, she turned back to the bacon sizzling noisily in the skillet.

They were just finishing the meal when Milly walked in, her arms laden with two sacks of groceries. "You found somethin' to eat, did ya?" she asked, glancing at the table.

"Plenty," Denver replied.

Tessa helped Milly unload the sacks. "By the way," Milly said, stacking two loaves of bread in the bread box, "that attorney called yesterday afternoon."

Denver's head snapped up. "Ross Anderson?"

Milly nodded. "He said that he was sure they'd found your brother."

Tessa's heart nearly stopped. "Colton?"

"Where?" Denver asked.

Milly shrugged. "Said you knew about it."

Dumbfounded, Tessa stared at Denver. Why hadn't he mentioned that Colton had been located?

"I knew some private investigator *thought* he might have found Colton in Northern Ireland. But since I hadn't heard anything in days, I figured he was wrong."

"Doesn't seem that way," Milly said, glancing from Tessa to Denver and back again. "He said he'd call back tomorrow. He's in court today."

"Great," Denver grumbled, his countenance changing. "Did he say if Colton was returning?"

"Nope. That was it."

The phone jangled, and Milly answered it, then handed the receiver to Tessa. "Nate Edwards."

Tessa's nerves tightened. "Good morning," she said, forcing a smile into her voice.

"Same to you. I've been thinking, and I've decided I want the stallion and those two mares—the black and the chestnut."

"Both?" she repeated.

"If you're willing to sell."

She swallowed back the urge to tell him no, that she wanted to keep all three. "I am," she said, though a pain slashed deep into her heart.

"Good. Now, I know the mares are both with foal, and I'll buy 'em as such and keep the offspring, but if you'd rather, you can have the foals after they're weaned. I'll sell 'em back to you at a fair price."

"I'd appreciate that."

"I'll give you fifty thousand for the whole lot. I figure the stallion's worth twenty-five and the mares in their condition are between twelve and thirteen apiece."

She couldn't argue. She'd already decided that she wouldn't take less than forty; the extra ten thousand was a godsend.

"I'll give you a couple days to think on it."

"What was that all about?" Denver asked as Tessa slowly replaced the receiver.

"Nate Edwards has offered to buy Brigadier and the mares. It's enough money for the down payment on this place."

"And the rest?"

"The bank will loan the difference, I think," she said, sitting carefully in the nearest chair. Now that her dream was so close, almost in hand, she was scared.

"And Colton's been found." Denver didn't smile as he stared at her. "It looks, Ms. Kramer, as if you're on your way to owning a ranch." The words were said without malice, but there was an empty note in his voice. Denver finished his coffee, placed his dishes in the sink and turned toward the door. "I think I'll get cleaned up and drive into Helena. Maybe I can catch Ross when he gets out of court."

"I don't suppose you'd want company?" Tessa asked boldly.

His eyebrows shot up. "Don't you have things to do around here?"

She lifted a shoulder. "Mitch and Dad can handle everything. We may as well give them a trial run, don't you think?" she added, ignoring the quizzical look on Milly's face.

He grinned and drawled, "That might not be a bad idea. I'll be ready to go in about twenty minutes."

"I'll be waiting."

"And I'll tell your brother and father they're in charge," Milly said.

While Denver showered and changed, Tessa walked outside. The morning air was brisk, the grass still covered with dew. From his paddock, Brigadier whistled softly, tossing his head. Sunlight gilded his red coat as he hoisted his tail high in the air and raced around the fence with long, sweeping strides.

"You know this is killing me, don't you?" Tessa asked, delving in her pocket for a bit of apple. As the big stallion nipped the morsel from her palm, she wrestled with her conscience. Caught in a vicious circle, she found no answers. If she didn't sell her best horses, she wouldn't have money to buy the ranch, and if she couldn't buy the ranch, someone else would. Then she and her animals would have to find a new place—a place they could afford, a place that might not be big enough to support her growing herd. Besides, Nate Edwards was a good horseman and he'd treat her horses well.

But the crux of the problem was Denver. As it always had been. If she bought the ranch from him, he'd surely leave. If she didn't buy the McLean place, he might stay longer, but only for a while. Then he'd be forced to return to L.A. For good. Without her. She had agreed to a weekend trip to California, but not a lifetime in L.A., which, she reminded herself, he hadn't asked her to share.

Her brows drew together in vexation. "Damned if you do, damned if you don't," she murmured, eyeing Brigadier fondly. There was just no perfect answer.

"Ready?" Denver called as he crossed the yard.

Tessa whirled and her breath caught in her throat. Clean-shaven, his hair neatly combed, he was dressed in a gray business suit—no longer the man she loved, but a stranger— an engineer who owned a firm of his own in Los Angeles.

"As ready as I'll ever be," she quipped. She walked to Denver's rental car just as her father and Mitchell drove in.

Mitchell was out of the cab before the truck had rolled to a complete stop. "Going somewhere?" he asked.

"Into Helena. It looks as if Colton's finally surfaced," Tessa explained.

"Has he?" Mitchell's lips tightened. "I suppose he's coming back here, too?"

"We don't know yet," Denver cut in.

Tessa caught the anger in her brother's eyes, and she understood it. It had been Colton McLean's horrid words that had turned Denver away from her. Colton hadn't held his tongue after the fire. In his outrage and fury, his false accusations had cut deep, wounding everyone in her family.

She didn't blame Mitch for hating him. But soon it would be over, and soon the McLeans would be out of this part of Montana. At that particular thought, her stomach churned. After these past few weeks, she wondered if she would find any joy in life without Denver. "We'll work things out," she said to Mitch.

Shoving his hat on his head, he muttered, "I wonder."

Denver's lips drew tight. "Let's go."

Tessa slid into the passenger side of the car, turning a stiff shoulder to the anger smoldering in her brother's gaze.

"When Colton gets back here, the fireworks are really going to start," she predicted, slanting a glance at Denver as he drove down the long lane and turned onto the main road.

Denver's answer was a grimace.

By midmorning the rolling hills had given way to the city of Helena. Denver drove toward the heart of the city and past the copper-domed capitol building before parking near the courthouse.

"You're going to wait for Ross here?" she asked, eyeing the building.

"Maybe. But first we'll check with his secretary; find out when he's supposed to be out of court. Then we'll have lunch."

He linked his fingers through hers and started across the street. A few minutes later they were standing in front of a huge oak desk in the reception area of a steel-and-glass building. The names of O'Brien, Simmons and Taft were mounted on the wall in chrome letters, and a petite woman with shining copper hair and a wide, friendly smile had waved them into the high-backed chairs in the waiting room. "Mr. Anderson's in court, but his secretary is in."

Within minutes a tall svelte blonde with striking dark eyebrows and a midnight-blue dress swept through the doors. Her glossy lips curved at the sight of Denver. "Mr. McLean," she said, extending her hand, her silver bracelet jangling a little. "I'm sorry but Ross isn't in right now."

Denver took her hand for a second, then let it fall. "This is Tessa Kramer," he said quickly.

"Nancy Pomeroy," the blonde replied.

"Nice to meet you," Tessa said woodenly.

Denver explained, "Tessa runs the ranch."

If that surprised Nancy, she managed to keep her face expressionless.

Denver added, "Yesterday Ross called and said he'd located my brother. I wasn't at the house and didn't get the message until this morning."

"And you're anxious to know what's going on," Nancy guessed. "I don't blame you."

"When will Ross be back?"

"Not until late afternoon."

Denver scowled, but there wasn't much he could do, Tessa realized. "We'll be back," he said, taking Tessa's hand again. "Don't let him slip away."

Nancy nodded, her brown eyes twinkling behind thick, mascara-blackened lashes. "I'll tie him to the desk if I have to."

"I'd appreciate it," Denver said with a lazy smile.

Inwardly, Tessa groaned. She saw the look of playful longing in Nancy's eyes and the easy response of Denver's grin. How many other women did Denver smile for? How many pairs of eyes had gazed longingly into his? Los Angeles was a big city—much larger than Helena—and so near Hollywood, it was practically oozing with beautiful women, actresses and models....

"Something wrong?" Denver asked as he shouldered open the glass door and squinted against the sunlight reflecting on the sidewalk and windows of the buildings lining the street.

"Nothing serious," she replied, fighting to repress the jealousy that coiled around her heart when she considered the fact that Denver might have a dozen women waiting for him in Los Angeles.

"You're worried about Colton, aren't you?"

"That's part of it, I suppose." It wasn't really a lie. Facing Colton wasn't going to be a bed of roses.

"And the rest?" There was a break in traffic and he pulled gently on her hand. They jaywalked across the street to a park.

"I was just wondering about your life in L.A."

"What about it?"

"I won't fit in. Not even for a weekend."

"Sure you will." They were walking more slowly now, the branches of the shade trees stirring lazily in the warm summer breeze. The noise of the traffic faded away. Children scampered down the worn paths to a playground and dogs bounded across the grass. She had to ask the question that had been with her ever since seeing Nancy Pomeroy's response to him. "Isn't there a woman in L.A.?"

"Thousands of them."

"You know what I mean."

He laughed loudly, startling a bird in the lacy branches overhead. The jay flapped noisily away. "A woman," he repeated, amused, "as in a lover?"

It sounded so childish. She couldn't meet his eyes. "It doesn't matter," she lied.

"Or mistress? Or fiancée?" he prodded.

"It was just a question," she retorted, angry with herself. "Don't make a federal case of it."

One side of his mouth curved upward, and he pulled on her wrist, tugging her off the path and around the broad trunk of a maple tree. "What do you think?" he asked, pinning her against the scratchy bark, his eyes delving deep into hers.

"I think it would be stupid of me to believe that an attractive man, who's not quite over the hill—"

"Over the hill?" he hooted, his blue eyes filled with mirth. "Me?"

"I said 'not quite over the hill'. Anyway, it's very possible that there's some woman waiting for you back in L.A."

"Not one," he corrected, touching the line of her jaw familiarly. "Dozens."

"You're impossible!"

"That's why they all love me." His arms were on either side of her head, effectively imprisoning her against the bole while the wind sifted through the leaves overhead.

"Be serious!"

"I am." His lips, thin and sensual, twisted in amusement. "Don't you know me better than to think I'm ready to bed any woman who shows some interest?"

"I used to think so."

"Don't you still? Didn't last night mean anything?" he asked, his smile fading as he touched the end of her braid with his fingers.

"It meant a lot. To me."

"And to me." His breath was warm against her face, his gaze sincere. She could see the pinpoints of light in his eyes, the perspiration beading on his brow.

She swallowed hard, and he noticed the movement, his gaze shifting to her throat. "I can't lie and say there haven't been other women, Tess. Seven years is a long time. But there haven't been all that many, and none of them, *none*, can hold a candle to you."

Absurdly, she wanted to cry. But she fought her tears. His lips rubbed lightly over hers. She wrapped her arms around his neck, mindless of the mothers with young children in strollers, the adolescents on bikes, the older men and women sitting together, shoulders touching, on park benches.

His arms circled her and he held her close, the kiss deepening, his lips as hot and hungry as they had been the night before. When he finally lifted his head, his breathing was ragged, but a smile tugged at the corners of his mouth. "Not that your jealousy isn't flattering," he said.

"Jealousy?" she retorted, wanting to deny what was so patently obvious.

"Admit it, Tess, you were jealous!"

"I hate jealous women."

"And I love them." He laughed again and dragged her from the relative privacy of the trees. "How about some lunch?"

"You're changing the subject."

"I'm hungry."

Cajoled out of her worries by his good mood, she laughed. "I am, too."

"Good. If things haven't changed too much, I remember a great little café with a view of Mount Helena."

The café was long gone. But they did find a small Italian restaurant not far from the courthouse. As the waiter brought pasta and Chablis, Denver sat across from Tessa at the table and clinked his glass to hers. "Here's to . . . a long and successful business arrangement."

Tessa almost choked. "Business arrangement?"

"Umm. You said you wanted to buy the ranch."

"I do."

"Well, now that Colton's been found and you've sold your horses—you have sold them, haven't you?"

Swallowing with difficulty, she set down her glass. "Nate's made a generous offer," she admitted.

"Then all that's left is to draw up a contract, sign it and take it to the bank. Right?"

Suddenly feeling depressed, she nodded. "If Colton agrees."

"And if he doesn't—you still want my half?"

"Yes," she said firmly, though inside she was dying a little. All her dreams of owning the ranch, of being mistress of the McLean spread, seemed to shrivel in front of her very eyes. Without Denver, the ranch meant so little. She shoved her fettuccine around on her plate and tried to eat. Her appetite had disappeared.

"But first you have to pay off your bet," he reminded her.

"And then what happens? When everything's signed, sealed and delivered, will you just head back to California?"

"What else?" He eyed her quietly, sipping his wine, his jaw thrust forward.

"Nothing, I guess," she whispered, then gave herself a quick mental kick. She wasn't about to let go without a whimper. "You said last night was something special," she said, meeting his gaze again.

"It was."

"But it doesn't have to go on forever, is that it?"

"I didn't say—"

Her anger sparked. "Were we just 'experimenting' again, Denver? Seeing if it was as good as when we were kids?"

"What're you getting at?"

"Last night was more than a one-night stand. At least for me. I didn't wait seven years just to be used and tossed aside again!"

A muscle jumped in his jaw. "I never intended to use you."

"But it happened." She felt her cheeks flame, but she couldn't control the rage and hurt deep inside. "I don't want another affair, Denver," she snapped. "I had enough trouble living through the last one."

"You were only nineteen."

"And now I'm twenty-six, but my values haven't changed," she said angrily, tossing her napkin into her plate and stalking out of the restaurant. Outside the sun was blinding. She marched down the street, but Denver caught up with her on the second block, grabbed her hand and whirled her around.

"What do you want from me, Tessa? A marriage proposal?" he fumed.

Yes! "I'm not trying to manipulate you, Denver."

"Aren't you?"

She wanted to slap him and tell him to take his hands off her. But her dignity wouldn't allow this fight to be aired to all the good citizens of Helena. "Leave it alone, Denver," she said between clenched teeth, wrenching her arm away from him.

"That's the problem, Tess," he said, sighing. "I can't leave it alone. Just like I can't leave you alone. But, by the same token, I can't lie to you or promise you things that just won't happen."

"Look, you don't have to go on about this. I didn't ask you to marry me, did I?" She started up the street again and he kept up with her, stride for stride, until they reached the car. At that point she had to stop. The car was locked and there was nowhere she could run—no place she could hide.

"We need to talk," he growled, shoving his scarred hand through his ebony hair.

"Maybe we should've done more *talking* last night!"

Tense as a panther ready to strike, he paced from one end of the car to the other. "I just don't know what you want from me—"

"Denver?" Ross Anderson's voice boomed over the sound of traffic.

Denver's head jerked up. He watched in mild surprise as the wiry young attorney, briefcase tucked under one arm, dashed down the courthouse steps. "We'll discuss this later," he said from the corner of his mouth.

"Right." Tessa was disbelieving.

"Later!" Then, forcing a tight smile onto his face, he observed Ross zigzagging through the traffic.

"I called the office and Nancy said you were waiting for me," Ross said as he extended his free hand, "but I didn't think you'd be camping out on the courthouse steps."

"We weren't—we were just having a...discussion. Ross, I'd like you to meet Tessa Kramer. Tessa—Ross."

Ross grinned, his narrow face cracking with a smile. "I've heard a lot about you, Ms. Kramer. John McLean was one of your biggest fans." He offered his hand and Tessa shook it. But her gaze traveled past the expensive weave of his jacket to clash with the anger in Denver's eyes.

"John was good to me and my family. We miss him."

"Don't we all?" Ross shot a glance at Denver, whose lips had tightened until they were white.

"Have you heard anything else about Colton?" Denver demanded.

Ross reached into his pocket and withdrew a long, thin cigar. "Is that what this is all about?"

"Ms. Kramer, here, wants to purchase the ranch—all of it. We need to talk to my brother, then work out a purchase agreement. Since you're involved in the probate of his estate, I'd like you to iron out the details."

"If Colt agrees." Ross snapped his lighter over the end of his cheroot and puffed furiously, sending up a stream of small, blue clouds.

"Even if he doesn't, she wants my half."

Ross squinted thoughtfully through the smoke. "Unless Colt wants the entire place. There's a provision in John's will, you know. If one brother doesn't want his share, the other has the option to buy him out at fair market value."

Tessa's heart sank. Not only was she losing Denver to the bright lights of Los Angeles, but even if she did sell her horses and the bank approved her loan, Colton might want the place! Though he'd been overseas for years, he might want to quit his dangerous job, give up his wanderlust and settle back in the valley where his family had lived for generations.

"Colton won't want the ranch any more than I do," Denver said tightly. "He left right after the fire, too. Hasn't been back since."

"A man could change his mind when he owns the land."

"I didn't." Denver stared pointedly at Tessa.

"You're not your brother. Come on, we can talk more comfortably in my office."

Puffing smoke like a steam engine, Ross led the way, and within minutes they were seated around his desk. "So you're here about Colton."

"Have you heard from him?" Denver asked, leaning back in his leather chair and eyeing the attorney.

Ross shook his head. "Not Colton himself. But the P.I. called again. He's sure the man he's seen is Colton—though his looks have changed. He just hasn't gotten close enough to talk to him yet. It's touchy, you know."

"Touchy?" Tessa asked. "How?"

"Dangerous. No one wants to blow Colt's cover," Denver explained, drumming his fingers on the arm of his chair.

"You make it sound like he's a spy."

"Close enough," Denver muttered. "Close enough."

"I don't know when we'll actually hear from Colton," Ross said, "but the investigator's supposed to call back in a few days. Hopefully he will have contacted him by then."

Denver's face muscles were tight. "Tell your man I want to talk to my brother."

"I'll try."

"And if by some fluke Colton himself calls, let him know what's going on; explain about John and the land. Let him know we have a buyer."

Ross scribbled himself a note and Tessa's name leaped off the clean yellow page.

"Maybe you shouldn't tell him who wants to buy," Denver decided, surveying Ross's notes.

"Why not?"

Denver glanced at Tessa. "He and the Kramers have never seen eye to eye."

Tessa's mouth went dry. Dealing with Denver's accusations had been bad enough. She couldn't imagine what Colton would say if and when he returned. No amount of arguing had changed his mind before he left Montana. She doubted anything would now.

Secretly Tessa had wondered if Colton had been behind the accident. Though he was supposed to have been in town with John when the blaze started, he hadn't been. John had admitted as much later. And Colton had arrived at the ranch quickly—just as the explosion had rocked through the stables. However, she'd kept her thoughts to herself. Pointing fingers without proof was a McLean trait, and she wasn't about to lower herself to that level. But the thought of seeing Colton again hung like a pall over her. First facing Colton—then watching Denver leave for Los Angeles. Déjà vu, she thought wearily.

"—I'll let you know the minute I hear anything," Ross was promising Denver.

"Good. Just make sure we don't put Colt in any jeopardy." Denver stretched his arm toward Ross.

"I'll give it my best shot!" The wiry attorney shook Denver's hand, but looked at Tessa. "Nice meeting you, Ms. Kramer."

"You, too."

On the way home, she barely said a word to Denver. They stopped for dinner at a restaurant owned by a young couple who served "family-style" meals. The room was crowded, the table big enough to hold four couples, which it did, but there wasn't one bit of intimacy.

Tessa ate the chicken and dumplings and didn't taste a bite. She couldn't think of anything save the fact that Denver was planning to leave her again. Not that he'd ever promised anything else, she knew. And there was some time left—time to be shared here and in California. But the prospect of living the rest of her life without him was more depressing than she'd ever imagined. The past seven years she'd known that somewhere, sometime, she'd see him again, but now it seemed that once he left for Los Angeles, the only contact she would have with him would be quarterly statements about the ranch—property tax statements, income taxes and such—until he was completely bought out.

And what then? Would he return to the ranch whenever he wanted, to check up on her? Take her to bed for one night only to leave the next day? Her head was swimming, her eyes hot. She could barely breathe.

Shoving her chair away from the table, she scrambled to her feet. "I need some fresh air," she explained, not waiting for Denver's reaction. She struck out through the restaurant's front door and didn't stop until she was in the parking lot, breathing in huge gulps, mentally kicking herself for loving him.

She heard his footsteps thudding on the boards of the front porch. Before she could turn around, she felt his arms surround her waist, his breath on her nape. "I've been an ass," he decided, and she clenched her fists impotently.

She couldn't agree more. "This is all coming down too quickly. The ranch, Colton, you. It's not turning out like it was supposed to."

"No fairy-tale ending?" he mocked.

"I suppose I deserved that."

"What is it you want, Tessa?"

You, her heart thundered. *Just you!*

"If you want the ranch, I'll sell it to you. If you want Colton's share, I'll convince him you're the right buyer. If you need money, I'll loan it to you. Whatever it is that will make you happy..."

She tried not to shake. Her heart wrenched. "The ranch is all I've ever wanted," she whispered, her tongue tripping on the lie. *Tell him! Tell him you love him!* a part of her cried, but pride kept her silent.

"Then there's nothing to worry about. Let me handle Colton." He kissed the nape of her neck. A shiver darted quickly up her spine to linger at the spot where he'd brushed his lips across her skin.

"Let's go," she murmured.

Denver yanked viciously on the tie still knotted at his throat, then threw his jacket into the back seat. After rolling his sleeves over his forearms, he helped Tessa into the car, then slid behind the wheel.

For most of the drive, they didn't speak. The late-afternoon sun descended slowly behind the rocky peaks to the west, streaking the sky in a blaze of pink and gold.

Tessa closed her eyes. She pushed her worries aside and leaned back in the seat, letting the heat of the day settle around her as Denver drove steadily north. Dusk had just shaded the sky when they passed her father's cottage and the lane to the McLean ranch came into view.

"Almost home," Tessa murmured.

"Not yet." Denver said quietly. He stepped on the throttle, passing the lane.

"What're you doing?" Tessa asked, surprised.

He smiled crookedly. "I thought we deserved a detour." A quarter of a mile past the lane, he cranked hard on the wheel. The car responded, lurching onto the old silver mining road. Barely more than twin ruts in the bleached grass, the tracks curved, snaking along the banks of the Sage River and the Aldridge property before climbing the gentle slope of the surrounding foothills.

"Where're we going?" Tessa asked, though she had already guessed. This road led not only to the abandoned mine, but to the ridge where she and Denver had first made love. Nervously she reached for the handle of the car door, wrapping her fingers around the armrest.

The little car bumped and spun, leaving a cloud of dust. Denver had to flip on the lights as shadows lengthened stealthily through the trees. "I just wanted to see this place again."

"Nothing's changed," she said, her stomach knotting, her palms beginning to sweat. She'd been up to the ridge more times than she wanted to count, remembering how wonderful that afternoon had been before the smell of smoke and the crackle of flames had clouded the clear air and altered the course of their lives forever.

The road gave way to a clearing, and he parked, switching off the lights. Only the moon and stars illuminated the night, turning the dry grass opalescent. Two small shacks, sagging now from disuse, were the last reminders of the silver that had existed only in John McLean's dreams.

Denver climbed out of the car and stretched, rubbing his shoulder muscles.

Tessa joined him. "What is it they say about never going back?" she asked, hoping to sound lighthearted though her heart continued to beat unevenly.

"If *they*'re talking about L.A., *they*'re wrong." He strode swiftly through the stubble, ignoring the rambling blackberry vines and weeds clutching at his pants. He made his way up a short path to the ridge.

She scrambled after him. "I was talking about coming back here." A bramble pulled at her skirt, a branch tugged at her hair, but she closed the distance, catching Denver just at the edge of the cliff.

Majestic pines towered high overhead, their long needled branches soughing in the soft summer breeze. And the valley floor, in contrast to the dark trees, shifted restlessly under the moonlight. Cattle dotted the landscape, dark lumbering shapes against the moonlit grass. Its windows glowing with square patches of light, the main house was visible, as was the winding Sage River, a moon-washed ribbon reflecting a wide canopy of twinkling stars. Far in the distance, the lights of her father's house shone gold in an otherwise silvery night.

"How can you leave this place?" she wondered aloud.

He stared down at her. "It's not the land I'm leaving," he said quietly. "Nor the work. Leaving the ranching life behind is easy." His fingers were gentle on her arms. "What's hard is leaving you."

Tessa's breath expelled in a rush. She could barely believe her ears. And she wouldn't. Words were easy. Too easy. She'd heard them before. "You don't have to leave."

"What I don't have to do is repeat a conversation we had a long time ago."

Her heart squeezed wretchedly at the memories of their arguments, long dead. Now, as before, nothing she could say would stop him. He was willing to sell her this part of his past, the dust, the trees, the stream and buildings, but he couldn't, wouldn't, give her the one thing she wanted most—his love.

Angry with herself for loving him when he didn't care, she turned, unable to face him. She stared across the valley floor. But he placed one finger under her chin and pushed it upward, forcing her gaze to meet his. Her pulse trembled in her throat, and before she could say a word, he lowered his head and kissed her. Long and hard and hot, the kiss touched the very deepest part of her soul. His tongue slid familiarly past her teeth, his hands unwound her braid.

Her hair tumbled free in a twisted cloud that fell past her shoulders.

She knew in her heart that she should stop him, but the night and her senses were against her. She couldn't pull away from him any more than she could stop breathing—or still the wretched pounding beat of her heart.

Just once more, her mind screamed, drowning all her doubts. *Just love me once more.*

As his weight pulled her downward, onto that very patch of ground where they'd made love so long ago, she didn't protest, but fell willingly, accepting his passion for what it was and meeting that delicious desire with her own driving needs.

For as long as he stayed, she would be with him. And she would cherish each moment even as she knew that as surely as the sun would come up in the morning, Denver would leave.

Chapter Ten

I saw it happen," Mitchell said, as he and Tessa examined Brigadier in his stall the next day. The stallion's head hung low and he favored his right front leg. "He picked up a loose piece of gravel in the yard."

Tessa's brows drew into a worried frown. "Poor baby. Let's take a look." Tessa lifted the hoof, then moved quickly when Brigadier tried to nip her. "Hey, watch it!"

"I'll hold his head," Mitchell offered, stroking Brigadier's sleek neck. "I hope he doesn't turn up lame. That could spoil your deal with Nate Edwards."

"It doesn't matter," Tessa said sharply, her fingers running expertly along the edge of the stallion's tender hoof. Brigadier rolled his eyes and his ears flattened as she worked. "Looks like a bruised sole," she thought aloud. Brigadier snorted and jerked hard on the lead rope. "Find the toolbox and help me get this shoe off."

Together they removed the shoe and Tessa pared out the bruised area of the inner hoof. "I'll pack it with a poultice, but we'd better call Craig Fulton and have him take a look at it," Tessa said quickly.

Craig was a young veterinarian who lived on a ranch nearby. He operated a clinic for large animals and house pets that was located on the outskirts of Three Falls.

"I'll call him," Mitchell offered.

"Good. I'll finish here."

Mitchell left the barn to phone the vet while Tessa cleaned the bruised area of Brigadier's hoof then packed it with a poultice. Once assured that the stallion was comfortable, she rubbed his jagged white blaze and handed him a piece of apple. The fruit was whisked out of her open palm before she had time to blink.

"Thank goodness you still have your appetite," she said, patting his soft muzzle before closing the gate to his stall behind her.

The barn door squeaked open and Tessa, expecting Mitchell, glanced over her shoulder. Denver! She'd left him less than an hour ago in the study, but her heart tripped at the sight of him.

Tall and masculine, he winked at her. "I thought I'd find you here."

Her pulse leaped.

Dressed in a gray sport coat, black slacks and a crisp white shirt, he was dashing and handsome and, unfortunately, looked as if he belonged in a high-rise office building in some huge city.

She, on the other hand, was wearing dusty jeans and a checked blouse. Not exactly haute couture.

"Brigadier's favoring his right foreleg. I think it's a bruised sole," she explained.

"I know. Mitch was on the phone in the kitchen."

"Eavesdropping?" she teased.

"About horse ailments? Hardly. I'm on my way back to Helena. Jim Van Stern called. He has some legal papers he wants Ross to draw up." He reached her and wrapped his arms comfortably around her waist. "I thought you'd like to join me." He flashed her a devilish grin and his blue eyes danced irreverently.

"I'd love to," she admitted. She wanted to be with him every minute of every day.

"Then do it." He whispered into her ear. "Just this once, indulge yourself. We could spend the night, order room service for dinner and never leave the hotel again."

"Now who's the dreamer?" she quipped, though she tingled inside.

He kissed her neck, his lips warm and inviting. "Come on, Tess."

More than anything she wanted to go with him. "You know I can't, not with Brigadier lame."

"The vet will take care of him."

She shook her head and toyed with the buttons on his shirt. "How about a rain check?"

One side of Denver's mouth lifted engagingly. "You've got it. How about tomorrow night?"

"You're willing to drive all the way to Helena again?"

His blue eyes twinkled. "For a night alone with you? You bet."

"We're alone here at night."

"It's not the same. Any minute I expect your dad or brother or Milly to show up and interrupt us." His lips pressed against her forehead. "I'd like to be alone with you where no one could find us for days."

A shiver of anticipation swept up her spine. "Sounds wonderful," she whispered. Denver lowered his head and kissed her softly on the lips. Responding, Tessa wound her arms around his neck just as Brigadier stuck his head over the stall gate and shoved her.

She lost her footing and fell heavily against Denver, who laughed in surprise.

"Someone's jealous," Denver observed. "Be careful, my friend," he said to the stallion, "this one's mine."

Brigadier tossed his great head, and Tessa felt a lump fill her throat. She rubbed the stallion's nose fondly. "I'm going to miss you," she said, her voice low.

"Then the sale is final?"

She nodded. "Nate plans to pick up Brigadier and the mares tomorrow."

As if understanding the conversation, Brigadier whinnied plaintively.

Denver's arms tightened around Tessa's waist. "You don't have to sell him, you know."

"I don't want to talk about it." She tried to extract herself, but Denver wouldn't let go.

"I know how fond you are of your horses."

"They're like family," she admitted.

"That's why you should keep them."

"Is this a way of getting out of selling the ranch to me?"

"I didn't say that. But maybe we could come up with some other way of financing the sale."

"I don't see how."

"I could waive the down payment—in effect loan the money to you without interest."

"And how would Colton feel about that?"

Denver's jaw hardened. "I'll deal with Colton, *if* I ever see him again."

Tessa considered her alternatives. Leaning against the power of Denver's chest, hearing the steady beat of his heart, feeling his breath stir her hair, she was just about willing to do anything he suggested. Except become beholden to him. "I don't think I should borrow money from you," she said softly. "People might get the wrong idea."

She felt him stiffen, saw a flash of anger in his eyes. "You mean the way some people might have gotten the wrong idea about you and John."

Her emotions, already strung tight, snapped. Tessa scrambled out of his arms. "That was different and you know it!"

"How?"

"I wasn't sleeping with John!" Bristling with injustice, she gave her hot temper free rein. "I thought we settled this."

"We have," he said tightly. "I just don't understand why you can work a deal with John and not with me."

"Because you and I—we're... *involved!*"

"All the more reason to help each other."

"Not like this," she said. "I can't accept gifts from you, Denver, or loans without collateral."

"Why not?"

"Don't you know?" she asked in wonder. "Don't you realize that I don't want to be obligated to you—that I wouldn't want you obligated to me. You're the one who doesn't want any strings attached in this relationship. You're the one hell-bent to run back to L.A."

"I thought you were coming with me," he said slowly.

"That would only make it worse! I can't borrow money from you and then follow you like some moon-eyed calf to California! I no more belong on Rodeo Drive than—"

"*I* do in a hick town the size of Three Falls, Montana," he cut in, the edge in his voice sharp.

"You were born and raised here!"

"An accident of my birth."

She sucked in a swift, disbelieving breath. "Do you hate it here so much?"

He bit back the urge to say Yes! I hate this goddamned ranch and all the memories it brings—memories of pain and suffering and thick yellow smoke and flames. Instead he sealed his mouth shut. He didn't hate this valley or this ranch. His aversion to it was long over. But it wasn't the land that beckoned him. It was Tessa.

"I've got to leave," he said quietly, his face a mask. "You coming?"

Shaking her head, she said, "I'd better stay. The vet's probably already on his way."

"Then I'll see you tomorrow." He turned and walked quickly down the concrete corridor between the rows of stalls. Nearly colliding with Mitch in the doorway, he muttered a curse under his breath without breaking stride.

Mitch stared after him. "What was that all about?" he asked.

"Don't ask me."

Mitch frowned. "I am asking you. And you'd better tell me what's going on between the two of you."

"Nothing, Mitch."

"Sure."

"I told you—it's just business."

Mitch scowled, raking stiff fingers through his hair. "Okay, you win, Tess. Play it close to the vest. If you want Denver McLean, there's nothing I can say that will change your mind." His mouth compressed into a crooked smile. "I just hope he'll make you happy."

"I am happy," she said, turning back to Brigadier and changing the subject. "Did you call the vet?"

Mitch nodded. "Craig's busy. But his assistant's on her way."

"*Her* way?"

A slow grin spread across Mitchell's stubbled jaw. "That's right. Cassie Aldridge. Remember her?"

"How could I forget?" Tessa smiled faintly. Cassie was a couple of years younger than Tessa, and rumor had it, seven years before, that young Cassie had thrown herself at Colton McLean, making a fool of herself over Denver's headstrong younger brother much the way Tessa had made a fool of herself over Denver.

"Good thing Colton isn't back yet," Mitch remarked.

"It's been a long time," Tessa said. "Cassie's probably changed a lot."

"Well, she isn't married yet—or if she is, she hasn't changed her name.

Tessa turned back to Brigadier and scratched him fondly under the forelock. "It doesn't matter if she's married or not. Let's just hope she can take care of our boy here."

An hour later, Tessa realized that Cassie Aldridge had changed a lot in the past seven years. No longer a teenager with a wild crush on one of the McLean brothers, she was a full-grown woman with shiny black hair and intelligent gray eyes. Thin and athletic, she handled Brigadier expertly as she examined his hoof.

"Doesn't look too bad," she announced, once she'd closed the stall gate behind her. "The poultice should work. Just make sure he rests for a week and keep the hoof clean."

Relieved, Tessa walked with Cassie out of the stallion barn. Outside, the sky was hazy. Low clouds hung over the ridge surrounding the valley floor. The air was still and hot.

"Brigadier's a good-looking stallion," Cassie said. She opened the door of her beat-up truck but paused before climbing into the sun-baked cab.

"The best. But you should know that. I bought him from your father."

"That's right," Cassie replied, her smooth forehead creasing a little. "Call me if Brigadier gets any worse—or better. I like to know the good news with the bad."

"Will do," Tessa promised.

Cassie hopped into the cab of her dusty old Dodge truck, ground the gears and took off.

The next day Tessa opened the door of the barn and was greeted with an excited whinny. Brigadier pawed the straw on the floor of his stall. His eyes were clear, his ears pricked and he barely favored the sore leg.

"A medical wonder, aren't you?" Tessa teased, scratching his ears fondly before giving him a carrot, which he ground noisily between his teeth.

Relieved, she brushed his rust-colored coat until it gleamed like polished copper. While she ran the currycomb across his hide, her thoughts drifted, as always, to Denver. Ever since he left the day before, she'd replayed their argument over and over in her mind. The fight had been silly and pointless, as arguments usually were. Still she was angry with him.

"He looks better," Mitchell said from somewhere behind her head.

Tessa nearly jumped out of her skin. "You scared me," she said with a nervous laugh.

"Didn't you hear me come in?"

She shook her head. "I . . . was thinking."

Mitchell poured oats into the manger, then walked outside with his sister. "Let me guess, you were thinking about Denver McLean." His green eyes were shadowed with worry, and deep grooves tightened the corners of his mouth. But he held his tongue and Tessa was grateful for that. She'd done enough soul-searching without having to be reprimanded by her brother. She wiped the sweat from her forehead and rinsed her hands in the cold water from a spigot near the barn. "I'm gonna run into town for some more wire for the fence bordering the Aldridge property. Want to come along?" he asked.

"I can't."

"Why not?"

"I've got things to do."

"Like wait for Denver to show up?"

"Like work on the invoices."

"Oh, come on. Lighten up a little. The bills aren't going anywhere."

"True, unfortunately."

"I'll buy you a hamburger." He offered her a smile and a wink. "Or I'll let you buy me one."

"And why would I do that?"

"Because I'm such a great brother."

She laughed. "Give me a break. Look, I can't go now. Nate Edwards is supposed to show up this afternoon."

Mitch's smile turned sad. "So this is it. You're really going to sell part of your herd. Unbelievable."

"It is hard to believe, isn't it?" she said, her voice gone rough at the thought. She shrugged her shoulders. "But it's almost done. Nate'll be good to them."

"Just make sure it's what you want," Mitch said before ambling toward the machine shed. "And if you change your mind and discover you can't live without a double-cheese bacon burger, let me know."

"I will."

She heard the sound of Nate Edwards's truck before she saw the big rig lumbering down the drive, a long horse trailer in tow, dust clouding behind.

Forcing a smile she didn't feel, Tessa waved as Nate ground the truck to a stop. He hopped out of the cab, and his daughter, Sherrie, unbuckled the straps from her car seat and jumped to the ground. "Tessie!" she squealed delightedly as she ran pell-mell into Tessa's waiting arms.

"How're you, sugarplum?" Tessa asked, hoisting the spirited child into the air.

"I want to see my new horse! Where is he?" she demanded. Her plump arms were crossed firmly over her chest.

"She," her father said, laughing. "You get one of the mares, remember?"

"Where is *she* then?"

"Over here." Tessa carried Sherrie to the fence beyond which Red Wing switched her tail, her body already round with the foal growing inside.

"I want to ride her!"

"You will."

"Right now!"

"Not on your life," Nate said, grinning widely as he plucked Sherrie out of Tessa's arms. "Maybe later, when we get home."

"But Tessa promised she'd teach me how to ride!"

"I will," Tessa vowed. "When your mom and dad say it's okay."

"That'll be never," Sherrie grumbled, her lower lip protruding unhappily.

"'Never' has a way of coming back to haunt you," Tessa said. "Sometimes when you least expect it or don't want it." *How many times had she promised herself she would never fall in love with Denver McLean again?*

Sherrie regarded Tessa mutinously, as if her special friend had turned coat and joined the enemy camp.

"I should have called you," Tessa said to Nate. "Brigadier's got a bruised sole. Cassie Aldridge looked at the hoof and told me it would be fine if we kept up the poultices and let him rest, but if you'd rather wait—"

"No way. Just let me take a look at him."

Tessa's heart nearly dropped to the ground. Until this moment, she hadn't realized how much she wanted Nate to change his mind—or at least put off his decision.

In the stallion barn, Nate examined the rather spirited Brigadier and laughed when the stallion tried to nip him.

"He looks fine to me," Nate drawled as they walked outside and stood near the fence next to Sherrie. He reached into his inside jacket pocket and withdrew a check. "Have we got a deal?" he asked.

Tessa felt numb inside, but shoved her worries out of her mind. "We will as soon as we sign the papers. Everything's in the house."

"I want to stay out here!" Sherrie declared as her father turned toward the front door. "With my Red Wing."

"All right, dumplin'," Nate replied. "Just make sure you stay on *this* side of the fence."

"I will." Clucking her tongue softly and calling to Red Wing, Sherrie climbed the rails and peeked through. Aside from the flick of her pointed ears and the swish of her tail against a few bothersome flies, the mare didn't move.

The house was cool inside. Tessa led Nate to the study and sat behind the desk so recently vacated by Denver. She could smell his after-shave in the air.

Nate scribbled his signature on the bill of sale for each horse. "So where's McLean?" he asked, pushing the paperwork across the desk.

"In Helena," Tessa replied. "He should be back soon."

"How much longer is he planning to stay around here?"

"I—I don't know," Tessa answered quickly.

"Probably not too long. He couldn't wait to move away from here before. The fire just gave him a head start."

"I suppose," Tessa said woodenly.

"Well, this should make it easier for him," Nate said, thumping the paperwork with one thick finger. "Now that you've got the down payment on the ranch, he can take off for the bright lights of L.A."

"Right." Tessa wasn't about to think of impending departure. Not today. Not when she was giving up Brigadier and the mares for the sole purpose of buying a ranch Denver had no use for.

By the time she and Nate returned to the paddock, Len had loaded the mares into the trailer and Brigadier was being led across the yard by one of the younger hands. Brigadier nickered when he noticed Tessa and tossed his magnificent head as he pranced up the incline to the trailer. He barely favored his right foreleg.

Tessa's throat grew hot and thick and her eyes misted. Feeling like a traitor, she turned toward Sherrie just as Curtis hobbled across the yard.

"Howdy, there," he called to Sherrie. He tipped his hat and his weathered face cracked into a broad smile.

Sherrie squinted up at him. "Who're you?" she demanded.

Curtis chuckled. "Well, now, I could be askin' you the same question, couldn't I?"

"I'm Sherrie!" the little sprite said proudly, folding chubby arms across her chest.

Curtis glanced up at Nate. "You must be proud of this one."

"I am," Nate agreed, his gold tooth flashing as he scooped Sherrie from the ground.

"I want to ride Red Wing!" Sherrie cried.

"Later," her father said.

"That's what you always say," Sherrie pouted, staring longingly at the mare.

"You'll have plenty of time." Nate turned to Tessa. "You come and visit the horses anytime you like."

"And teach me to ride!" Sherrie commanded.

"I will," Tessa promised.

"Thanks a lot," Nate said, clasping Tessa's hand, "and good luck."

"You, too. Take good care of them," Tessa replied, despite the fact that the back of her eyes burned and her throat seemed nearly swollen shut with hot tears.

"I will." He nodded at Tessa's father. "See ya around."

Nate climbed into the cab of his truck and rammed it into gear.

Standing in the middle of the yard, Tessa watched as the rig carrying her precious horses rolled slowly down the lane in a plume of dry dust.

"You didn't have to sell them," Curtis said softly.

She refused to cry, though she felt a part of her had left in that trailer. "Of course I did. How else was I supposed to pay for this place?" she asked, dashing back the lingering tears in her eyes. Sniffing, her eyes red-rimmed, she faced her father.

"No one put a gun to your head, Tessa. Neither Mitch nor I—nor Denver McLean for that matter—expected you to buy the ranch." He slung an arm across her shoulders and hugged her. "I'm proud of you, y'know. But you shouldn't carry the world on your shoulders."

"I don't."

"Don't you?" He cocked his head toward the lane and Nate's truck and trailer. "You could take a lesson or two from Paula Edwards."

"Meaning?"

"Meaning being mistress of your own house—raising me a passel of grandkids."

Tessa thought about the baby she might be carrying. What would her father say? Surely he would figure out that the child was sired by Denver. She steered her thoughts clear of such dangerous ground and said, "So where were you during the women's movement?"

"Right here watchin' 'em burn their bras and what-have-you, protestin' and carryin' on. And all the time I'm wonderin' why they don't have the sense to know a good thing when they see it."

"I guess it depends on your perspective," Tessa said, squinting. Nate's rig turned away from the lane and rumbled out of view.

"All I know is that I'm almost seventy and haven't got one grandson to ride on my knee."

"Talk to Mitchell," she advised.

"I already have. But you—you're the one who should be thinking about settlin' down."

"I'll remember that," she said dryly, her lips pressed together.

"And I'm not talking about Denver McLean."

"Give me some credit, Dad. I know how you feel about Denver, and I know how Mitch feels about him." *Besides,* she thought, *he hasn't asked me.*

"And what about you?" her father asked gently, touching her shoulder. "How do you feel about him?"

"Denver's an enigma," she whispered, her voice catching.

"You think you're in love with him again," her father deduced, sighing loudly. "And don't deny it. I can see it in your eyes."

"I don't hate him, if that's what you mean."

"That's not what I mean and you know it, Tess. But there's just no reason for you to go pining for the likes of Denver McLean."

"I'm not *pining* for anyone."

"Good," he said, sounding unconvinced. He swatted at a yellow jacket buzzing near his head. "I guess I'd better see if Mitch needs some help with the combine."

Relieved that the conversation was over, Tessa walked through the back porch and into the kitchen, which smelled of spices and simmering meat. Milly was busy ladling gravy over pot roast.

"Denver with you?" she asked, without looking up.

"He's still in town."

"Well, if he gets back after I leave, tell him to call that partner of his."

"Van Stern?"

"Right. He called a half hour ago. Left a message. Denver's to call him immediately." She paused to look over her shoulder. "He sounded real upset."

"About what?"

"Didn't say, but I gathered it was important."

Great, Tessa thought, frowning to herself. *Now what?*

Chapter Eleven

Tessa flung off the covers, snatched her robe from the foot of the bed and glared at the clock. Four-thirty. She'd gone to bed at eleven and hadn't slept a wink.

Where was Denver? she wondered. *Still in Helena?* Cinching her belt tightly around her waist, she walked to her open window. Streaks of gray rimmed the mountains surrounding the valley floor, casting the buildings of the ranch into black shadows. In a few days, she realized, these old buildings, the equipment, the acres of land and the cattle and horses would all be hers.

If the bank approved the loan.

If Denver located Colton.

If she could stand to stay here without Denver.

"If, if, if," she said to herself as she hurried downstairs and thought about her future—a future without Denver.

She heard Marsha mewing at the back door. "I'm coming," she called, unlatching the lock and opening the door a crack as the old cat trotted to her milk dish. "So where're your babies, hmm?'' Tessa asked as the calico rubbed against her bare leg. "Still hidden?"

Marsha mewed loudly again and followed Tessa into the kitchen. After starting coffee, Tessa poured some milk into a clean dish and set it on the back porch. "There you go, girl," she whispered, petting the cat's arched back.

The sound of a car's engine cut through the early-morning stillness. *Denver!*

Clutching the lapels of her robe together, Tessa hurried outside. Denver parked the rental near the garage, and Tessa ran down the path barefoot. She reached the car just as he opened the door and stretched out.

He looked as if he hadn't slept in the two days he'd been gone. His jaw was dark with shadow, his eyes sunk deep into his head and the lines near his mouth seemed to have deepened.

"I thought you'd be asleep," he said when she flung her arms around his neck.

"I couldn't. I missed you," she said in a rush, glad just to be in his arms again.

His hands clasped behind her back and he held her close, his breath fanning across her hair. "I missed you, too," he admitted. "Maybe I should leave more often."

"Maybe you should stay." She could hear his heart drumming, feel the warmth of his body surround her. A slight breeze, cool from the night, played with her hair and ruffled his.

"Van Stern caught up with me. He needs me in L.A."

"He called here, too."

"I know. There's a problem with a project at work."

"So that's why you came back," Tessa said, disappointed.

"That, and the fact that I couldn't let you off the hook. You owe me, Kramer."

Cocking her head to look up at him, she asked, "Owe you what?"

His teeth gleamed in the dark. "A trip to L.A."

Tessa groaned. "I hoped you'd forgotten."

"No way. A bet's a bet." His arms tightened around her. "I've come to collect."

"Now?"

"Now. Get ready. *We're* leaving in—" he checked his watch "—less than an hour."

"But I can't—" she said, suddenly panicked. Though she longed to go with him, this was too soon. She couldn't just abandon the ranch—a ranch she'd worked so hard for. Nor could she leave her family for the sake of a whim...or a bet.

"Sure you can. I've already bought the airline tickets. Come on, Tess, it's only a few days." He took her face between his hands, forced her to stare up at him, and the laughter died in his eyes. "Come with me, Tessa. See how I live—stay with me."

Her throat closed. Hadn't he asked her once before to leave this ranch and follow him to Los Angeles? On the afternoon of the fire, he'd begged her to go with him, and then seven years later he'd told her that the love they'd shared, the love she'd cherished, had meant nothing to him.

"I have responsibilities," she said, her voice husky. She tried to take a step backward, but his arms were strong and unmoving, his features set.

"So do I. In L.A."

"But—"

"I'm not asking for a lifetime commitment," he reminded her, and her heart wrenched. *If only you were, Denver.*

His gaze delved deep into hers and she felt herself drowning in the liquid warmth. "It's payoff time, Tessa."

"Why now? What's this all about?"

The teasing light disappeared from his eyes. His skin tightened over his cheekbones, pulling taut, stretching over now-invisible scars. She sensed something had gone wrong—horribly wrong. She felt suddenly cold inside.

"Colton gave the P.I. the slip. He's not in Northern Ireland—or at least he's not where Ross's private investigator thought he was." He squinted against the rising sun. Golden rays touched his face, but his features remained strained. "The investigator thinks he's in trouble. Big trouble."

"Isn't he always?"

Denver shrugged. "Probably. But I've got a bad feeling about this," he murmured, almost to himself. "If Colton needs to reach me, he'll try to get hold of me in L.A."

"Why would he want to get in touch with you now?"

"Because of the private investigator—because of John's death—"

"He didn't care about John."

"It's just a feeling I have," Denver whispered, and a shiver darted down Tessa's spine. "There's been a lot of trouble in Northern Ireland—a lot of unrest."

"There has been for years."

"But lately—" He shrugged, as if to shake off a sense of foreboding.

"What good would it do for me to come to L.A.?" she asked.

"I need you," he said, wincing a little, as if the words actually hurt. Exhaling slowly, he added, "Besides, you and I are at an impasse, Tessa. I think it's time we found out a little more about each other."

"And we have to do that in California?"

"Yes."

She studied the tired lines of his face, the tiny inflexible lines near his mouth, his black hair, falling fetchingly over his forehead. "And who will run this ranch?"

"Your father."

Inside, Tessa panicked. Though she was loath to admit it, she was afraid to leave the ranch in Curtis's hands. What if something went wrong? What if there were another accident? Dear God, what if he really had caused the fire all those years before? "I just can't."

"Mitch will be around to help him."

"Mitch is getting ready to go to college in Seattle."

"He's not leaving for a few more weeks. I'm only talking about a couple of days." He touched her tenderly on the cheek. "I need you, Tess," he said again, and he didn't have to say another word.

Within twenty minutes, Denver had showered, shaved and changed. Tessa threw a couple pairs of slacks, two cotton sweaters, a pair of shorts, T-shirts and a skirt into her old suitcase, then dressed in a billowing white skirt and pink sleeveless blouse. She plaited her hair into a French braid and snapped on small gold earrings and a matching necklace before meeting Denver downstairs.

"Do I look So Cal?" she asked, her dimple showing a bit.

"If that stands for sensational."

"Southern California," she said, laughing. There was something exhilarating and carefree about taking off with Denver and leaving the worries of the ranch behind. Even Denver's concerns for his brother seemed far removed. "Come on. We don't want to keep the Beach Boys waiting." With a wink, she breezed out the back door.

Denver locked it behind him. "You're enjoying this, aren't you?" he accused, tossing her suitcase into the trunk of his rental car as she slid into the passenger seat.

"Enjoying what?"

He grinned as he climbed behind the wheel and shoved the key in the ignition. "Harassing me at every chance."

"Me?" she asked innocently. "Never." But she couldn't stop the giggle that bubbled in her throat.

"Sure."

"You ask for it," she said as the car bounced down the lane. She relayed the message from Van Stern, then felt her lighthearted mood dissipate as they neared the foreman's house. Denver turned off the engine and she stared at the dark little cabin. "Dad won't like this," she thought aloud.

"Does that bother you?"

"A little."

"Enough to change your mind?"

She stared at him then, studied the crease furrowing his brow, the narrowing of his eyes, the way his fingers drummed against the steering wheel. "No," she whispered, touching his hand before climbing out of the car. When he reached for the door handle, she shook her head. "Let me handle this."

Brittle yellow grass brushed her ankles as she crossed the yard, rounded the corner and rapped on the back door. "Mitch?" she called through the panels. "Mitch?"

"What the hell?" her brother mumbled, stumbling to the door and poking his head through the crack. His hair stuck up at odd angles from his face and he had to blink a couple of times. He was bare-chested and wore nothing but jockey shorts and a wrist watch. "Tess? What're you doing here?"

"Saying goodbye."

"What?" He rubbed a tired hand across his face and focused. "Good Lord, where're you going?" he asked, before glancing at his watch. "It's barely five-thirty."

"I know. But I've got a plane to catch."

"A plane?" he asked, cobwebs of sleep still fogging his mind as he stretched, yawned and leaned against the doorframe for support. "What're you talking about?"

"I'm going to California. With Denver."

A half a beat passed. The sleep faded from Mitch's eyes. "To California," he repeated. "You're kidding, right?"

"Wrong."

For the first time he seemed to notice her clothes and hair. He rammed stiff fingers through his hair, only adding to the spikes already sticking straight up. "Why?"

"For a vacation."

"A what? Oh, no, Tess. This is wrong. All wrong."

"Why?"

"Why? Because you're trying to buy the place from McLean. Because you just sold your horses to Nate Edwards. Because Dad'll never be able to run the ranch without you—"

"You can help him."

"I know, but—" His shoulders slumped, and he suddenly seemed to age ten years. "Are you sure this is what you want?"

"Positive."

Mitch frowned, his green eyes sad. "You've got it bad, haven't you, Tess?" he whispered. "You never really got over him, did you?"

"It's not a question of—"

"Just be careful. Don't let him hurt you again."

"He won't," Tessa said, wondering at the conviction in her words.

Mitchell's entire body flexed. "He'd better not," he growled, his lips thinning. "Because if he does, he'll have to answer to me!"

Tessa nearly laughed. "I'll tell him," she said, smothering a smile.

"Do that. I'd love to have a crack at McLean."

She couldn't help laughing then, eyeing his shorts and wristwatch. "I'll warn him. You just take care of Dad."

"I'll try," Mitchell said, crossing his arms over his bare chest as Tessa dashed back to the car.

"So how did he take the news?" Denver asked, once Tessa was in her seat and he'd rammed the car into gear.

"As well as can be expected."

"That well?" Denver asked dryly.

"Actually, he implied that he'd do you bodily harm if you hurt me."

"Did he?" Denver's crooked smile stretched across his face. "Protective bastard, isn't he?"

"Maybe he just doesn't want to pick up the pieces again," she said softly.

"He won't have to," Denver swore. He turned the car onto the main road and slipped a pair of aviator sunglasses onto his nose. "I won't hurt you, Tessa. Never again."

A lump swelled in her throat when he linked his fingers with hers. "Don't worry about it," she whispered, blinking back hot tears. "I won't let you."

The California sun blazed hot in a hazy blue sky. The fronds of tall palms moved in a whisper-soft breeze as Tessa and Denver pushed open a courtyard gate and walked together along a flagstone path to the front door of his Spanish-style condominium. Vines, laden with fragrant purple flowers, climbed across the overhang protecting the door.

"It's beautiful here," Tessa commented, wishing she could hate the place.

"It's home." Shoving open the door, he carried her bag inside.

The interior was bright and airy. A staircase curled upward on one side of the entry, while two steps led to an expansive living room. The western side of the building was walled in two-story high panes of glass that offered a panoramic view of the sun-washed Pacific Ocean. "This isn't anything like I'd imagined," Tessa remarked, walking across the gleaming hardwood floor to French doors. A redwood deck stretched across the back of the condominium with steps leading down to the beach.

Tessa kicked off her shoes and grinned as she felt sand between her toes. "How did you find this place?" she asked, when Denver joined her. The tide lapped around her toes, frothy water swirling around her ankles. Salt spray misted in the air, carried inland on a warm Pacific breeze.

"I bought it from a friend of mine—a guy I went to school with. He and his wife divorced and he wanted to sell it fast. I'd been living in an apartment and this place seemed more permanent."

"And that was important?"

Unconsciously he rubbed the back of his scarred hand with the fingers of the other. "It seemed to be at the time," he whispered. "I'd been out of the hospital about six months and was working for a big firm not far from here. I decided it was time to grow some roots."

"So you'd never have to go back," she guessed, her heart constricting.

"There wasn't a reason to go back. Mom and Dad were dead, Colton was God only knew where, and you—" He sighed loudly, then gazed deep into her eyes. His own were shadowed with an intense pain that sliced to the bone. "I couldn't deal with you," he added.

"Why not?"

"Everything was too fresh, I guess." Frowning, he stared at the ocean, watching as sailboats, dark against the horizon, skimmed along the smooth surface of the sea. "Colton had convinced me that you were part of your father's scam."

"My father's *what*?"

"His embezzling."

"My father never took one dime from the ranch that didn't belong to him!" she hissed, instantly infuriated. She couldn't believe that after everything she and Denver had shared, he would still believe the lies—the horrid, hateful lies! "He's not an embezzler, or a thief, or an arsonist! As for the fire, you don't know that Colton wasn't behind it," she said, her mind spinning. "He was supposed to be in town with John during the blaze, wasn't he?"

"Yes, but—"

"Yes, but nothing. He wasn't with John. He didn't have an alibi. Said he'd been riding, but he showed up in a pickup. For all anyone knows he could've been in the stables, started the blaze and managed to escape!"

Denver's eyes narrowed. "Why, Tessa?"

"I don't know. Maybe for the same reasons he uses to blame Dad. Maybe he was skimming money off the top—"

"No way!"

"Maybe he didn't mean to start the fire," she went on, her thoughts ahead of her tongue. "It was probably an accident—he didn't intend to hurt anyone...."

Denver's hands tightened over her bare forearms. "Do you honestly think he would accuse you, accuse your father, blame them for something he'd done!"

"Maybe," she accused. "He didn't stick around too long afterward, did he?"

"But he had no reason—"

"Neither did Dad! But you seem to think it's all right to accuse him! Think about it, Denver. Think about it long and hard. Why was Colton so adamant, so damned insistent that my family was involved!"

Turning, she tried to escape from the manacle of his hands, but he wouldn't let her go. "You're forgetting something, Tessa," he said, his eyes as dark as midnight.

"What?"

"Your father was found drunk at the fire. He really couldn't remember what had happened. Colton, on the other hand, had been riding the back fields—"

"He claims."

"His horse was still saddled."

"But he drove up in the truck. Isn't that odd? Just because his horse wasn't in the barn isn't any proof he wasn't involved."

"And it doesn't get your father off the hook!"

Gasping, Tessa arched her hand upward intending to slap him, but she didn't. She stopped just before her palm connected with his cheek. "I knew I shouldn't have come here," she said, fighting the urge to break down completely.

A gamut of emotions contorted his features—hate, anger, sadness, love?

To her surprise, he folded her into his arms. "Shh. Of course you should have," he said, his face becoming gentle. "Let's not argue about it. Not now."

"But you don't trust us."

"I trust you."

"And Dad?"

"I'm not sure about him, Tessa. Face it. Your father has a problem—a serious problem. We have to do something about it."

"We?" she whispered, disbelieving. Denver wanted to help Curtis Kramer? She couldn't believe it—wouldn't.

"There are places he could go—hospitals and clinics. But first he's got to admit he has an alcohol problem."

Tessa swallowed back the urge to argue. "I—I'll talk to him when we get back," she said. She'd come to the same conclusion herself, but hated discussing her father's private life with Denver. "Mitchell seems to think he drinks to block out the fire."

Denver's lips twisted. "It doesn't work," he said. "I should know. I tried to pour myself into a bottle the week after I got out of the hospital."

"Why?"

He let out a long breath. "To forget you, Tessa," he said. "To forget you, the fire, everything." He glanced down at the scars on his hand and his mouth tightened. "Unfortunately I couldn't, and alcohol didn't make a damned bit of difference. So I gave myself a swift kick, picked up the pieces as best I could and threw myself into my work." He kissed her crown as the ocean breeze snatched at her skirt. "And I did my best to forget you."

"I didn't have anything to do with the fire," she said slowly. "I would never, *never* have done anything to hurt you."

His arms slid upward and he took her face between his palms. "I know that now," he whispered, his eyes shining as he slanted his mouth over hers.

His arms tightened and she fell against him, tilting her face upward, her lips eager for his. He pulled her against him, the length of his body protection against the stiff ocean breeze. "Make love to me, Tessa," he whispered against her hair.

"Here?" She quivered inside. The beach was deserted, but houses and condominiums curved along the shoreline.

He grinned wickedly. "Inside." He scooped her into his arms and carried her up the few steps to the deck. She had to cling to him to keep from slipping as he shouldered open the door and climbed the stairs to a loft that shared a view of the ocean with the living room below.

"Here," he said, tossing her onto a huge bed with a patterned spread of forest green and pearl gray. Twining his fingers through her hair, he leaned over her, his weight causing the mattress to sag. "You don't know how many nights I've dreamed of you," he said. "Wished that you were here in my bed." His voice was low and throaty, his breath hot against her ear. Lying beside her, he guided her hand to the buttons of his shirt. "Make love to me, Tessa."

She slid the first two buttons through the holes, then pressed the flat of her hand to the hard muscles of his chest. She could feel his heart pounding wildly, knew its erratic cadence matched her own.

He moaned softly and his lips crashed down on hers, stealing the breath from her lungs and forcing liquid fire through her veins. She tingled expectantly and felt his hands slide beneath the elastic waistband of her skirt, slowly sliding the soft cotton down her legs and calves.

The bed creaked as he finished undressing her and rolled onto his back, guiding her to rest atop him. He watched the gentle sway of her breasts, nipples dark, above him. "Now," he said, letting his tongue rim her lips.

She moaned, wanting more. Heat coiled deep within.

Denver slid lower, capturing the tip of one breast with his lips then circling the firm bud with his tongue. "Make love to me, Tessa," he whispered. His breath was hot against her wet, taut nipple. "Make love to me all night long."

She had no choice.

The next morning Tessa was up before Denver and had dashed down to a local market for groceries. She'd already poured beaten eggs into a pan and grated cheese for an omelet before she heard his familiar tread on the stairs.

"What's going on?" he asked, poking his head into the kitchen. Sleep still clouded his eyes, his chin was dark with beard and his jeans hung low on his hips. His chest was bare and muscled and she had trouble dragging her gaze from him.

"When in California . . ." she said, motioning to the table, where fresh slices of oranges, melons and berries filled fruit cups and warm muffins were piled high on a small plate.

She was working at the stove. Slowly he sauntered over to her, slid his arms around her waist and clasped his hands over her abdomen, pressing her buttocks into his hips. She felt the bulge in his pants and her throat went dry.

"You should wear shorts more often," he growled into her ear, his hands reaching upward to cup a breast through her T-shirt. The scent of recent lovemaking still clung to him and she felt like a bride on her honeymoon.

"Not very practical on the ranch."

"Maybe you should stop being so practical," he rasped.

"Maybe I already have."

Twisting her in his arms, he slid his hands down her ribs, feeling each small indentation and watching as her T-shirt stretched across her breasts, displaying beneath the cotton fabric the hard buttons of her nipples.

"Hey, wait," she breathed, her mind swimming under his magical touch. "Breakfast—"

"Can wait." He turned off the burners and hoisted her upward, balancing her back against the wall, forcing her legs to wrap around his hips. Her arms circled his head as he pressed his mouth over her T-shirt and suckled, wetting the fabric and drawing on the sweet nubbin hidden deep in the cloth.

"Denver, please—ooh—" she gasped as his hands cupped her bottom and she felt her shorts being dragged over her hips. Together they tumbled to the floor and she forgot about breakfast as he stripped them both of their clothes and made love to her with a passion that tore through her soul and left her trembling in its wake.

For two days, Tessa learned the secrets of Denver's life in Los Angeles, she saw the wonder of Western sunsets blazing magenta and violet as the sun settled into the ocean. She smelled the salt of the sea and felt the ocean's spray against her face. They walked hand in hand through the streets of Venice, exploring the shops and boutiques, sipping drinks in shaded patios or walking barefoot near the ocean, playing tag with the waves.

"You love it here," she finally said as they trudged through the warm sand and up the steps to his deck.

"It's peaceful." One black eyebrow cocked. "Though some people have the impression that I live in a pressure cooker—that my life in Southern California has to be hectic."

"Okay, okay," she said, laughing and holding up her palms. "I'm guilty."

His arms circled her waist and he kissed her eyelids. "Guilty and beautiful," he whispered. His lips promised so much more.

The phone rang. "Go 'way," Denver growled.

The ring seemed more shrill the second time.

"You'd better answer it," Tessa said, pushing him away. "It might be Colton." *Or Mitch—or Dad.*

Grumbling, Denver threw open the French doors, crossed the room and picked up the living room extension by the fourth ring.

Tessa strolled to the far end of the deck and placed her palms against the railing as she stared for one last moment at the sea. Salt air pushed her hair from her face and she breathed deeply of the tangy air.

Her flight back to Montana left in three hours.

"Second thoughts?" Denver asked as he reached her. From behind, he wrapped his arms around her waist and balanced his chin on her crown.

"Second and third and fourth and so on," she admitted.

"California's not so bad, is it?"

"It's wonderful." *As long as I'm with you.*

"You could stay longer."

Torn, she shook her head. "I have to go back. Everything I've ever worked for is there." She smiled wistfully. "But you could come with me."

He sighed, his breath stirring her hair. "Not for a while. That was my partner on the phone. He needs help on a project that's hit some snags. And then there's Colton."

"You really think he'll call you here?"

"I don't know."

"It's been so long," she pointed out before she wondered if waiting for Colton was just an excuse for him to stay. "If he really wanted to find you, he could. My guess is that he doesn't."

"Probably," Denver whispered, his voice barely audible over the roar of the sea. Placing his hands on her shoulders, he turned her, forced her to look in his eyes. "I'll fly back to Montana next week—then we can settle everything."

Her lungs constricted. "Such as?"

"You still want to buy the ranch, don't you?" he asked and her spirits dropped. "I'll call Ross and tell him to find some way for me to sell my part of the ranch to you."

"I thought you couldn't do that without Colton's consent."

Denver frowned. "There's got to be some provision—some loophole. Ross is a lawyer. It's up to him to figure it out. That's what he gets paid to do."

"Of course," she said sadly. "Well, I guess I'd better make sure I've packed everything," she said, her heart sinking at the thought of leaving.

"Or you could stay," he invited, leisurely tracing the column of her throat.

She shuddered, torn. All she'd ever wanted was Denver—on any terms. But now she realized he'd have to meet her halfway. One-sided love always died.

"No, Denver," she finally said, meeting his gaze dry-eyed, though the prospect of separating from him loomed dark in her horizon. "I have to go back."

Chapter Twelve

Mitchell was waiting at the airport. Shaved and dressed in clean slacks and a cotton shirt, a crisp Stetson pushed back on his head, he waved to Tessa as she pulled her suitcase from the baggage carousel. "I'll take that," he offered, eyeing her closely. "You okay?"

"I'm fine," she said, struggling with a smile.

"You don't look fine." Mitchell took her bag and slung one arm familiarly over her shoulders.

"Thanks a lot." She blew a strand of reddish-blond hair from her eyes as they wended through the crowded terminal. Mitchell showed her the way to the old pickup and held the door for her. "What's going on?" she asked suspiciously.

"Why?"

"The last time you opened a door for me was in high school. You wanted me to write a report on *Macbeth* or something."

"You're a jaded woman, Tessa Kramer," he said, his green eyes glinting in the afternoon sun.

"And you're holding out on me." She tapped her fingers on the sun-baked dash until he climbed into the cab, flicked on the ignition and threaded the old truck through the traffic in the parking lot. Tessa stared out the dusty windshield. "What's been going on while I've been gone?"

"Denver called."

"Today?" She snapped her head around, eyeing her brother.

"Just before I left. He thought you'd be home. He didn't know your flight was delayed in Salt Lake."

"And you did?"

"I called the airport and found out there were mechanical difficulties with your connecting flight." He grinned at her and winked. "I'm smarter than I look."

"Good thing," she teased, trying to keep the mood.light, though she sensed something was wrong. "What did Denver want?"

"To talk to you. He said he probably won't come back here as soon as he'd originally planned."

"No?" Dread stole into her soul. Deep in her heart she'd feared that he would leave her again. Maybe their weekend in California had been a diversion for him and nothing more. But she hadn't expected his rejection so quickly. The force of it washed over her in an ice-cold shower of reality. Her hands curled into fists and she tried to drive the ugly thoughts aside. "Why not?"

"He didn't say," Mitchell said, driving through town and stepping on the gas. "I guess something came up."

"He must have told you something."

Mitchell frowned. "He said he'd call back as soon as he could."

Relief chased her fears away. "Did he say when?"

Mitchell's lips compressed and his fingers tightened over the wheel. "The conversation wasn't all that long."

"Why not?"

Mitchell stared through the dusty glass to the road ahead. "You may as well hear it all, I suppose. Dad answered the phone."

"So?"

"He wasn't in very good shape, if you know what I mean."

"He was drunk."

Mitchell's jaw clamped shut. He didn't look at Tessa. "He'd had a few. And he told McLean just what he thought of you going to California."

Tessa groaned. "How bad did it get?"

"Bad. Dad wasn't crazy about you flying off to L.A. with Denver, or any man for that matter, I suppose. The fact that it was McLean only made things worse. By the time I got on the phone, Dad had told Denver what he thought and then some. Dad was red in the face and Denver wasn't very communicative."

"Great," Tessa murmured.

"He'll call back," Mitchell said without much conviction. "And when he does, just make sure you answer the phone."

"I will." Leaning her head against the window, she sighed and said, "We've got to talk to Dad, you know."

Mitchell's shoulders stiffened. "About what?"

"You know what. His drinking. He needs help."

"I've talked until I'm blue in the face. It doesn't help."

"Something's got to. Not only is it unhealthy, but it's dangerous." She swallowed against a lump forming in her throat. "It won't be easy, but we've got to help him."

"He drinks because of the fire, damn it! Everyone blamed him, the town was against him, Colton and Denver all but accused him of murder."

"He drank before the fire, Mitch. We both know it. When they pulled him out of the stables, he was out cold, and it wasn't just from the smoke."

Mitch tossed her an angry glare. "You're beginning to sound like a McLean."

"I'm not—"

"A few days in California and Denver's got you convinced that Dad started the fire, Dad's got a drinking problem and Dad was ripping off the ranch," he grumbled, the back of his neck dark with rage. "Just remember who stuck by you, Tess. When you were torn apart. Where was Mc-Lean?"

Tessa clamped her mouth shut and seethed in silence.

Mitchell cranked down the window. Cool air swept into the warm cab. "The only other things that have happened on the ranch are that one of the tractors broke down—the clutch went out, and there are a couple of calves that turned up sick. I think they might have gotten into something— probably turpentine poisoning. Several branches from a pine tree near the barn blew down and the calves got into the needles. I called Craig Fulton and he said he'd be over as soon as he could."

"How serious?" Tessa asked.

"Not too bad, but I can't tell." He glanced at her. "Look, I'm sorry I got on you about McLean, but that guy has a way of getting under my skin."

Mine, too, Tessa thought, sighing. *Mine, too.*

Before she changed, Tessa thought she'd check on the two sick calves. She found them in a corner of the barn, lying on straw, rolling eyes up at her as she entered. "How're you?" she asked, rubbing her hand along one ruddy hide.

The calf bawled, his head drooping, but he struggled to his feet. As well as she could, she examined him, noting that though he was listless, he seemed sturdy. The other calf, a heifer, was worse. She barely moved when Tessa examined her. "Come on," Tessa said, rubbing the heifer's white face. "Hang in there."

Dusting her hands, Tessa walked toward the south end of the barn, but stopped as the odor of stale liquor filtered through smells of horses, cows and dust.

Then she saw him. Lying facedown on a bale of straw, an empty bottle dangling from the fingers of one outstretched arm, her father, dead to the world, snored loudly.

"Oh, no!" Tessa whispered, swallowing hard. "Dad, no." She touched him gently on the shoulder.

He didn't move.

"Wake up, Dad," she said, shaking him. Why couldn't she help him? Why couldn't he help himself? What demon possessed him that forced him to seek comfort in a bottle of Scotch?

Her stomach tightened painfully.

He snorted.

"For God's sake, Dad," she muttered, hauling him to a sitting position before shaking his shoulders so that his eyes rolled open and he coughed.

"What the devil?" he growled, rousing a little. He shoved her hands aside. Wincing and squinting one eye, he grumbled loudly. "Wha—what's goin' on?"

Tessa sat on the edge of a nearby bale. "My guess is that you passed out."

"What time is it?"

"About eight-thirty."

Curtis let out a long whistle and winced a little as he sat up. "I just came in to feed the stock…" he said, but avoided her eyes and dropped the bottle in an empty oak cask that had been shoved against the wall. His grizzled jaw hardened and he rubbed his chin. "Looks like I overdid it a mite."

"More than a mite."

"Maybe." He rubbed his forehead, then pinched the bridge of his nose between his thumb and forefinger as if to ward off a tremendous headache. "It's McLean's fault. He called and got me all riled." Blinking rapidly, he fixed his eyes on his daughter. "So now you're back from California." Sighing loudly, he asked, "What's gotten into you, Tessa? Taking off for three days and nights with Denver McLean. Living with him just like you were married! It's a good thing your mother's not alive."

She inhaled sharply, wounded by his words. "My relationship with Denver has nothing to do with you."

"I'm the one that raised you—taught you right from wrong."

"I haven't done anything wrong," Tessa said.

Curtis squinted. "That's probably a matter of opinion. Look at you." He wagged a finger at her linen skirt, silk blouse and eelskin pumps. "You already look different—like those damned mannequins you see on a Hollywood game show."

"I haven't changed, Dad, and I didn't come in here to fight about Denver," she said slowly, biting back the urge to scream that she loved Denver McLean. "I came to talk about you."

"Me?"

Tessa sat on the bale next to him. "You've got a problem, Dad. With this." She reached into the oak cask and withdrew the bottle.

"A problem? Me?" He barked a short, uncomfortable laugh. "No way. Sure, I have a drink now and then—"

"Every day. And it's not just one drink." She saw the pain in his eyes, the despair, and she had to fight to keep talking. Her own insides were shredding. This man had raised her and Mitchell alone, had done everything he could to give them a good life, had provided for them and cared for them when their mother died. He'd been mother, father, provider and friend—at least he had been until that horrid night when the stables were engulfed in flames.

Curtis's already flushed face reddened, his watery gaze drifted away from hers. "So now you're tellin' me how to run my life," he whispered, running one work-roughened hand over the worn denim covering his knee.

Tessa's eyes burned. "I only want to help," she said, placing her hand on his shoulder.

He flinched. "You've been listening to McLean."

"No—"

"Then why now, Tessa? Huh? Why now—right when you're fresh off the plane from Los Angeles and Denver McLean!" He eyed her speculatively. "And just when is he coming back here? Let's hope it's soon. Then he can sign the papers and we can all be rid of him."

"It's not that easy," Tessa said.

"Why not?"

"No one's heard from Colton."

"Bah! If you ask me, Denver's just stringin' you along. If he wanted to sell his part of this ranch, he'd be on the phone to his lawyer in a minute. Where there's a will, there's a way."

"Denver's already called Ross."

"Has he now? Does that mean he is or isn't coming back here?"

"I don't know," Tessa said. "Maybe you can tell me. He called, and you talked to him."

"It wasn't much of a conversation." Curtis shook his head, then reached into his jacket pocket, searching for cigarettes. He pulled out the pack, found it empty and crumpled it in his fist. "All he said was that he's been delayed. There was some kind of emergency."

"Emergency? What happened?"

"He didn't bother sayin'. If ya ask me, it was an excuse—a way to avoid comin' back here." His gaze turned sad and some of the fire left his eyes. He looked suddenly old and weary. "You know, Tess, there's a chance McLean's double-crossing you."

"Double-crossing me?"

"I'm just pointing out the facts," he said, his weathered face softening. "Doesn't it seem strange that he showed up just after John's funeral, stuck around long enough to find out what was going on—just to make sure the ranch was on its feet—and then took off?"

"He had work in California—"

"Sure he did. But my guess is that he found out you'd turned this ranch around, that it's making a profit, and he's decided there's no reason to sell."

She wouldn't believe it. "I went back with him."

"And now you're here alone," he pointed out. "Denver's called, already made up an excuse about not bein' able to come back here."

Her lungs felt tight and some of her old fears took a stranglehold on her heart. "You think he used me."

Curtis's eyes shifted to the hay-strewn floor. "It wouldn't be the first time."

"No!" Her small fist clenched. She wouldn't believe that Denver had so callously and calculatingly seduced her! They had shared too many wonderful days and nights for it all to have been a lie. "Denver lov—cares for me."

Tears filled the corners of her father's eyes. "If you say so, Tess," he said, his voice raw. He touched her hair and sighed. "You're too good for him, you know. Too damned good."

"Denver doesn't want this ranch," she pointed out, trying to come up with reasons, explanations, excuses, *anything* to refute her father's accusations. Denver loved her—though he'd never said it. He had to!

"Maybe he changed his mind," Curtis said. "I checked the books—we're not in bad shape. In fact, this ranch is in the black. Think on it, Tessa," her father whispered, his old eyes squinting thoughtfully. "Why should he sell to you, when he could probably run the place from L.A. and make a handsome profit?"

"Because he gave me his word!"

The door to the barn swung open and Mitchell, his hands and shirt black with grease, entered. "The clutch is shot on the John Deere. I think we'll need to—" As if seeing Tessa for the first time, he stopped and glanced from his sister to his father. "What's going on here? Why haven't you changed?"

"We were just discussing Denver McLean," Curtis said.

"So we're back to him again, are we?" Eyeing his sister cautiously, Mitch leaned casually against the manger. "Don't tell me—you're defending McLean and Dad won't buy it?"

"Something like that."

"Well, you know where I stand."

"Stay out of this, Mitch," she warned. "We've been over it before."

Mitchell wiped a grimy hand over his brow, leaving a streak of grease. "Maybe someone should remind you that

Denver doesn't have what you'd refer to as a sterling track record.''

"Enough!" she shouted. She wouldn't listen to these lies a minute longer.

Her father sighed. "Mitch's right. Now that Denver knows this place is worth more than he originally thought, why wouldn't he try to sell it to a higher bidder?"

"Because we had an agreement," she said testily.

"In writing?" Mitchell asked.

"No, but—"

"Don't tell me," Mitch cut in. "He promised to sell the land to you, convince Colton to do the same, and then, once his brother was out of the picture, he'd come back, marry you and hand you your money back."

"Of course not!" she blurted, though deep in her heart, Mitch's scenario was just what she'd hoped for.

"Tessa," Mitch said softly, spreading his hands. "Open your eyes."

"I have!"

Pity stretched across Mitch's features. "Oh, Tess—"

Tessa wanted to run from the barn. Her words sounded strangled and forced. "Don't 'Oh, Tess,' me—okay? Things are going to work out just fine!"

"I hope so," Mitch said fervently. "I just don't see how. You know, there's a chance Denver won't locate his brother. Or that Colton won't come back here. He's got himself a hotshot photography job all full of glitter and danger. He won't want to come back."

"But he might sell."

"And he might not."

Tessa's world was breaking apart. If only Denver were here! If only her brother and father could see the real Denver, the man hidden deep beneath his scars from the fire. And yet, her family's accusations held a ring of truth. Inside, her heart was shredding. Hot tears clogged her throat. "You two are as bad as Denver and Colton," she accused, her voice a whisper. "You don't trust them, and they don't trust you."

"So whose side are you on?" Mitch asked.

"Believe it or not, there doesn't have to be sides."

"Oh, Tess, grow up. This isn't some female fantasy."

She gasped, feeling as if she'd been kicked in the stomach. Hadn't Denver said just the same thing—hadn't he accused her of being a dreamer, a hopeless romantic? Sick inside, she ran from the barn, leaving her family and their horrid accusations of Denver behind. She'd call Denver, and if he didn't answer, she'd call his office. If that didn't work, she'd call Jim Van Stern. Once she heard from Denver everything would be all right.

Desperate, she ran into the house and dialed Denver's number in Venice. The phone rang twelve times before she hung up. It was late, but she called Denver's engineering firm. A tape machine answered on the third ring. She left a message for Denver and told herself not to worry. She'd hear from him in the morning.

"I'm sorry, Ms. Kramer, but all I know is that Denver took off in a hurry. He left a message on the recorder and said that he'd call in as soon as possible. I assumed he was in Montana," Jim Van Stern said over the hum of the long distance connection.

Tessa's heart sank and the headache behind her eyes began to throb.

"Have you called his attorney in Helena?" Jim asked. "I don't know all the details, but he was hell-bent to sell the ranch. I just assumed this had something to do with the sale."

"I've spoken with Ross Anderson," Tessa said, remembering her telephone conversation with the young lawyer. "He hasn't heard a word."

"It's not like Denver," Van Stern remarked.

Tessa knew she was grasping at straws, that the possibility that Denver had heard from Colton was remote, but nothing else made any sense. She asked, "Could he have left because of his brother? He said he wanted to stay in L.A. until he heard from Colton."

"Maybe, but I doubt it. I don't think they've seen each other in years. Ever since that fire."

"Right," Tessa said, sick with worry. She stared out the kitchen window and wondered where Denver was. Why hadn't he called again? "If he phones you, please ask him to call me."

"Will do," Van Stern said before hanging up.

Tessa leaned against the wall. Her stomach rumbled. Her head was pounding, she ached all over. She hadn't slept well. She'd only dozed, and her dreams, when she had drifted off, had been filled with Denver. They'd been lying on the sand, the sea breeze ruffling his hair, the water lapping at her skirt, and he'd kissed her, long and hard, only stopping to vow that he loved her—

"Tessa?" a female voice called, accompanied by pounding on the front door.

"Coming!" Tessa hurried down the hall, swung open the door and found Cassie Aldridge standing on the front porch.

"Hi. Mitch called Craig yesterday."

"He did?" Tessa said before remembering.

Cassie nodded. "He had a couple of calves he wanted me to check out."

"Oh, right. They're in the barn. I'll come with you."

"I can find my way," Cassie offered with a smile. "Isn't that where I examined Brigadier?"

"Yes."

Cassie's black hair gleamed in the afternoon sun. "I was at the Edwards ranch the other day," she said as they walked toward the barn. "Brigadier's as good as new."

Tessa's heart turned over. "Ornery as ever?"

Cassie laughed. "He tried to take a bite out of my back side. Fortunately, I'm quick."

Chuckling, Tessa opened the door and snapped on the lights. The two calves were still in the stall, but they were both on their feet. At the sight of Tessa, they began to bawl.

"Hungry?" she asked.

Cassie opened the gate and caught the first calf. He tried to struggle free. The heifer, too, backed away. "They look good to me," Cassie said, examining first one calf, then the other. Both animals tried to escape, running into each other and nearly knocking Cassie down. "Mitch said he thought they'd eaten pine needles."

"No one said they were Rhodes scholars," Tessa replied, and Cassie smiled—a wide feminine smile.

"Well I don't see any reason to keep them penned up any longer."

"Good."

Together, they herded the rambunctious calves outside. The ruddy heifer and steer took off, tails switching, galloping through the dry field toward the rest of the herd.

"Thanks for stopping by," Tessa said as she walked Cassie back to her truck.

"No problem. I'll send you a bill." Cassie's hazel eyes gleamed and her mouth curved into a feminine smile. She climbed into the cab and leaned out the window. "Is Denver around?"

Tessa rammed her hands deep into the pockets of her jeans. "I don't know where he is," she admitted, wondering at the ease with which she confided in a woman she barely knew. "He was in California, but he left."

Jamming her key into the ignition, Cassie asked, "Has he heard anything from Colton?"

"Not a word," Tessa said.

"I guess that's not a big surprise." Cassie slid a pair of sunglasses onto her nose. Her mouth twisted wryly. "I don't think there's enough adventure or danger in this world to keep Colton McLean satisfied."

"Probably not," Tessa agreed, her thoughts with Denver, wherever he was.

"I'll see you around. Let me know if those calves relapse." Cassie stepped on the throttle and waved as she drove away. Tessa watched the white truck ramble down the drive and wished she had some inkling about Denver. Where was he? Frowning, she walked back to the house.

Get up! she told herself nearly a week later, but couldn't find the energy. She hadn't heard a word from Denver. Not one lousy word! "A lot he cares," she grumbled as she tossed off the sheets, then gasped when she felt the overpowering urge to vomit. She barely made it to the bathroom where she retched for a full ten minutes.

Sweat collected over her brow and the sensation slowly passed. She cleaned her mouth with water, then leaned against the sink. She'd suspected for two weeks she might be pregnant, this morning nearly confirmed it. She smiled wanly at her white-faced reflection in the mirror. Maybe she and Denver would never be together, but at least, God willing, she would have his baby.

Her heart bled at the thought of Denver. He hadn't wanted a child. Hadn't he asked her if she were protected on the first night they made love? Since then, he'd forgotten about birth control, but she knew in her heart he wouldn't want this baby. Nor did he want her.

Why else would he avoid her?

If Denver had wanted her, he would have called. If he had intended to sell the ranch, he would have returned to Montana to meet with the bank. And if he had loved her, he never would have left. Aching inside, she glanced at her reflection. Her eyes were shadowed with dark circles and her skin had paled. She looked every bit as miserable as she felt.

"Idiot," she accused, yanking the brush through her hair until the golden-red strands crackled. How could she have been such a fool—*and for the second time?* She tossed her brush onto the bureau, changed into clean jeans and a T-shirt and muttered, "Some people never learn."

By the time Milly arrived a half hour later, Tessa had convinced herself that Denver had conned her. Though part of her wanted desperately to trust him, the reasonable side of her nature wouldn't let her fall for his lies all over again.

"Trouble?" Milly asked as she entered through the back porch.

Tessa felt like a fool. She poured herself a glass of orange juice. "A little," she admitted grudgingly.

"Let me guess. This has to do with Denver, doesn't it?"

Tessa nodded. "You could say that. He had no intention of selling this place to me."

Milly's eyebrows raised a fraction. "And just how have you figured this out?" She tucked her purse in the pantry, hung up her jacket and whipped on an apron. "Didn't he try to call you?"

"Yes, but who knows why?" Tessa asked.

"At least give him the chance to explain."

"I will—if I ever hear from him again." She drank one sip of juice and her stomach revolted. Carefully, she set her cup on the counter.

"Oh, bah!" Milly started chopping onions. "Say what you want, that man loves you. Any fool could see it when he was here."

"That's just the point. He's not here anymore, is he?"

"He'll be back."

"When?"

"Hasn't anyone told you patience is a virtue?"

"Over and over again," Tessa mumbled, unconvinced that Milly knew what she was talking about. "As soon as I'm finished around here, I'm going over to the Edwards ranch. If Denver calls—" Mentally kicking herself, she snapped her mouth shut. Denver wouldn't call. Nor would he return. He was gone again. Tears threatened her eyes and clogged her throat.

"I'll give him the number," Milly said, "right after I give him a piece of my mind!"

"I thought you were just singing his praises, telling me to be patient."

Milly's eyes glimmered. "Haven't you ever heard the old expression, 'Do as I say, not as I do'?"

"Too many times to count. But I always thought it was a crock," Tessa said, forcing a wan smile despite the stone-cold feeling that she'd lost Denver forever.

She went through the motions of doing the chores, but her mind was on Denver. Where was he? Why hadn't he called? If he loved her, and that was looking like a bigger "if" as each second passed, why had he left her? "It's over—face it!" she told herself, feeling positively wretched as she tossed hay into the manger. *And now you might be pregnant. What will you do? How will you tell him?* "I won't," she said aloud. She couldn't. Denver would twist things around, think she'd tried to trap him into a marriage he didn't want.

It hit her then with the force of a northern gale. Denver had used her, hurt her intentionally, lied to her. And he was probably now enjoying the fact—he'd gotten back at the family that had ruined his.

Dropping onto a bale of hay and drawing her knees to her chest, she let the tears that had been building for weeks fill her eyes. "No," she whispered, denying even now what was so evident.

Trust him. Give him time, one part of her argued.

Why? So he can drag out your heart and stomp all over it again? another part screamed.

Dropping her head to her arms, she cried from the depths of her soul. Deep racking sobs convulsed her small frame, and she sat rocking alone in the dark barn, the musty smell of hay mingling with the moist, fresh scent of her tears. Desperation ripped through her heart, and all her faith in love died as quickly as the flame of a candle in the rain. "Never again," she whispered, the words strangled, her voice raw with pain. "Never again."

"Tess? Is that you?" her brother called as the barn door creaked open.

Not now, she thought wildly. *I can't let him see me like this—not again!*

"I—I'm just leaving," she said, wiping her eyes and ignoring her quivering insides.

"Where're you go—" Mitchell rounded the corner, took one look at Tessa and groaned. "Oh, no, Tess. Don't tell me—"

"I'm not telling you anything."

"What happened?"

"Nothing. I, uh, just decided you were right about Denver." Refusing to meet the pity in his eyes, she swept past him. "But it's okay," she lied, "I'm going to straighten things out right now."

"How?"

I don't know! "I—I'm going to start with Nate Edwards," she said, then, before he could ask any more questions, she raced out of the barn, climbed into the pickup and shoved the old rig into gear. The truck lumbered out of the drive, lurching through potholes, kicking up dust and roaring loudly because of a hole in the muffler. Tessa didn't mind. Setting her jaw, she slid a pair of sunglasses on her nose and decided just how she was going to get her life back on track—without Denver McLean!

She drove to the Edwards ranch as if her life depended upon it. Knowing that Denver had left her as he had before—without a word or explanation—clarified things. The fact that he had called once didn't change things. He'd stripped her of her most precious possessions, then abandoned her. Well, she wasn't going to lie down and die! And maybe she'd get back at him. She'd never tell him about the baby—*if*, indeed, she was pregnant.

She coasted to a stop at the yard, then pulled hard on the emergency brake.

Her heart squeezed at the sight of Brigadier, prancing proudly in one small paddock, his ears pricked forward, his tail raised like a banner as he stared over the top rail of a whitewashed fence to a pasture of mares grazing nearby. He nickered softly, intent on the small herd, and ignored Tessa's repeated attempts to get his attention.

"Traitor," she murmured, dusting her hands as she approached the huge white house.

Nate answered the door in his stocking feet. "Tessa! Good to see you," he exclaimed. "You just missed Paula and Sherrie—they're in town doing the grocery shopping."

"That's okay," she said, though she would have liked to have a heart-to-heart with Paula and had hoped to give Sherrie the riding lesson she'd promised. "Actually, I came to see you."

"Me?" he asked, smiling. "I'm flattered. Come on in." He led her into the kitchen where the smell of coffee lingered in the air. "What can I do for you?" he asked as he motioned her onto a bar stool and held up the coffeepot. "How about a cup?"

"I'd love one."

She accepted a brimming mug. The coffee was strong and black and hot. It warmed her throat but couldn't take away the frigid cold that had settled so deep in her soul.

"What's on your mind?" Nate climbed onto the stool next to hers.

"Business, I'm afraid. I came over to offer to buy back my horses. I was hoping you'd sell Brigadier and Ebony back to me. I'd like Red Wing, too, but since she's Sherrie's horse..."

"You want the horses back?" Nate scowled as he took a long swallow of coffee.

"Yes. But I'm willing to pay you more than you paid me—for all your trouble."

"I just can't help you, Tessa," he said, confused.

She had expected to haggle. Nate was a businessman. Leaning closer to him, she said, "This is very important to me."

"I know."

"Name your price."

"I can't."

"You *can't*?"

His eyebrows drew together over his eyes and his mouth turned down at the corners. "I already sold the horses, Tessa. I thought you knew about it."

Tessa's heart fell so far she was sure it would hit the floor. "You didn't," she whispered, feeling betrayed. She had no reason to feel Nate had deceived her. She'd sold him Brigadier and Ebony with no strings attached. And yet... "I—I just saw Brigadier out in the paddock."

"I'm keeping him and the mares until the trailer comes. Sometime today."

Sick inside, her world spinning, Tessa had to set her cup on the counter. It took all of her concentration to stay upright on the stool. "Wait a minute," she whispered. "You thought I'd know about the sale? How?"

"I sold the horses through Ross Anderson."

"Denver's attorney?"

Nate met her eyes. "Right. Denver bought the horses from me, Tessa. Even Red Wing. He paid top dollar, too. I made fifteen thousand on the deal, and he promised to sell me another horse for Sherrie."

Tessa grabbed the edge of the counter. She could barely breathe. "You spoke to Denver?" she whispered, her thoughts jumbled and confused.

"No—just Anderson. But believe me, Denver wanted your horses. I had no intention of letting them go, but I'm not fool enough to turn down a quick fifteen grand."

"Of course not," Tessa replied, blinking.

"Look, Tessa, I'm sorry—"

She waved off his apology. "I guess I'll just have to talk to Denver," she said, forcing a calm edge to her voice, though her mind was burning with accusations, her insides tied in knots of betrayal.

"He's not around."

"Don't worry," she vowed, as much to herself as to Nate. "I'll find him." *If I have to chase him to the ends of the earth. I'll find him, demand answers and then nail his handsome, lying hide to the wall!*

Chapter Thirteen

Furious, though her heart was breaking into a thousand pieces, Tessa drove back to the McLean ranch. She stomped on the throttle, dying to tell Denver just what she thought of his crooked, underhanded dealings. How could she have been so stupid as to trust him again?

Not only had he reneged on the ranch deal, but he'd stripped her of her horses, her means of support—the animals so dear to her heart. Her fingers clenched around the wheel, knuckles showing white. Brigadier meant nothing to Denver except as a source of profit for the ranch.

"Black-hearted, vengeful son of a—" Downshifting, she wheeled the old truck into the lane. The pickup bounced and jarred. Tessa barely noticed. If she ever saw Denver again, she'd personally wring his neck!

And then what! Denver had all the cards. He owned the ranch, owned the horses, owned her own foolish heart. She had nothing, *nothing,* to fight him with. She'd lost everything, she realized as she drove past the acres of summer-dry ranch land—*McLean* ranch land. Except, perhaps, the baby.

And if she stayed here, let Denver know he might become a father, there was a chance, just for the sake of vengeance, he'd want the baby, too.

Tears drizzled down her cheeks. She couldn't stay here a minute longer. Without Denver, without the horses, she had no reason to stay at all.

Her gaze swept the surrounding hills, foothills she'd seen every day of her life. Mountains she'd naively believed would someday be hers. Pain welled from deep inside. She ached to belong, to be a part of this land, to be a part of Denver's life.

She blinked hard against the horrid tears. Even this damned beat-up old truck, she realized angrily as she cranked on the emergency brake, belonged to Denver. "He can have it," she murmured, hoping to sound strong though she was dying inside. Wiping her face, willing the red blotches to disappear, she jumped out of the cab and strode across the yard to the house—Denver's house.

"Something wrong?" Milly, elbow-deep in flour, asked. She was kneading bread at the counter, while Curtis, smoking and sipping coffee, sat in a chair at the table, a newspaper spread in front of him.

"Something? Try everything," Tessa said, pride lifting her chin, though her throat was still swollen.

Her father stubbed out his cigarette. "Everything?"

She braced herself for another lecture. "Everything. You were right, Dad. About Denver. About this ranch. About me. This place belongs to the McLeans. Always has, always will!" Tessa met her father's worried gaze and fought the overwhelming urge to break down and cry all over again. "It's over, Dad." Stripped bare, her very soul raw and aching, she whispered, "Just like you knew it would be. I don't belong here."

"Hey, slow down," her father said. "Start at the beginning. Of course you belong here. More than anyone. You run this place."

"That's right," Milly agreed, wiping the flour from her hands on the hem of her apron.

"Not anymore."

She was shaking all over, and she had to battle a fresh flood of tears. "I'm leaving, Dad," she said, half apologizing. "I thought I could hold this place together—make something of it. But I was wrong."

"Now hold on—"

"Don't try to talk me out of it," she said firmly. Her mind was made up, her eyes glittering fiercely with standing tears. "It's time."

"Just because—"

"It's time," she said again. She turned on her heel before her emotions got the better of her. Willing the sobs in her heart to stop, she took the stairs two at a time and dashed into her room—Denver's parents' room.

She dragged out her old suitcase, the same suitcase she'd tried to pack on that humid summer night—the night Denver had returned. The very suitcase she'd taken with her to California.

Dear God, how did I let this happen?

"Don't," she told herself, refusing to think of aquamarine water, white beach and Denver. Always Denver. "He's not worth it!"

As she banged open the bureau drawers, she caught a glimpse of her red-rimmed eyes, her straggling hair, her pale cheeks. Furious with herself, she tossed her clothes recklessly into the tattered old case.

"Tess?"

Oh Lord, not now. She couldn't stand her father's pity. "I'll be down in a minute," she called, her fingers fumbling with the locks on her case.

He pushed open the door. Wearily, he surveyed the room. "Where you plannin' to go?"

"Doesn't matter."

"Sure it does."

"Alaska, then. Or Brazil. Or Singapore. I really don't know, and I sure as hell don't care!" she lied.

He sat heavily on the edge of the bed. It groaned beneath his weight. "It's not like you to quit."

"I'm not quitting, Dad. I was defeated." She held her palms out, silently pleading with him. "Don't try to talk me out of this."

"That's exactly what I'm gonna do." Offering her a gentle smile that would have broken her heart if it hadn't been broken already, he said, "You didn't give up on me, did you?"

"Of course not. But what—"

"I haven't had a drink in three days." He frowned and rubbed the back of his neck. "Though, I got to admit, it feels more like three hundred. I'm goin' to my first A.A. meeting on Tuesday."

She swallowed hard and blinked against fresh tears. Would she ever stop crying? "Good for you," she murmured. "I knew you could do it."

"Not without you I couldn't."

"I had nothing to do with it."

He stared at her dusty old suitcase. "You know, if you leave, I might just reach for the nearest bottle."

"Nah." She shook her head, sniffing. "Not you. Not when you set your mind to something."

"That's what I thought about you."

"Oh, Dad, I'm just so tired of fighting." Her throat clogged even tighter when she witnessed the naked pain in her father's eyes. She had promised herself she would never cry for Denver again, but she couldn't seem to stop.

"What happened?" he asked.

"Denver bought the horses, Dad. He bought Brigadier and Ebony and even Red Wing. Right out from under my nose! He plans to use them here, on this ranch, for his own profit. You were right. Denver never intended to sell this place to me. Never. I was stupid and crazy and just plain dumb to have listened to him."

She heard the screen door slam downstairs. Yanking her bag from the bed, she said, "I don't want to explain this all to Mitch, all right? He wouldn't understand." She started for the door, but her father caught her wrist in his gnarled fingers.

"You can't just run, Tess."

"Watch me."

"At least stay at my place for the night. You're upset. You need time to think things through. Sometimes things are a lot clearer in the morning."

"That's the problem, Dad. Things are too clear already." She heard the sound of footsteps on the stairs and yanked her hand from her father's grasp. She had to get out now, before she changed her mind.

She took two steps just as he strode in.

"Look, Mitch, I've got to—" Her eyes clashed with Denver McLean's curious blue gaze. Big as life, his expression guarded, he blocked the door. "Oh, no," she whispered, wanting to shrink away from the magnetism in his blue eyes, from the handsome angles of his face. He looked tired and drawn, his hair long against his collar, his features more gaunt than she remembered. Despite the pain, despite the anger, despite the fact that he'd wounded her shamelessly and she was still bleeding deep inside, she felt an overwhelming urge to run to him, to suffer any ridicule, to feel his arms wrap around her again.

Denver's gaze darted from Tessa to Curtis and back again.

"What're you doing here?" she whispered, her pride surfacing. "Don't you have some horses to steal, some old men to beat down or a woman to stomp on?"

His gaze fastened to the fury in hers. "What's going on here?" he asked, his voice so low, she barely heard it.

"You tell me."

"It looks like you're leaving."

"I am."

His eyes narrowed. "I don't think so." Dressed in a wrinkled shirt and slacks, his jaw dark with three days' growth of beard, his eyes sunken, he looked as if hadn't slept in a week. Tessa told herself she didn't care. It didn't matter what he'd been through. He'd betrayed her, and any pain or remorse he might have suffered wasn't enough. It couldn't match the wretchedness slicing wickedly through her own heart.

"Why don't you start over," he suggested, "and tell me what this—" he motioned to her bag "—is all about?"

"It's simple. This place is yours, Denver," she replied coldly. "All of it. The horses, the machinery, the house and even the ridge! I don't want any part of it." Holding her chin rock solid, swallowing back hot, tormented tears, she tried to breeze past him, but he blocked the door.

"Wait a minute—where're you going?"

"Singapore or Brazil, wasn't it?" Curtis interjected, standing, trying to place himself squarely between his daughter and the man in the door.

Tessa said firmly, "I can handle this on my own, Dad."

"Just tryin' to help out."

"Thanks, but this is my problem."

"*What* problem?" Denver demanded, scowling savagely. "What the hell's going on here?"

"Move, McLean," Curtis said.

Denver refused to budge. His hard gaze landed on Tessa. "You and I have to talk."

"Too late."

"I don't think so."

"I'm leaving, Denver. There's not much to chat about!" She tried to squeeze past him.

He caught her wrist in his hard fingers, stepped quickly out of the door and met Curtis's gaze. "I'd like to speak to Tessa. Alone."

"Whatever it is you have to say, McLean, you can say to me."

"This is private."

Tessa's heart somersaulted. Denver's fingers tightened possessively over her wrist. "I can handle this, Dad," she said, her eyes as bright and furious as Denver's.

Curtis hesitated at the door, eyeing them both and shifting restlessly from one foot to the other. "I don't think—"

"I'll be fine," Tessa insisted. Now was her chance to tell Denver what a bastard he was, and she might not get another.

"All right," Curtis said reluctantly, his old face grim. "But I'll be in the kitchen." His lips pressed together until they showed white and he jabbed a gnarled finger at Denver's chest. "You've got fifteen minutes, McLean. Then I'm back up here and you're through with my daughter for good."

He pulled himself to his full five foot eight and glared up at Denver. "Fifteen minutes." Scrabbling in his breast pocket for his cigarettes, he turned and left the room.

"Okay, Denver, what is it?"

"You tell me. Why the hell are you leaving?"

"Why the hell do you care?"

"You're the most infuriating woman I've ever met."

"Good!"

With a growl, Denver kicked the door closed. It banged shut. Windows rattled in their casings and the whole house jarred. Tessa jumped. He clicked the lock into place. "I don't want to be disturbed," he said, when she started to protest.

His face muscles were tight, strained with leashed fury that sparked like blue flames in his eyes. Wrenching her arm, he nearly threw her into a chair and stood only inches in front of it, his arms crossed over his chest, his shirt stretched so tight at the shoulders the seams threatened to split. "Now, Tessa, you tell me just what's going on here."

"What does it look like?"

"It looks like you're taking a hike."

"I am."

"Why?"

"Why?" she repeated, incredulous. If nothing else, Denver had gall. She'd give him that much. But no more. "Because of you, Denver. Because of all the things you are and most certainly because of the things you aren't!"

"And what's that?"

"Honest."

"*You're* talking about honesty?" he said. "What about you? I spend the past week and a half going through hell for you and you're ready to walk out on me."

"*Me walk out on you!*" She leaped to her feet, tilting her head upward to meet the fury in his eyes. "Me walk out on you?" Laughing brittlely, she said, "You're the one who left me. You didn't call, didn't write, and now you're buying back my horses, *my* horses behind my back."

"Hold on a minute—"

"Why haven't you called?"

"I tried."

"Once."

"It was difficult," he hedged.

"I'll bet. And why didn't you show up, if for no other reason than to sign the papers at the bank?"

"I had problems. That's why I called. There was an emergency."

"Emergency? What? Did you find some other woman to put through an emotional wringer—accuse her and her family of horrid deeds and then buy her most precious possessions behind her back?"

"Is—is that what you think?"

"What else?" she jeered, wanting to hurt him as much as he'd wounded her. "Did you have to take a trip to Disneyland?"

His eyes narrowed angrily. "A little farther away than Disneyland."

"I don't really care!"

"By several thousand miles."

"Save it, Denver."

"I went to Ireland, Tess. Northern Ireland."

"Ireland?" she repeated dubiously, but some of her anger was already weakening as she guessed the answer. An icy chill ran down her spine. *Colton! Denver had gone looking for Colton!*

"That's right," he said, as if reading her thoughts. "I wanted to find my brother and convince him to come back here and sign the papers."

"No way."

"I just got a little sidetracked," he said.

"I'll bet."

Every muscle in his body coiled, and his lips thinned angrily.

She couldn't help goading him. "You expect me to believe that you flew all the way to Ireland to ask Colton to sell this place to me, when you didn't even call, didn't send a note, didn't so much as leave a message?" A traitorous part longed to believe him, wished that he could take away the pain of the past few weeks, that they could pick up where they'd left off, but she wouldn't let him fool her—not this time. Too much was at stake.

"That's what happened."

"I—I don't believe you."

"And just what do you think went on?"

"I think you've been conning me, Denver. This was all just a game to you. You don't have to deny it, because it just won't work. I'm done listening to your stupid lies."

"Lies?" he bellowed, sweeping her into his arms furiously, every muscle straining. He yanked her close against his rock-hard body, his nose nearly touching hers, his breath fanning her face, his eyes narrow slits. His fingers dug into her forearms. "The only lies I've told are to other people—people like my brother—to protect you!"

"Save it for someone who'll believe it."

His grip tightened. "I'm not lying, damn it!" Raw energy flowed from his body to hers—she could feel the anger coiling deep within him.

Tessa glared at him. "You never intended to sell this place to me! If you wanted to reach me, you could have. Instead you called Nate Edwards and bought my horses back so you could use them here."

"Why would I do that?" he growled.

"You tell me."

"Okay, I will!" Blue fire sizzled in his eyes. "Just after you left, I got a call from the private investigator."

"In Northern Ireland."

"Yes. He was worried about Colton. He'd spoken to him once and knew he was in trouble."

"So you flew over there?" she asked, doubting him.

"Yes, damn it. I went to Northern Ireland to find him and bring him back here to sign the papers. The trouble was, we didn't get that far because someone strolled into this cozy little bar and started taking potshots!" His eyes had grown cold, his face white beneath the black stubble of his beard.

"Don't lie, Denver!" But she'd begun to believe him, despite the voice in her mind that reminded her how often he'd lied.

His fingers clenched and he gave her a little shake. "That's what happened, Tess."

"I can't believe—"

"Because you won't!" The fingers digging into her flesh suddenly gave way.

"Why should I?" she demanded.

"Because it's the truth. Oh, hell." He shoved his hair out of his eyes impatiently and closed his eyes, as if trying to control his temper. He seemed weary and wrung out.

Seconds ticked by. Tessa edged toward the door.

When he spoke again, his voice was low—almost gentle. "You and I both know the kind of work he does, how he thrives on danger."

That much was true.

"Someone was trying to kill him."

She felt numb inside. "Why?"

He shook his head, his broad shoulders slumping. "I'm not really sure. No one would tell me the whole story and I don't think the authorities have everything pieced together—at least not yet. I had a hell of a time leaving the country." Denver stretched wearily, shoving his shirtsleeves over his forearms as he did.

"Go on," she said, disgusted with herself for even listening. He was a liar, a cheat, a man who had found her pride and stomped all over it. . . .

"As Dunkirk—he's the private investigator Ross hired—figured it, someone must have blown Colton's cover. Colton was in pretty tight with the IRA and had managed to take a few photos they wouldn't want published.''

"So the IRA had him shot."

"Or the other side, posing as revolutionaries—"

"I don't want to hear this," she whispered, holding up her palms and shaking her head. "This is too bizarre." She reached for her suitcase. Denver kicked it across the room. It slammed against the wall, springing open.

"Just hear me out, Tessa," he said, blue eyes flaming again.

She set her jaw, eyeing her suitcase dolefully. "Get on with it." She couldn't let herself believe him—not again. Not ever. But inside she was wavering. She had to get out fast—before he worked his treacherous magic on her all over again. She noticed the muscles flexing in his face and had to tear her eyes from his strong profile. Unnerved, her breath already whispering through her lungs, she clenched one fist around the molded brass of her bed and with her back to him, stared out the window. "I don't have all night," she reminded him.

"Right. You're on your way out."

She swallowed back a hot retort.

He stepped closer to her. The floorboards creaked. Tessa's every nerve ending fluttered as he spoke so quietly she had to strain to hear.

"The upshot is that one side—God only knows which— decided to use him for target practice. Probably as an example."

"While you were there?"

He didn't answer, but she understood from his silence that he had witnessed his brother being gunned down.

"If you don't believe me, you could call St. Mary's Hospital in Belfast."

"Oh, God—" She felt as if she might be sick. Denver wouldn't lie about his. He couldn't. She could find out the truth too easily. Images swam before her eyes—Colton McLean, a handsome if bitter man, stretched out in a pool of blood. Denver crouching over him—in danger himself.

Her hands shook, her insides roiled, and she forced herself to gaze up at Denver. "Is—is he all right?" she asked.

"He'll live."

Nauseated, she sank onto the edge of the bed. Her entire body was trembling. She could tell from his harsh expression, the tension radiating from his rigid muscles, that he was reliving that awful moment. Remorse tore at her soul. She felt like an utter idiot for a whole new set of reasons. "How badly was he hurt?"

"His shoulder will give him some trouble for a while."

"I'm sorry," she whispered, her voice trembling with genuine regret. If only she could call back the ugly words— if only she had trusted him more! How could she have stood there so damned self-righteously accusing him?

"We all are."

"Will he come back here?"

"As soon as he's released from the hospital and able to travel. My guess is that he'll show up in the next week or two."

"I owe you an apology," she said, her chin wobbling. "But you should have called."

"I couldn't. The authorities were highly suspicious of me. They grilled me for days."

"Why?"

"Because someone tried to kill my brother, as well as anyone else who happened to get in the way, only a few hours after I showed up. It looked a little too coincidental."

"I see."

"You believe me?"

Her throat so tight it ached, she whispered, "Yes—well, almost."

"Thank God for small favors." He dropped onto her bed, then sagged against the pillows. "I haven't slept in days." Rubbing the bridge of his nose, he let out a long sigh and closed his eyes. Black lashes swept the hollow circles over his cheeks.

Realizing that he might drift off, she had to ask a question that still nagged at her. "You managed to get through to Ross Anderson, but you didn't call me."

"I called Ross before I left for Belfast."

"So why didn't you tell me?"

"I tried to call. You weren't here. No one was." Blinking slowly, he forced his eyes open. "Besides, I wanted to surprise you."

"You managed that," she admitted, her fingers quivering as she brushed his hair from his eyes and tried to smooth the wrinkles from his brow. "I wanted to kill you."

"You and that idiot in Ireland."

"Did they catch him?"

Denver shook his head. "I don't know. I don't think so." He took her hand in his. "I guess I really blew it, handled the horse deal all wrong. I just didn't want you to sell stock. Those horses mean too much to you."

"I can't believe this," she murmured. Recognizing the lines of strain around his mouth, the weariness in his eyes, she almost trusted him again. Slowly, she pressed her lips to his cheek.

"Believe, Tessa."

"I want to—" Oh God, was she baring her soul to him again?

"Did I hurt you that badly?" he asked softly as he draped one arm around her waist, holding her close. The nearness of him, his smell and touch, caused her skin to tingle, her heart to race. "After the fire—did I hurt you that badly?"

Shuddering, she shut her eyes. "I was okay."

"Were you?" Levering himself onto one elbow, he pushed gently on her shoulder. She fell back against the pillows.

"I did this all for us, you know. I bought the horses and told Ross I wouldn't sign any real estate papers because I thought I'd come back here and marry you. I thought we could straighten everything out."

Her heart lurched, missing a beat. "How?" she asked, her palms beginning to sweat. She couldn't risk believing him again. Not completely. Not when it came to matters of the heart. She was too vulnerable. Just because he mentioned marriage wasn't any reason to run back to him, believe anything he said.

"I already talked to my partner. I'm thinking of splitting off—maybe starting a consulting firm in Helena."

"You'd hate living here."

"Maybe not. I had a lot of time to think things over in Northern Ireland. I did some serious soul-searching."

"And what did you find out?"

He cocked his head to the far wall, where her suitcase had landed. "That I want to be with you. No matter where you are."

She sniffed, her pulse leaping, her eyes shining.

"This ranch is only important if you're here. If you're leaving—so am I."

"And if I'm not?" she asked, twisting to face him. Her long hair fell over his arm, red-gold tresses spilling over wrinkled white cotton.

One corner of his mouth lifted. "Then I stay."

She swallowed hard. "Is—is this some kind of a proposal?"

His gaze flicked from her eyes to her lips and back again. Tessa's breath lodged deep in her throat.

"What do you think?" he asked, pushing up on his elbows, placing trembling lips against the side of her neck.

Her pulse played hopscotch. "I think I'm crazy to even consider it." But she leaned back, twining her arms around his neck, feeling his thick dark hair brush her fingers.

"Let me be the judge of that." His breath whispered across her face.

"What about the fire?" she asked quietly.

His grin twisted wickedly. "It's getting hotter by the second." Lazily, he kissed her. As if they had all the time in the world. Maybe they did.

"That's not what I'm talking about."

"I know." He covered her mouth with his and all thoughts of the past escaped her. Once again she was caught in the feel of him, the here and now, the promise of the future. The past, the fire, were but a distant memory.

A hungry warmth, deep and primal, uncoiled deep inside of her, spreading in radiant waves to her limbs.

She moaned, moving anxiously against him.

"Don't you want to see your horses? They're probably on their way," he said, kissing the tip of her nose and grinning.

"I'll wait."

"What about your father? Curtis should be back here any minute."

"Don't remind me," she groaned, moving reluctantly away from him. He caught her arm, yanked her back and pressed hot, eager lips to hers. Immediately, she turned liquid.

"That's just to remind you that I missed you."

"I missed you, too."

"And I love you, Tess," he said, his words husky and raw. "I always have."

"Oh, Denver. I love you, too!" she cried, letting her tears flow as she held him close, blinking rapidly and wishing this moment would never end.

A hard rap sounded on the door. "Tessa?" her father asked, his voice heavy with concern. "You in there?"

"I'm okay, Dad."

"You sure?"

"Positive." She glanced into Denver's eyes.

"She'd better be, McLean!"

Tessa smothered the urge to giggle. "Maybe we should go wait for the horses," she whispered. "I wouldn't want my father to get the right idea about us."

Denver's grin slashed across his face. "Not until you promise to marry me."

"Oh?" she asked, her eyebrows shooting skyward, the gloom in her heart disappearing. "And what are you going to do if I don't?"

"Hold you prisoner until you beg for mercy."

"Sounds interesting," she teased.

"Doesn't it?" He gazed deep in her eyes. "But I don't think your father would approve."

"Probably not, but he won't approve of the marriage either."

"Maybe I can change his mind."

She laughed. "If you can, you'll be the first."

"Watch me." He slapped her fondly on her rear.

"I will." She rolled off the bed and landed lithely on her feet. Denver was right behind her.

She unlocked the door, but before she could open it, he slammed it shut with the flat of his hand.

"One more thing," he said.

"What's that?" She turned and regarded him through a veil of gold-tipped lashes.

"About the fire."

Here it comes, she thought frantically, bracing herself. *This was too good to be true!* She leaned heavily against the cool panels of the door. "I thought we were through discussing the fire."

"Almost. But I thought I should explain."

"You don't have to—"

"Shh." He placed a finger to her lips, tracing her pout. "Just listen. I put everything into perspective in Ireland," he said. "I had a lot of time, sitting around hospitals and talking to the authorities. I thought things through, and I finally realized that I should never have blamed you for the accident."

"The accident?"

"Right. No matter what happened, the fire was an accident. It was no one's fault. Not yours. Not your father's."

"It was someone's."

"No. Let's not try to fix any blame."

Her throat closed around itself. Tears threatened to fill her eyes.

"I wanted to blame someone, Tessa. Mom and Dad were dead, I was in the hospital, and I thought there had to be some reason it happened—some person to blame. Your father was an easy target. So were you." His eyes were bright with unshed tears. "Can you ever forgive me?"

Blinking, she forced a quavering grin. "I think I can find a way."

"I'll talk to your dad and make it up to him."

"You'd better," she teased. "I expect him to give me away at the wedding. You'll probably have to do some fast talking. He's not too fond of McLeans. Neither is Mitch."

"When Colton gets here—"

"Oh, Lord, I hadn't even thought about that. He hates me!"

"He just doesn't know you." Denver shoved open the door. "I think it's time to start mending fences—and fast."

His fingers closed over hers and he pulled her downstairs. How, she wondered, would they ever mend the old rift between the two families? Time was supposed to heal all wounds, but the past seven years had only deepened the gap.

Her father would be easy. If Curtis saw how happy she was, he'd forgive Denver. And when they had the baby, Curtis Kramer would glide around this ranch on cloud nine. *The baby!* Should she tell him? She slid a glance at Denver and couldn't ruin the moment. She had to wait—at least until she was sure.

Besides, she and Denver had other hurdles. Mitchell and Colton would be more difficult to convince that she and Denver loved each other than would Curtis. Her brother and Denver were just too bullheaded and too much alike. *Heaven help us,* she silently prayed. God only knew what would happen when Colton McLean stepped back on Montana soil.

Chapter Fourteen

The sky was overcast, heavy with the threat of rain. Tessa glanced through her bedroom window to the shifting dark clouds and wished that the storm would hold off, if only for one more day.

Tomorrow she and Denver would be married. In a private ceremony in the Edwardses' rose garden, finally, she would become Mrs. Denver McLean.

If only rain didn't spoil the nuptials.

"I'm still not sure I approve," her father said. Standing stiffly in front of a full-length mirror in her bedroom, he surveyed his reflection with a jaundiced eye. His tuxedo fit perfectly, the white shirt in sharp contrast to his tanned skin. "I used to call these things monkey suits, and that's what I feel like—a damned circus monkey."

"You'll get over it." She adjusted his bow tie and grinned. "I know you don't want to hear this, but you look rather dashing and distinguished."

"Bah!" His fingers scrabbled across the front of his stiff white shirt for a nonexistent pocket. "Damned fool things," he muttered.

"It's only for one day."

Curtis's eyes grew sober. "You're sure about this marriage?"

"Positive."

"Mitch is fit to be tied."

Tessa remembered Mitch's volatile reaction. "That's Mitch's problem, isn't it?"

Her father smiled crookedly. "I suppose it is." He eyed the mirror harshly. "Can I take this thing off now?"

"As long as you promise to put it back on tomorrow." She breezed out of the room on the same cloud that had carried her, floating in happiness, for the past week. Never once in that time had any of the old doubts surfaced, and Denver had been wonderful. In only seven days, he'd rented an office building in Three Falls, had Ross Anderson draw up the papers to sell off his half of the engineering business to Jim Van Stern, straightened things out with her father and even planned a honeymoon in the Caribbean. The only glitch had been that the activity within the house at all hours while planning the wedding had left little time for them alone. But tomorrow that, too, would change. And then, she thought smiling secretly, she'd tell him *her* news.

If Mitchell was still harboring grudges, he'd have to work them out himself, she decided.

The kitchen smelled of cinnamon and chocolate and fruit. Milly had decided a bakery wedding cake wasn't enough and had taken it upon herself to make enough pies, cinnamon rolls and fudge for the entire third battalion. All neatly wrapped for the next day, the spicy confections were spread upon the counter of the kitchen.

The first drops of rain began to spatter the windowpanes, but Tessa told herself she didn't care. If it rained, the guests would just have to suffer a few cool drops drizzling down the back of their necks. Nothing could spoil her wedding day.

"You think this is enough food?" Denver mocked, startling her. Turning, she saw him standing in the archway between hall and kitchen, one shoulder propped against the wall as he gazed at the overladen counters.

"Maybe."

"Maybe, my eye. We'll have to raffle off pies at the reception. Each guest will win five."

"You're exaggerating," she teased.

His smile was slow but suggestive as he sauntered across the room, rested a hip against the edge of the table and drew her into his arms. "Maybe a little." Placing his forehead against hers, he sighed. "One more night. And then three weeks of warm water, hot sun and white sand."

Her eyes sparkled. "Hard to believe, isn't it?" She heard her father's footsteps on the stairs.

"I can't wait!"

Curtis walked into the room dressed in his dusty Levi's, checked shirt and boots.

"More comfortable?" Tessa asked.

He snorted and lit a cigarette. "You'd better take some pictures tomorrow, because it's the last time you'll catch me in one of those damned suits again."

The back door creaked open and Mitchell tossed off his jacket before flopping into the nearest chair. "Don't you think you could cut your trip down to one week?" he grumbled.

"Too much work for you?" Tessa asked.

"I hate to admit it," Mitch said, offering an off-center smile to his sister, "but for a little thing, you do pull your weight around here."

"I'll be back," she reminded him.

"I'm going to run into town for a while—"

"You need to try on your tux," she reminded him.

"It'll fit."

"Let's find out tonight."

"Okay, okay. I'll be back in a couple hours. Don't get all bent out of shape. Just remember who's filling in for you while you're busy playing baccarat and drinking mai tais on the beach.''

"I won't forget," she said as he left again.

"I'd better be shovin' off, too," Curtis said, eyeing his daughter fondly. "Big day tomorrow."

"The biggest."

Curtis glanced up at Denver. "I thought Colton might show up."

"So did I." Denver checked his watch. His forehead was grooved with worry. "He's still got a few hours."

"Not many," Curtis said tightly, and Tessa wondered if the bad blood between her father and Denver's brother could ever really be cleansed. Colton had been released from the hospital two days before, and Denver had hoped his brother would make it back for the wedding.

Colton, Denver had warned her, hadn't been thrilled at the prospect of Denver's marriage. Tessa figured there was nothing she could do to change his mind. That would take time.

"See ya tomorrow," Curtis said, waving as he shoved open the back door.

Tessa watched through the window. Her father ambled down the path and hunched his shoulders against the rain. "Do you believe in bad omens?" she asked as Curtis's old pickup drove away, the taillights barely visible through the zigzagging drops trailing on the glass.

"I've never thought of a summer storm as a bad omen." He wrapped his arms around her waist and kissed her neck. "In fact, I take it as a good sign. You know, a fresh start— that sort of thing."

"I don't know," she whispered leaning against him heavily. His arms were so strong, so protective.

"Don't borrow trouble." He turned her to face him. "Here we are, finally alone, the night before our wedding, and you're worried." He smoothed the lines furrowing her brow with one finger. "How about a toast?"

"A toast—with what?"

"A bottle of champagne." He eyed the pantry, where two cases of effervescent wine were stacked near the door.

"Milly will kill you."

"Milly will never know." Grinning devilishly, he strode into the pantry, pulled a jackknife from his pocket and deftly sliced the top case.

A conspiring smile twisted her lips. "I guess it is our wedding—our champagne."

"I doubt if we'll find many parched throats tomorrow. Not with this much champagne. We can spare a bottle, don't you think?"

"Well, maybe just one."

He poured them each a drink, clinked his long-stemmed glass to hers and said, "Here's to the most gorgeous bride in Montana."

"And California?"

"Most definitely California." His blue eyes danced. "And probably all the states west of the Mississippi."

"How about east?" she teased.

"Don't know about that." He wrapped one arm around her. "There might be one or two girls who are prettier than you."

"I'll remember that," she said with a laugh, sending him a wicked, provocative look.

Together they sipped champagne and shared chaste, wine-flavored kisses on the living room couch. After a week of self-imposed celibacy, Denver was about to go out of his mind. "I could carry you upstairs," he said, his eyes moving slowly down her neck to rest at the hollow of her throat.

"Then why don't you?" she teased. Half-lying across him, she poured the last of the bottle into each of their empty glasses.

"Because that damned brother of yours said he'd be back."

"He probably forgot. And he's not my 'damned brother,' he's your damned brother-in-law," she reminded him.

"Well, whoever he is, he'll show up the minute we go upstairs—"

Headlights cut through the night, flashing against the rain-spattered windows.

"What did I tell you?" Denver asked, his lips twisting wryly. "Right on schedule."

They heard boots clatter against the porch steps. The back door squeaked open. Footsteps paused in the kitchen and the refrigerator door clicked open.

"In here," Denver called over his shoulder.

"We thought you'd be back," Tessa said. She peeked over the back of the couch just as Colton McLean, one arm supported by a sling, his free hand clenched around the neck of a beer bottle, appeared in the hallway. Tall and lean, with suspicious gray eyes, an unruly beard and a rain-speckled suede jacket, Colton walked into the room as if he owned the place. Which he did. Or, at the very least, half of it.

Denver's muscles became rock hard as he slowly straightened. "Well, you finally made it! About time," he drawled, clapping his brother fondly on his back. "And from the looks of it, you're not too much the worse for wear."

Colton's glance slid to Tessa. "So tomorrow's the big day," he said without inflection. Grimacing a little, he twisted off the cap of his beer.

Tension crackled in the air. Tessa sat up quickly, smoothing her denim skirt and feeling very much like a sixteen-year-old virgin caught in the backseat of a car. Reminding herself that Colton was just Denver's brother, nothing more, she forced a smile. "I'm glad you made it. We were worried you might not get here in time for the ceremony."

"Oh, I wouldn't miss it for the world," Colton drawled, sweeping his gaze back to Denver. "The day that Tessa Kramer finally traps you into marriage is a red letter day for the McLeans."

"No one trapped anyone." Denver's eyes became slits, and his affable smile tightened into a thin line of frustration. Crossing the room, he draped his arm possessively around Tessa's waist.

Tessa, thinking of the baby within her, wanted to die. Would Denver think she'd tried to trap him? Colton would surely hammer the point home.

"So you've said," Colton replied, his gaze drifting through the house where he'd grown up.

There was a fight brewing—as intense as the storm outside. Tessa could feel it in the tightness of Denver's muscles, see it in the pulse throbbing at his temple. She tried to intervene. "How's your shoulder?"

"Just great," Colton muttered. He leaned against the windowsill, staring at the black night beyond. His gray eyes were dark, his lips drawn tight. "Anyone else around?"

Denver shook his head. "Just us."

"So where's the rest of the Kramer clan?"

"Why do you want to know?"

"It's been a long time," Colton said slowly. "I just wanted to talk with my new *family*."

"Leave it alone, Colt," Denver commanded.

Tessa was in no mood for Colton's snide insinuations. She tilted her chin up proudly. "Dad's down at his place and Mitchell's due back any time."

"Good."

"You know," she said, watching as he crossed the room, dropped into a chair and rested the heels of his boots on a coffee table, "my family wasn't too thrilled about this marriage."

"I'll bet."

"But they came around."

He lifted skeptical dark brows. "And why's that?"

"For the same reason you came all the way back here," she said, "because they care about me. Just as you care about Denver."

Colton took a long swallow of beer. "I didn't come here just to give you a wedding present," he said, wincing a little as he shifted in the chair. His face grew taut and white from pain. "I want to know how you can reconcile yourself to all this, Denver. How you can give up your life in L.A. and marry a woman you can't trust?"

Denver stepped between Tessa and Colton. "It's simple."

"Is it?"

"We love each other."

"Bah! Love?" Colton laughed. "You? Give me a break!" His insolent gaze moved to Tessa. "You conned him again, didn't you? He's always been weak where you're concerned."

"Leave it alone, Colt," Denver growled.

But Colton's mouth curved into a cynical smile. "At least she's smart enough to get what she wants, isn't she? She always wanted this ranch, Denver, and now she'll have it."

Tessa's chin inched upward. "Believe what you want, Colt. I'm sure I can't change your mind. But just to set the record straight, I'm marrying Denver because I love him."

"Sure you do." He took another long swallow. His eyes slid to his brother. "Have you ever explained what happened the afternoon of the fire?"

Denver crossed the room and loomed, huge and furious, over his brother. "It's a closed subject."

"Not with me." He took another long swallow, ignoring the storm in Denver's eyes.

"If you just came here to cause trouble, you may as well leave. Now."

Beneath his beard, Colton grinned roguishly. "Now that's not very hospitable of you, Denver. I traveled all this way—"

"To mess things up."

Colt's smile faded. "To straighten things out. I owe you one, and I'm paying you back right now."

Denver's voice was low, threatening. "I appreciate your concern. Now, either you're here with good wishes or you're history—if I have to throw you out myself."

"Stop it!" Tessa intervened. Outside, thunder cracked. "If you two want to fight like a couple of twelve-year-olds, for God's sake, wait until after the wedding—after Colton's recovered."

She heard the whine of an engine and her heart dropped. Glancing through the windows, she saw the truck roaring up the lane. So Mitchell was back. Maybe he could stop the fight simmering between the two brothers.

"God, Denver, open your eyes, for crying out loud!" Colton said just as the back door banged open. His voice had taken on a slight Irish accent—as if he were used to slipping into brogue. "The woman's been playing you for a fool from the first time she set eyes on you."

"That's enough!" Denver growled. "Tessa is going to be my wife and nothing you can say—"

"What the hell's goin' on in here?" Mitchell asked. Standing, dripping, in the front hall, his wheat-colored hair plastered to his head, he surveyed the room with surprised green eyes that landed with an almost audible thud on Colton.

"Well, if it isn't Denver's future brother-in-law," Colton drawled.

"Colt?" Mitchell whispered, eyeing the bearded man. All the color drained from his face.

"In the flesh." Colton stood and ignored the fire in Denver's eyes. "Tell me, what do you think about Denver and Tessa tying the big one?"

"I figure it's Tessa's life."

"And my brother's," Colton added.

"Knock it off, Colt," Denver warned.

"Not until I get to the bottom of this. Not until I convince you that the woman you're planning to marry betrayed you and the whole family. Don't you remember the fire, Denver?" he asked, clutching Denver's scarred hand and raising it high in the air like some sort of medal.

Tessa took one step toward Denver, wrapped her arm through his.

"It's over." Denver yanked his hand back.

"It'll never be over, Denver. How can you forget all those days in the hospital—all the surgery?" Colton spit out. "And the fire. You remember that, don't you? And Mom and Dad didn't make it out of there, for Christ's sake! All because Tessa, here, and her old man, were ripping us off!''

Mitch's face washed with horror. "Don't—" he rasped.

But Denver moved as quickly as a cat. He shoved his brother against the wall and pinned him there.

Colton's shoulder slammed against the wall and he winced.

Face set, Denver curled his fingers around the sodden lapels of Colton's jacket. "You want to settle this, Colt, then let's settle it. Between us."

"A fight?" Colt drawled, his face tight with pain but his hard smile flashing beneath his beard. "How chivalrous!"

"No!" Aghast, Tessa wedged herself between the two brothers. "Stop this right now! I had nothing, *nothing* to do with that fire—"

"Like hell!" Colton hissed.

"But maybe you did," she went on defensively. "You didn't have an alibi—"

"Are you crazy?" Colton asked incredulously.

"Leave her alone!" Mitch commanded.

Denver gave Colton a shake. "And get the hell out."

"Not until she admits what she and her father planned—"

"No!" Mitch cried, shaking. "She had nothing to do with it!"

"Then who—" But the question died on Colton's lips, and Tessa, horrified, met Mitch's tortured gaze.

"No—Mitch—"

Denver swung around, staring at Tessa's brother.

"It—it was my fault." Mitch's voice cut through the anger simmering in the air.

Tessa couldn't believe her ears. Wouldn't. "No, Mitch—"

"It's the truth, damn it!" Mitchell's face was pale, his eyes clouded with self-loathing.

"What the hell?" Colton said as Denver dropped his hands.

"I altered the books," Mitch admitted slowly, "I—I was ripping off the ranch."

"No!" Tessa cried, walking to him. "Don't—"

"It's true."

"I won't believe it."

He turned pleading eyes to Tessa. "I'm sorry, Tess. So sorry."

"Don't even say it," she whispered, disbelieving. Not Mitch—not the brother who had helped pull her out of her own emotional rubble.

"It's true, damn it!"

Colton's eyes fixed on Mitchell.

"I was in trouble—gambling debts—and so I started taking some money, a little here and there. Denver's father was catching up to me. I didn't mean to start the fire—it was an accident."

"You bastard! You lying, cheating, murdering bastard!" Colton growled, starting across the room.

Denver held him back. "Let him finish," he said, but his voice was harsh, his blue eyes frigid.

"Don't do this," Tessa whispered, "You don't have to—"

"I do, Tess," he said, his eyes pleading with her to understand. "It's been too long. I should have told everything right up front, but Dad insisted that it would only be worse for me." Mitch's body was shaking. "God, I'm sorry!"

"Curtis was in on this?" Denver hissed.

"Not really."

"What the hell is that supposed to mean?"

"He didn't know. I'd been stealing from the petty cash in the office, and I knew old man McLean was on to me." His eyes turned dark with the memory, his breathing irregular. "I—I was going to rip the ranch off one last time and take off. But something happened, I don't know what."

"Oh, God," she murmured.

Colton tried to break away from Denver's grip. "You were paying off gambling debts, and it cost my family their lives?" he roared. "Christ, what kind of man are you?"

"And you 'accidentally' caused a fire that consumed the whole damned stables and everything in it?" Denver hissed.

"Stop it! Please, all of you," Tessa commanded. "Stop it!"

But Mitch wasn't finished. "I used to smoke," he said. "I was nervous, and I guess I must have dropped my cigarette in the straw in the stables before I went up the office. By the time I took the money and changed the books the downstairs was already in flames. I opened all the stalls I could and left."

"You bloody bastard!" Colton lunged again, but Denver held him back.

Tessa's eyes were bright with tears, her insides ripping apart. Her world was out of kilter on its axis, spinning crazily out of control. "You could have told me," she whispered.

"You were already destroyed because of Denver!" he spit, then lost some of his fire. "Dad thought it best if no one said anything. I'd already had a couple of scrapes with the law.... Oh, hell, Tess, why do you think Dad drinks so much? Why do you think it's been worse since the fire? Because he took the rap for me, damn it!"

Denver released Colton. "Two people died in that fire, Kramer!" Colton thundered. "Two people!"

"I know it."

"What kind of a miserable bastard are you, Kramer?" Denver demanded, his temper exploding. "My parents and seven horses burned to death! And all this time, you knew. Your father knew! Why the hell didn't you say anything?"

"Denver," Tessa whispered, seeing the anguish in his eyes, the throbbing of the arteries at his temples.

"Oh, God, I don't know," Mitch whispered, his eyes red. "I'm sorry, I'm so sorry."

"Sorry?" Colton bellowed. "Sorry?"

Denver's teeth clenched. "Why the hell didn't you tell anyone? And don't give me that baloney about doing what your father wanted! That's just plain crazy. You ran because you were scared. Because you were a coward."

"Yes!" Mitch choked out, his eyes swimming in tears of remorse.

"Just listen to him!" Tessa yelled, defending her brother. "Can't you see how hard it is?"

"Harder than this?" Denver asked, stretching his fingers wide, his webbing of reddish scars more visible than ever before.

Mitchell was shaking. "Dad was sure that I'd be sent to prison for...involuntary manslaughter. He told me to join the Army—to get away. Let things die down."

"And so your dad poured himself even deeper into a bottle," Denver accused. "All because of you!"

"You miserable, lying murderer!" Colton hissed. He lunged at Mitchell, drawing back his fist. He connected with a right cross. Mitchell's head snapped back, and he reeled backward to land against the wall. His skull crashed into the wainscoting and he slid to the floor.

"Stop this!" Tessa screamed, running to Mitchell's side. "Get out, Colton! Just get out!" She dropped to her knees as Mitchell, holding his jaw, struggled to a sitting position. "It's over! Can't you see it's over?"

"It'll never be over," Colton snarled, as he kicked at an end table, sending it crashing against a far wall, then stalked out of the room.

Tessa's eyes flew to Denver. His face was taut, his eyes filled with accusations. He stood poised over Mitchell, muscles coiled, nostrils flared, as if he, too, would like to beat the living hell out of her brother.

"So that's it, Tessa," Denver said. "Your brother is a murderer and your father a drunk. Hell of a family I'm marryin' into!"

"No one's twisting your arm," she threw back at him.

His lips thinned furiously before he turned, shoved open the front door and stalked outside into the driving rain.

All the pain of the past—the lies, the treachery, the mental anguish of the days after the fire—burned bright in Tessa's mind. Denver had walked out on her before. And now she, because of Mitch, was linked to the fire. No doubt he blamed her. No doubt he thought she had known the truth all along.

"I'm sorry, Tess," Mitch said, biting his lip and rubbing a hand over the bruise already showing on his chin. "I should've told you a long time ago. I should've gone straight to the sheriff. God, it's been hell."

She saw him more clearly then, the relief that seemed to wash away his scowl, the pride that held his chin upward. Obviously Mitch had suffered every day since the accident.

"It's all right."

"It's not, Tess! Two people died. People Denver loved." He blinked rapidly. "It cost so many people so much. But it's over. Thank God, it's finally over." Standing, he forced pride back into his shoulders. "I think I've got a few phone calls to make."

"Can't you wait till morning? Give yourself time to talk to an attorney."

His green eyes were calm when they met hers. "I've waited seven years. It's time to face the music." Wincing, he reached for the phone.

But Tessa snatched the receiver from his fingers and slammed it back in the cradle. "Just stop and think a minute—call Ross Anderson."

"Forget it, Tess. This time I do what I should've done seven years ago. Don't you have a few things to do, to get ready for tomorrow?"

Tomorrow—the wedding!

"I don't know if there will be a wedding," she whispered, shaken to her roots. She ran quivering fingers through her hair while her mind spun out of control, trying to sort out everything that had happened in the past ten minutes—as well as the past seven years. "Denver and I have a few things to iron out," she said shakily. She forced her shoulders square, took in a deep breath and told herself it was now or never. "Will you be all right?"

Mitch smiled tiredly. "Better than I've been for seven years."

"I'll be right back," she said. "Don't do anything foolish."

"I can handle it, Tess." He reached for the phone and waved away the protest forming on her lips.

"Okay, Mitch, do it your way."

"You just worry about McLean."

"That I will," she vowed, thrusting open the front door and dashing down the rain-slickened steps. Wind tore at her hair. Rain drizzled relentlessly from the sky to run down her neck and cheeks. Squinting, she scanned the yard. Denver was nowhere in sight.

Maybe he's already left, she thought, her heart thudding painfully.

Then she saw him. Tails of his shirt flapping in the wind, his hair ruffled, he sagged against the bole of an old apple tree near the burned-out remains of the stables. She took off running, her heart in her throat. This time she wasn't afraid. This time she would force the issue. This time, come hell or high water, she was going to put out those last smoldering ashes of the fire no matter how long it took!

"What're you doing here?" he growled as she dashed through the wet grass.

"Looking for you."

"Why?"

"Because we need to talk."

His face was lined and strained, his shoulders set. He didn't look at her, just glared at the ugly black timbers. "What did you know about the fire, Tessa?"

"Nothing more than I told you."

"Your brother didn't fill you in?" he asked sarcastically.

"Not until tonight."

"You expect me to believe that?"

Wind howled through the valley, chilling the air. In the distance, thunder rumbled across the hills.

"You can believe what you want to," she said, shivering. "But you'd better listen to what I have to say. I've taken a lot from you, Denver. More than I should have. And I've done it for only one reason. Because I love you. I've let you humiliate me, degrade me, use me and accuse me, but I won't take it anymore."

She saw him flinch, but still he didn't look her way.

"Go back to Los Angeles, Denver. Run away. It's what you're best at! But don't expect me to be here if you return, because this is the last time I'll let you walk away from me, the last time I'll ever let you drag my heart through these damned ashes!"

His jaw worked angrily. His fingers clenched and flexed only to clench again.

She wanted to drop to her knees and beg him to love her, to forget the past, but she stood ramrod stiff, letting the rain and wind lash at her face and hair, bracing herself for the worst. "This is it, Denver. Either you love me forever, or you walk away. It can't be anything else."

"You've always been a dreamer," he said cuttingly.

"And you've always been in my dreams."

He blinked rapidly. Rain slid down his face and neck, past his wet collar. "And you've been in mine, Tessa," he admitted. "But maybe that's all we had. Dreams. Ashes. Nothing solid."

With a boldness she'd never felt before she planted herself in front of him and poked one long finger at his chest. "You listen to me, Denver McLean, we can make our dreams come true. And it doesn't matter what Colton or Mitch or the whole damned world thinks or does. All that matters is here and now. Me and you. What's it going to be?" She steadied herself, ready for the rejection she felt hanging in the air. *So be it,* she thought, *there's no going back.*

His throat worked. "What I want," he said, his voice as rough as the stormy night, "is you. Nothing more. Nothing less. But it has to be forever."

Tears burned behind her eyes. She could barely believe her ears. "You're sure?"

"Yes," he whispered, his voice nearly lost on the wind.

"Well, it can't just be us."

His jaw tightened, his features twisting in torture. "Why not?"

"Because I'm pregnant, Denver. I found out for sure this morning. You're going to be a father."

For a second he didn't speak. "You're sure?"

"Positive."

"Oh, God."

"You can have me and the baby—or you can take a walk and never look back," she said, her heart frozen at the thought, though she loved him enough to let him go. "I won't tie you down."

"Like hell," he murmured, his lips curving into a smile of wonder. "You're never getting away from me again."

"But the baby—"

"Makes it all the better," he said, blinking rapidly. "A baby?" Rain slid down his collar and his arms wrapped securely around her. "Marry me, Tessa. Be mine the rest of my life."

"I wouldn't have it any other way," she vowed, just as his rain-soaked arms tightened around her, strong, possessive and warm.

His lips crushed hers hungrily. "Neither would I."

"Welcome home, Denver," she said with a sigh.

A shudder ripped through him. Thunder cracked in the dark sky. "I don't think I ever really left."

"You may kiss the bride," the preacher announced, and a whisper of approval swept through the guests standing on the wet lawn behind Nate and Paula Edwards's manor.

"Amen," Denver murmured. He lifted Tessa's ivory veil and stared deep into her wide hazel eyes. His lips covered hers in a familiar warmth, and for a minute he was lost in her, aware only of her fingers on his shoulders, his arms circling her waist, the eager promise of her mouth molding to his.

"I love you," she whispered, when at last he lifted his head. Her eyes were bright with wonder, her cheeks flushed.

"Let's leave."

"Soon," she promised as they strolled among the guests, arms linked, smiles wide.

Denver caught his brother's eye and winked. It had taken long hours of convincing, but finally Colton had agreed to attend the wedding, albeit reluctantly. Even Mitch had decided to attend, though earlier he'd spent hours with the county sheriff and insurance people. Things would work out, though, Denver decided, glancing again at his gorgeous bride. Mitchell might have to do some time. But then again, maybe not. No one, not even Colton, was pressing charges. As for Colton, he was trapped in Montana, at least until his arm healed.

"You take care of her," Curtis said as he approached.

"I can take care of myself." Tessa laughed.

"Lord, am I tired of hearin' that!" Curtis grinned at Denver. "Now maybe you can listen to it."

"I'll take care of her," Denver said, his eyes glinting mischievously. "In more ways than one."

"Talk is cheap," she quipped.

"Just you wait, Mrs. McLean," he replied, but he laughed just the same. For seven years he'd carried a burden deep in his soul, and now, beneath a cloudy sky, he felt as if he were finally free.

"Come on, let's get out of here," he said.

"And where will we go?"

"How about Brazil? Or maybe Singapore," he mocked and she jabbed him playfully in the ribs.

"How about the Caribbean and then Three Falls, Montana?" she suggested, as her new brother-in-law, looking uncomfortable and stiff in his formal suit, approached.

"Congratulations," Colton said, forcing a smile. "Isn't it a custom to kiss the bride?"

Denver's lips twisted. "I'm not too keen on tradition."

Colton raised his eyebrows, then touched the bouton-
niere pinned to Denver's black tuxedo lapel. "You
could've fooled me," he said with a genuine smile that
slashed white against his beard. He glanced at Tessa. "When
you get tired of this guy, maybe you should give me a
call—"

"Don't even think it," Denver warned, but he laughed
when he caught the teasing glimmer in Colton's gray eyes.
"The man's incorrigible," Denver decided as his brother
strolled uncomfortably through the crowd.

"A McLean family trait," she observed. "Let's just hope
it's not passed on to the next generation." She smiled then,
a knowing smile that caused his heart to lurch.

A warmth spread through Denver like none he'd ever felt
before. "No regrets?" she asked, cocking her head coyly.

"No regrets."

* * * * *

FOUR UNIQUE SERIES
FOR EVERY WOMAN YOU ARE...

Silhouette Romance

Love, at its most tender, provocative, emotional... in stories that will make you laugh and cry while bringing you the magic of falling in love.

6 titles per month

Silhouette Special Edition

Sophisticated, substantial and packed with emotion, these powerful novels of life and love will capture your imagination and steal your heart.

6 titles per month

Silhouette Desire

Open the door to romance and passion. Humorous, emotional, compelling—yet always a believable and sensuous story—Silhouette Desire never fails to deliver on the promise of love.

6 titles per month

Silhouette Intimate Moments

Enter a world of excitement, of romance heightened by suspense, adventure and the passions every woman dreams of. Let us sweep you away.

4 titles per month

READERS' COMMENTS ON SILHOUETTE SPECIAL EDITIONS:

"I just finished reading the first six Silhouette Special Edition Books and I had to take the opportunity to write you and tell you how much I enjoyed them. I enjoyed all the authors in this series. Best wishes on your Silhouette Special Editions line and many thanks."

—B.H.*, Jackson, OH

"The Special Editions are really special and I enjoyed them very much! I am looking forward to next month's books."

—R.M.W.*, Melbourne, FL

"I've just finished reading four of your first six Special Editions and I enjoyed them very much. I like the more sensual detail and longer stories. I will look forward each month to your new Special Editions."

—L.S.*, Visalia, CA

"Silhouette Special Editions are — 1.) Superb! 2.) Great! 3.) Delicious! 4.) Fantastic! . . . Did I leave anything out? These are books that an adult woman can read . . . I love them!"

—H.C.*, Monterey Park, CA

*names available on request

You'll flip . . . your pages won't!
Read paperbacks *hands-free* with

Book Mate • I

The perfect "mate" for all your romance paperbacks

Traveling • Vacationing • At Work • In Bed • Studying • Cooking • Eating

Perfect size for all standard paperbacks, this wonderful invention makes reading a pure pleasure! Ingenious design holds paperback books OPEN and FLAT so even wind can't ruffle pages — leaves your hands free to do other things. Reinforced, wipe-clean vinyl-covered holder flexes to let you turn pages without undoing the strap . . . supports paperbacks so well, they have the strength of hardcovers!

Pages turn WITHOUT opening the strap.

SEE-THROUGH STRAP

Reinforced back stays flat

Built in bookmark

BOOK MARK

BACK COVER HOLDING STRIP

10 x 7¼ opened
Snaps closed for easy carrying, too